Estelle Ryan

The

Léger Connection

The Léger Connection
A Genevieve Lenard Novel
By Estelle Ryan

First published 2015

Acknowledgements

I am so deeply honoured to be standing on the shoulders of giants. It's a growing list of people without whose support, interest and love I would not have achieved as much as I have.

To all of these amazing individuals, a huge thank you. Charlene, words fail me. Linette, for your support. Moeks, for being my biggest cheerleader. R.J., for editing that makes my books stronger and better. Anne Victory for your friendly professionalism. Maggie, Krystina, Julie, Anna, Kamila, Jola, Ania B, Ania S, Alta and Jane – knowing you guys are always there for me is invaluable.

And I could not do any of this without fantastic readers. Every email, Facebook and blog comment means the world to me. I'm so deeply honoured to have your love and support.

Dedication

To Tomek

Chapter ONE

Francine Bianchi frowned at one of her high-definition monitors. She was looking at real-time footage from security cameras placed in the viewing room in Rousseau & Rousseau, an insurance company catering to the one percent. On the monitors, Doctor Genevieve Lenard was sitting on her ergonomically designed office chair. She appeared frozen as she watched recordings of interviews on the bank of monitors in front of her.

To anyone else, Francine might be spying. Not to her. She was keeping a close eye on her best friend in case Genevieve needed help.

Francine had met Genevieve two and half years ago. In her thirty-three years on this planet, Francine had met many people. Most of them were on the fringes of society, moving around the grey areas of legality. But never before or since had she come across someone as unique as the dark-haired woman intently staring at the top left monitor in front of her.

"What on God's green earth are you doing, supermodel?"

Francine jumped in her chair when Colonel Manfred Millard spoke right behind her. She swivelled around and glared at him. "Do you have to sneak up on me every single time?"

"Can't help if you are sleeping." Manny nodded at her desk. "Spying on Doc again?"

Francine lifted one eyebrow and flicked her hair over her shoulder. "I'm not spying."

"Let me guess. You're just concerned." Manny might have been sarcastic, but he'd hit the nail on the head. It had been four months since the last major case their team had worked on.

Genevieve, Manny and Francine were part of a team working directly for the president of France. More than two years ago, Manny had brought a case to Rousseau & Rousseau. A greedy Russian had been killing off art students and Manny had wanted to prevent another young life from being taken. By the end of the case, their small team had been formed and now they investigated art crimes or any other crimes the president might request them to look into.

Everyone considered Genevieve to be the heart of their investigative team, so when she had announced that she needed to take a break from investigating cases, Francine and the other three members had been shocked. For the last four months, it had felt as if they had been a car without an engine. It didn't matter that Francine was one of the top hackers in the world, that Manny was highly respected and successful, that Colin Frey had an international reputation as an uncatchable thief or that Vinnie had connections in the underworld that made law enforcement agencies salivate. Without Genevieve, their team wasn't a team.

"As a matter of fact, I am worried about her." Francine zoomed in on her best friend's face. As always, Genevieve's short hair was perfectly styled. Once, Francine had watched Genevieve spend ten minutes getting the messy look just so. Then she had spent another ten minutes applying minimal, but perfect makeup. The result was a natural look that emphasised Genevieve's cheekbones and drew attention to her all-seeing emerald-green eyes.

Genevieve had no idea of her beauty. A few times, Francine had pointed out the men turning their heads whenever Genevieve walked into the restaurant where they had their weekly lunch. Genevieve had explained it away as a primal reaction to seeing two women of childbearing age. Then she'd coolly analysed Francine's facial features and pointed out they both had prominent cheekbones, but Francine's lips were much fuller. According to Genevieve, men viewed women with lips like Francine's as more sensual than women with Genevieve's average lips. She'd dismissed the male interest as reptilian brain activity and a lack of frontal lobe stimulation.

It was a good thing Francine had a healthy self-image. She'd taken the smackdown for the clinical rationalisation it was. She knew those men were gawking at Genevieve because of the aloof beauty she exuded. And those reptilian-brained males were entertaining numerous fantasies about Francine because that was the closest they would ever get to her fabulous Brazilian-French self.

Onscreen, Genevieve's eyes narrowed and she leaned a bit closer to the monitors. She must have seen suspicious body language on the footage she was watching. As one of the world's top nonverbal communication experts, Genevieve really did see everything. From a recorded interview, Genevieve could spot when someone was trying to pull the wool over the interviewer's eyes. Or that they were sincere in their shock, sadness or outrage when talking about an insurance claim. On top of that, she could point out an anomaly faster than Francine could log in to her favourite online store. This had made her a great asset to the company, helping Phillip Rousseau, the owner of Rousseau & Rousseau, save millions of euros.

"Hey, supermodel." Manny snapped his fingers in front of Francine's nose. "I asked you a question."

Francine slowly turned towards him, rolling her eyes. He'd been asking her the same question every day for the last four months. "Yes, oh great one. I asked her how she was and she said she's fine."

Manny pushed his hands into his trouser pockets. "Then why the bloody hell is she not here with us?"

"Why don't you ask her that?" Four months ago, they had worked on a case that had ended in extreme violence. Many lives had been saved, but Genevieve had been caught in the crossfire. It had proven too much for her and had prompted her hiatus. As far as Francine knew, no one had asked her to return to her role in the team.

The physical and emotional distance between them had been exacerbated by the renovations to Rousseau & Rousseau. For the first two years, their team had operated from the offices of Rousseau & Rousseau. A few times, the security had been breached, but never as badly as in the last case, which had resulted in a shoot-out that had damaged one hallway and two conference rooms beyond repair.

Genevieve had shown no interest in discussions about renovations and security upgrades. After five minutes in the first meeting, she'd declared it a waste of her time and had left. No one had taken offence. Genevieve's high-functioning autism caused her to sometimes be quite abrasive. Since they were not only team members but friends, they accepted Genevieve's quirks even if they didn't always understand.

So they'd continued their brainstorming sessions until they'd found the perfect way to secure the premises. Once it had been agreed, things had happened very fast. Colin had bought the building next to Rousseau & Rousseau's under a company owned by one of his many aliases. Manny had been dismayed at the subterfuge, but had agreed it would add a layer of protection. As far as all official databases were concerned, none of them had any connection to Rousseau & Rousseau. Not anymore. Even Genevieve had been officially fired. Yet she hadn't joined them in their new team room, but continued to look into Rousseau & Rousseau cases.

Manny had muttered and cursed, but accepted the new arrangement. It had been at his suggestion that they'd kept on most of the businesses renting space in the building, but had cleared the top floor for themselves. Two weekends of intense renovations had given them a working space with security that very few would ever be able to penetrate. Francine had even moved most of her equipment from her basement workspace to their new team room.

"We should get Frey to ask her." Manny nodded to himself. Colin and Genevieve had been romantically involved for two years. Being his friend for over twelve years, Francine had been overjoyed for him when he'd found someone who accepted him for who he was. In the time she'd known him, he'd only had flings. Most of those women had dated an alias, never knowing the true person, never knowing the caring, gentle man Colin was.

Working undercover, retrieving stolen goods of great value, he'd always had to put on a performance. He was terrifyingly good at it—one of the reasons all law enforcement agencies should be happy Colin was working for them, not against them. It was only when he'd grown close to Genevieve that Francine had seen his true side as well. For the first time in their friendship, Colin had relaxed enough to reveal the side of him that wasn't calculating every sentence and action. He'd even proven to have a sense of humour.

One of Francine's monitors blinked and another window replaced the side view of Genevieve still staring at the monitors. Father Tomás Bianchi, priest of a large parish in the western outskirts of Rio de Janeiro—and Francine's dad—was squinting at her. No matter how many times she told her dad he was doing it right, he still doubted his Skype skills.

"Fifi? Can you hear me?" Her dad's whisper was barely audible. If he needed to whisper, he most likely also needed a quiet answer. Francine checked and saw the thin red cables from his earphones against his full beard.

She moved closer to her computer, to her webcam. "I can hear and see you, Daddy. How are you?"

"I can't talk much." He brought the phone closer to his face, giving her a view of his left eye and part of his nose. "Is that boyfriend of yours with you?"

"He's not my boyfriend, Daddy." Francine waved Manny closer. "But he's right next to me."

"Good. Good." Her dad's one-eyed squint intensified. "I can't see him."

Manny grunted, leaned down until his cheek was almost against Francine's. "Father Tomás. Pleased to meet you."

"About time too, boy." Her dad moved the phone away so they could see his whole face. "You're not a boy, are you?"

"No, sir." Manny's lips twitched. "I haven't been a boy in a long time."

"Good. Good. Hmm. Good." Only when he was distracted did her dad repeat himself like this. "I think we have a situation here, Manny."

"What situation, Daddy?" Francine didn't like the deep frown pulling her dad's grey eyebrows together.

"One of my parishioners died early this morning while eating breakfast. Mateas Almeida. He was so young." The absence of her dad's trademark smile that always made the corners of his eyes crinkle was telling. "It's a long story that I'll tell later, but now I'm worried. I'm in the cellar of his home looking at stuff I know you work with, Fifi."

Manny snorted when her dad called her by the only name he'd ever used for her. Francine pinched the skin on his hand until he made a growling sound in her ear. She smiled sweetly at the webcam. "What stuff are you looking at, Daddy?"

Her dad pulled the phone even further away from his face and waved his finger at the screen. "That smile means trouble. We'll talk about that later, Fifi. For now I need to figure out how to…" The view changed to the ceiling, then to her dad's collar and back to the ceiling before he managed to change to the front-facing camera and point it at what he was seeing.

"Holy hell!" Manny cleared his throat. "Father Tomás, what is that?"

"Paintings, son. Paintings. Are you recording this, Fifi?"

"As always." Francine recorded all calls, whether audio

only or video. A few times it had come in handy when a contact had tried to go back on his word. Today, it might serve a completely different purpose. "Try to go as slow as possible, Daddy."

The cellar her dad was standing in was a richly decorated space. It was the home office of a person who wanted to convey elegance and old money. A lot of old money. The walls were painted a dark green, yet it didn't make the space look dark. Well-placed lights brought the focus to the paintings her dad was aiming his phone camera at.

Manny left for a moment and returned with a chair. He sat down and pushed the chair until it was flush against hers. "Supermodel—"

"I'm already on it." Francine grabbed her tablet from her desk and took a screenshot when her dad stopped moving for a moment to focus on a large, colourful painting. In the time she'd been working on art cases with the team, she'd learned a lot. Looking at the lines and blocks depicting a still-life scene, she was confident identifying it as cubist in style. Changing windows on her tablet, she ran an image search and hit pay dirt a second later. "It's stolen."

"Oh, dear." Her dad's whisper was so soft, she barely heard him.

Her heart missed a beat, her hand clutching the tablet tighter. Her dad's congregation were from a suburb in Rio de Janeiro that housed both the disgustingly rich and the dirt poor. Most of the poor people attending her dad's services had minimum-wage jobs, but clung onto their dignity and faith in equal measure. The affluent were a different kettle of fish. A lot of them lived two lives—one as church-going, family-loving Christians, and the other a lot less benign. "Daddy? Are you in danger?"

"I don't think so."

"What are you doing in the cellar, Father Tomás?" Manny scowled at the video feed.

"The widow asked me to come down here and look for her husband's last will and testament. She didn't trust anyone else to come in here."

"Why not?" Manny asked before Francine could.

"I didn't ask." There was a slight pause. "But I think that she doesn't trust the men upstairs."

"There are men upstairs?" Francine couldn't keep the worry out of her voice. "What men?"

The video image shook as her dad shrugged. "They're all friends of the family. Apparently, they've been friends since school."

The image moved to another painting. Her dad moved quickly between paintings, but paused long enough on each one to get good screenshots. She took another one and did an image search on it. This time it took two seconds, but with the same results.

Manny leaned closer to look at her tablet screen. "Also stolen."

"These are the only paintings I can see." Her dad turned around slowly to give them a three-hundred-and-sixty-degree view of the room. "Should I look for more?"

"No!" Francine and Manny spoke at the same time. Rather loudly.

"I would prefer if you got out as soon as possible, Daddy."

"Not without the last will and testament." The video moved over to the large mahogany desk before it shuffled again to the ceiling, floor, walls and finally settled facing towards the desk again. "I've got this thing hanging around my neck now."

"Keep it on, but first turn off the flash, Daddy." Francine waited for the video to settle again. "We don't want someone to walk in on you and discover that you're recording anything."

For a few seconds, Francine and Manny watched her dad go through the contents of the desk. Manny leaned towards the computer. "Why didn't the widow get the last will and testament herself?"

"Her husband's sudden death has left her devastated. The doctor had to give her a sedative to calm her down and her sister is sitting with her at the moment." The image rose and fell as her dad sighed. "They had been parishioners for eleven years. Not once did I ever see them angry with each other. After twenty-three years of marriage, they still loved each other deeply. Aha! I got it."

Her dad lifted a green folder—'Last Will and Testament' handwritten in the top left-hand corner. He opened the folder to reveal three thick documents. The few sentences Francine caught as her dad paged through the first document revealed a detailed will. She guessed it to be around forty pages long. The second and third documents were certified copies of the first.

"Don't linger down here, Father Tomás," Manny said. "Go back upstairs, hand the widow the documents and pretend everything is normal."

"Everything is not normal." The view changed towards the

door as Francine's dad straightened. "A man died and I have to comfort the family."

"Daddy, please remember all our talks." Francine glanced at Manny and wasn't surprised to see his eyebrows rise in suspicion. She lifted her chin and looked back at the monitor.

"The talks or the sessions you forced on me?"

It took all her self-control not to look at Manny. Instead, she cleared her throat. "Um… yes. Those sessions."

The view shook and soft chuckles came over the speakers. "Manny doesn't know, does he?"

"No, I don't." Manny was glaring at her when Francine gave in and glanced at him. He didn't look away. "But if those sessions are going to keep you safe, I suggest you do as she says."

"Don't I always." The humorous resignation in his voice elicited deep longing in Francine.

"I miss you, Daddy."

He replaced the three documents and walked towards the door. "I miss you too, Fifi. I'm going to take the earphones out, but will keep the camera on. And before you say it, I'll be careful."

"I'll say it anyways." She leaned closer to the computer and wished she was leaning closer to her dad. "Be careful. And I love you, Daddy."

"Love you too, Fifi."

The noise over the speakers indicated that he'd removed the headphones from the phone. She wished he didn't have to. Speaking to him was one of her greatest pleasures. Not only was he one of the most selfless people she knew, he was also incredibly smart. Not on the same scale as Genevieve, but his insight into people always amazed her. His interest in international politics combined with his intellect made him the perfect debate opponent. They seldom agreed on topics, but always respected the other's opinion. And more often than not, she learned from him.

Francine watched wide-eyed as her dad climbed the stairs. His breathing increased and she made a mental note to ask him whether he was keeping to his New Year's promise that he would exercise more. At sixty-two, he was still healthy, but he'd become less active over the years. She hated that she'd only now remembered about his intention to strengthen his muscles and raise his fitness level.

"Fifi, huh?" Manny slumped in his chair and looked her up and down. "What's that all about?"

"Watch the monitor. My dad might need our help."

"Your dad will be just fine, supermodel. Tell me why he's calling you Fifi."

Francine glared at him for a second before she realised he was trying to distract her. Some of the tension left her body and she smiled at him. "You can be really sweet sometimes, you know?"

"Milena, may I come in?" Francine's dad's voice drew their attention back to the monitor. He was standing in the doorway of a large bedroom. A beautiful bed made of a solid dark wood only took up a third of the room. Across from it were sliding doors, very likely opening onto a terrace. Two women were sitting on a deep burgundy sofa in front of large windows. One woman had her arm around the other and handed the crying woman a tissue from the box on her lap.

"Oh, shit." Francine turned to Manny. "I forgot that he was going to speak Portuguese."

Manny slumped deeper into his chair. "Don't worry about me, supermodel. I'll get by."

"You speak Portuguese?" Why had he never told her this? Francine frantically tried to recall which insults she'd used when he'd driven her to lengthy tirades in Portuguese.

Manny pointed at the monitors. "Watch."

She narrowed her eyes at him and was sure his lips twitched. When he shook his index finger again at the monitor, she huffed and turned—just in time to see both women look up and nod.

"Please come in, Father." The crying woman blotted her eyes and blew her nose loudly. As Francine's dad walked closer, she took a few shaky breaths. "I don't know how I'm going to get through this. I never even entertained the idea of being without Mattie. Now he's gone. What am I going to do?"

"God will give you the strength, Milena. Just place your trust in Him." Francine's dad sat on one of the chairs facing the sofa.

"I'm sorry, Father, but at the moment I really don't understand how God can take away a healthy, kind, generous forty-seven-year-old man who did so much for his community."

"Being angry with God is normal." The sincerity in her dad's voice was the reason he was so loved. "I've also been angry with Him a few times. I know this is meaningless right now while you are in such pain, but time will bring you the peace that you need."

"I don't know, Father." It looked like Milena wanted to say more, but fresh tears fell from her eyes and she bent over, the sound of her wracking sobs filling the room.

They sat in silence for a few seconds, Milena weeping and her sister holding her close. Once Milena's crying lessened, her sister looked at Francine's dad. "Did you find Mateas' last will and testament, Father?"

"I did."

Milena looked up. "What does it say?"

"I didn't look, Milena. That is your privilege." Again, his answer was gentle, filled with compassion. Francine knew he dealt far too often with people's grief, with the pain accompanying the loss.

"I don't want this privilege. I want Mateas back." Her sobs started again.

Her sister looked at Francine's dad, her expression pleading. "I don't know how to help her."

"You are helping her. Hold her, give her more tissues and listen to her when she needs to talk." He held out the folder towards her. "This seems to be the most recent last will and testament. I'm going to give you both some space, but I will be available at any time. Just phone me and I'll be back."

The sister briefly tightened her hold on Milena before she got up. "I'll walk with you, Father."

Francine wasn't surprised when her dad didn't refuse the offer. Something in the sister's tone had also caught Francine's attention. "I wish Genevieve was here. She would give us so much more insight."

"We can show this to Doc later. I would also like to know what she makes of this." Before Manny could say anything else, Milena's sister and Francine's dad reached the hallway. The woman stopped just outside the bedroom door and hugged herself tightly.

"Is there something you would like to share with me, Gabriela?"

Gabriela cleared her throat twice then sighed heavily. "Milena refuses to believe that her healthy husband could've had a heart attack. We both know it happens, but she is convinced he was murdered."

"Did she say who she suspects?"

"That's just it. She can't imagine anyone who would've wanted to hurt her Mattie."

"But you don't agree?"

"I didn't say that."

"My dear"—Francine's dad's tone was regretful—"I deal with people's secrets every day. I can tell that you have one."

Gabriela held his gaze for a few seconds before looking away. "She loved him."

"And you didn't trust him?"

"I don't have any real basis for my distrust. There was just something about Mateas. Nothing I could ever put my finger on."

"Did he ever hurt Milena?"

"Oh, no! He would never do that." She shook her head vehemently. "That was the only reason I tolerated him. He loved my sister as much as she loved him."

"But you still think that someone could've wanted him dead?"

She raised both shoulders before dropping them with a

sigh. "I don't know. Maybe I'm just overwhelmed with all this emotion. Ignore me, Father. I will make sure Milena is okay. If she needs to speak to you, I'll call."

Gabriela turned around and walked into the room, out of sight. The view didn't move for a few seconds. Francine's dad was most likely contemplating his next move. She was extremely glad when he didn't plug his headphones into the phone, but continued down the hallway towards the staircase. Whether Milena's suspicions were right or not, Francine didn't want her dad to draw attention to himself, possibly putting his life in danger. She let out the breath she hadn't realised she'd been holding when he reached the foyer without any incident.

When he took his light coat from the housekeeper and put it on, Francine dropped her head into her hands.

"He's covering up the camera." Manny pointed at the monitor. "Why is he covering up the camera?"

"Because my absentminded dad has forgotten about the phone hanging around his neck." She had lost count of the times she had reminded her dad to widen his attention. He was the perfect example of living in the moment. "I wonder if he even remembered it was on when he went into the bedroom."

Manny lifted his hand to stop her from saying anything else. Male voices were coming over the speakers. Francine turned up the sound and frowned. "They're speaking French."

"Shh." Manny made a chopping motion with his hand. Francine wanted to grab the offending hand and bend his fingers backwards. Nobody shushed her.

"Quiet. The priest is coming," a deep voice said.

"Nah, it's just the local yokel. He only speaks Portuguese." This voice had a whiny quality to it. Francine immediately disliked this man.

"Are you sure?" Deep Voice asked.

"Yeah. He's been here for the last thirty-something years and I've never heard him speak anything but Portuguese. The old man doesn't even travel."

"I don't know about his linguistic skills, but I do know that he's never even taken a holiday." The third voice held an authority the others didn't. "The locals all talk about it. He's always here. He's harmless."

"What's he doing?" Whiny asked.

"Waiting. What does it look like, idiot?" It sounded as if footsteps were coming closer. "Can we help you, Father?"

"Oh. I'm sorry. Do you speak Portuguese?" Francine's dad sounded calm and friendly.

"Yes, of course," Deep Voice answered in Portuguese. "Can we help with something, Father?"

"That's very kind of you to offer. I'm waiting for my driver. He should be here any minute now."

The pause that followed made Francine nervous. Were they studying her dad to make sure he wasn't lying? And since when did he have a driver?

"Very well. We were also leaving." Footsteps sounded again—leaving. "Good day, Father."

"God bless, son."

"Arsehole," Whiney said in French as they walked away. "I never understood why Mateas was so religious. Such a crock. Hey, maybe he confessed to this old guy. We should take the priest and find out if he knows anything. We can't risk a hint of our… project coming out now."

Francine's hand flew to her mouth, her heart pounding.

"Nah. Didn't you see how relaxed he was? He doesn't know squat. He…" The third voice was too far away to hear anything else. Francine played with the sound settings, but there were no other sounds to capture. Just her dad's breathing. A long, uneventful minute later, a rumbling car came closer until it stopped. Her dad grunted as he got in the car and the door slammed a second later.

"I'm sorry you had to wait for me, Father. I tried to get back as soon as possible."

Francine recognised the voice. In the last three years, her dad had admitted to being overwhelmed by work. Enrico Diaz had started working as his assistant and apparently now also as his driver.

"No problem, Enrico. You were just in time."

"How is Mrs Almeida?"

"As one could expect. One can only pray for them."

"Indeed." It sounded as if they were on a main road. "Any problems? Other than the obvious, of course."

"Not at all. Just the sadness of losing a loved one."

Francine jerked away from the computer. "He lied!"

"Of course he did, supermodel. He can't exactly go around telling everyone he's found stolen artwork and that someone might have been murdered."

"But he lied." She turned to face Manny. "Daddy doesn't lie. He might mislead like he did when the guy asked him a question in French. But he doesn't tell big whoppers like this.

He must have seen something in those three men that has him worried. Oh, God. I have to speak to him."

She was still on video call with her dad, but it was no good if he couldn't hear her. Her dad and Enrico were discussing the agenda for the rest of the week, so she felt comfortable disconnecting. She called his mobile and listened in frustration as the call went to voice mail.

After the third time, Manny put his hand over hers. "He probably put it on silent, supermodel. Does he have a house phone?"

"Yes."

"Then phone him there later. Let's go through the stuff you recorded." He shifted in his chair. "Dammit. I wish Doc would get her butt here. We could really do with her insight."

Francine agreed, but didn't want to impose on Genevieve. They would look through the footage and if they got stuck, they'd get Genevieve involved. Francine opened the software programme she used for videos and opened the recording she'd just saved.

Chapter TWO

"I love you too, Daddy." Francine ended the call and turned to Manny. They'd watched the footage twice before she'd phoned her dad again at his home. He'd picked up and had chuckled when he'd admitted to forgetting about having his phone's camera on. The five-minute conversation she'd had with him had done nothing to soothe her mind.

"So? What did he say, supermodel?"

Francine forced her frustration back and relaxed her facial muscles. "He said there were four men. He recognised them as friends of Almeida's who have been there a few times when my dad visited. He never met them and only ever saw them from a distance. Until today. One of the men didn't say anything, not until they'd reached their cars and my dad couldn't hear anything. But my dad said he is the guy we should look out for. All four were wearing expensive clothing."

"How does your dad define expensive?"

"The same way I do. He recognised one man's shoes as a pair of Bruno Maglis. And Daddy knows how to spot a bespoke suit. All of them looked like they were about to put on their ties and walk into a board meeting."

"Interesting." Manny rubbed his chin. "What else?"

"Daddy visits the local prison once a week as part of his duties. He said the man with the high voice had the same look in his eyes as some of the thugs he ministers to in prison. He also said the cars they got into were a Mercedes and a Porsche."

"Did he get the number plates?"

"I didn't ask. I'll phone him again, but I don't think so. He hates taking off his reading glasses, which means he can never read anything which is not in front of him." Every time Francine had confronted him about it, he'd told her that he spent most of his time reading and looking at people right in front of him. He didn't need to see detail far away.

"Supermodel?" Manny lifted both eyebrows.

"What?" Manny staring at her was unnerving and she didn't need it right now.

"You're not telling me everything."

"I am. I did." She threw her hands in the air. "I've told you everything my dad just told me."

He tilted his head. Whenever he did that, he always said something that made her want to reach for a weapon. "What aren't you telling me? What's wrong?"

For a second, Francine considered telling him how mistaken he was. It annoyed her endlessly that he would know she was lying. She shook her finger at him, the jingle of her bracelets filling the room. "You're annoying."

"Not more than you. Now tell me what's wrong."

She dropped both hands on her lap in defeat. "My dad. That's what's wrong. He's the most stubborn, nosiest person I have ever laid eyes on."

Manny's bark of laughter surprised Francine. Manny didn't laugh. Not often. Francine realised why he was laughing and folded her arms, glaring at him.

He laughed harder. "So rich, supermodel. Coming from you of all people."

"It's not funny." She really wanted to stay annoyed, but the laughter was making Manny look younger. Happier. And it was contagious.

Manny shook his head. "Yes, it is funny. To hear the most obstinate and nosy person I know accuse her dad of the same."

"At least I'm smart enough not to put my life in danger when I check into something."

"What the hell?" All laughter disappeared from Manny's face. "You think your dad is going to investigate these men? Or the paintings in that cellar?"

Francine pushed her fingers through her hair. "I wish I could tell you he would never do it."

"But you know he's going to."

"Yo, yo, yo! Vee and Cee are in da house!" Vinnie's deep voice boomed through the large space. Francine and Manny turned towards the elevator in time to see the doors close behind Colin and Vinnie. The latter walked towards them, his smile wide. "Whaddup, my peeps?"

"Another reason Doc needs to come back." Manny's top lip curled. "At least people speak normal English then."

"Aw, old man, you're just jealous that you don't have my way with words."

"No, criminal. I'm *thankful* I don't have your way with words."

Colin's smile disappeared when he noticed the image on the computer monitor behind Francine. "What's that? Where did you get that?"

"My dad saw it in the basement of a parishioner's house. We have more footage."

"What do you know about this, Frey?" Manny lifted his chin towards the cubist painting on the monitor.

"This?" Colin pointed at the monitor. "This is Fernand Léger's *Still Life with Chandeliers*, stolen in 2010 and not yet recovered. Francine, zoom in, please."

"Where?" Her hand rested on the wireless mouse, ready to enlarge any section Colin wanted to see. He was an expert in art forgery, frequently consulting with galleries and museums to help them authenticate artworks. Although most of those times he was wearing some form of disguise and never used his real name.

"Doesn't matter. I just need to have a closer look."

She zoomed in on the fork lying on the table and made space for Colin to lean closer to the monitor. For a few seconds he studied the monitor from different angles. Manny shifted in his chair, a sign that he was getting impatient. To his credit, he didn't rush Colin.

Vinnie did. "Dude. Are you going to make out with the screen or are you going to tell us whether it is the stolen painting or not?"

Colin straightened. Usually he would respond to Vinnie's baiting with his own sharp wit. He didn't even smile. "It's impossible to tell for certain from an image of this quality, but in my opinion this is the original Léger."

"Holy Mother Mary." Manny rubbed his hand hard over his face. "Supermodel, play the whole video."

"There's a video? Where's the popcorn?" Vinnie's grin increased when Manny glared at him.

"Vin." Colin's soft request was enough. Vinnie was still smiling, but he pressed his lips together. Colin took a step away from Francine's desk. "What video?"

Manny held up a hand the second Francine inhaled. "No. You're going to be too long-winded. And don't get huffy."

"I never get huffy!"

Colin and Vinnie laughed at her outraged tone. Manny only lifted one eyebrow and turned to the other men. In four sentences, he summarised what would've taken Francine at least four paragraphs. She wasn't surprised to see the concern on the other two's faces.

"Did you tell Franny's dad to stay out of this?" Vinnie nodded towards her, but looked at Manny. "This one is a chip off the old block. Nosier than my Aunt Helen's three cats."

Manny's blasted eyebrow rose again. Francine was ready to sneak into his house tonight and shave that eyebrow while he was sleeping. She tapped her foot and put one fist on her hip. "I'm not that nosy."

"Have you or have you not been spying on Genevieve?" Colin folded his arms and looked down at her. "Have you or have you not been reading all her email correspondence?"

"I'm worried! I was looking to see if there was anything in her emails that might tell us if she's not okay."

"She's okay." Colin's lips thinned. They'd had this argument before. "If you're so worried, why don't you ask her?"

"I have."

"And?"

"She said she's fine." Francine threw her hands in the air when Colin didn't say anything. "A lot of people say they're fine when they're not."

"As much as it pains me to say, Frey has a point, supermodel." Manny scowled at Colin. "Don't gloat, thief. I'm just saying that Doc has never said anything she didn't mean. She wouldn't lie about being fine or not."

"You are all far too careful around her." Colin unfolded his arms and placed his hands on his hips. "The last case threw us all for a loop. I don't see any of you tiptoeing around each other. Why are you treating her differently?"

"She said she needed a break, dude." Vinnie had always been gentle with Genevieve, but Francine had noticed that he'd taken it up a few notches since the last case.

"And she had her break." Twice they'd had this discussion and twice Colin had argued that there was nothing wrong with Genevieve.

"Yes, she did," Francine said. "And she's been reading all those friendship books."

Everyone groaned. Including Colin. "Yeah, that's something I'm trying to get her to lose interest in. She's convinced those books might teach her something, but she keeps deleting them from her e-reader."

"Why?" Francine thought that odd. During one of their lunches, Genevieve had been outraged that people would throw books away. Genevieve had said that she kept all her books.

Colin sighed deeply. "According to Jenny, the people who wrote those books have no idea what they are talking about. Their friendship advice is counter-intuitive, their writing skills are subpar, there are too many or too few commas, their knowledge about communication might be the reason the divorce rates are so high. I could go on—"

"But we get the gist." Manny pushed his chair back and stretched out his legs. "Why the hell is she reading those books, Frey?"

"The obvious reason." Colin shrugged. "Information-gathering. Her reasoning is that the books might give her insight into how neurotypical people might define friendship. She thinks it will help her be a better friend."

"She's a great friend." Vinnie picked up Francine's favourite pen before she could stop him. He was agitated. That meant the death of her pen. He flipped the pen between his fingers. "Why doesn't she get that?"

"Have you told her that?" Colin asked.

"Huh? Me?" Vinnie's grip tightened on the pen and a soft cracking sound came from his fist. "Of course I did. I tell her she rocks all the time."

"Seriously, Vin? After all this time, you really think Jenny will hear, 'You rock,' and understand, 'You're a wonderful friend'?"

It was silent in the team room for a long while. Francine thought back to the many lunches and shopping trips she and Genevieve had had. Not once had she told her best friend that she was a good friend. She'd only assumed Genevieve would know this because Francine called her 'my bestest friend'.

"Why doesn't she tell us how she feels?" Far too many times Francine didn't know what was going through her friend's mind.

"Whoa there." Colin raised both hands and took a step back. "I'm not Genevieve's spokesperson. If you have questions for her, ask her yourself. How many more times must I tell you that she's not as fragile as you think she is?"

"She's special, dude," Vinnie said after some time. "Even the old man doesn't want to fuck things up with her. We don't want her to…"

"Stop right there, Vin. You should be telling her this. Not me. I know how much you all love her. She knows how I feel about her, because I tell her. I tell her that I appreciate that she accepts me as I am. That it means a lot to me that she doesn't judge—not me, not my friends and not other people. I tell her when she says something hurtful and I explain to her why. Shit, man, I've seen you read those books on autism. You know her brain works differently than ours. You guys need to speak to her."

Francine's eyes widened at the anger in Colin's tone. She could count on one hand the times she'd seen Colin lose his cool. He was in so many ways the opposite to Vinnie's passion and open emotions. If Genevieve was the foundation of the team, Colin was the pillar. No matter what a case threw at them, he remained level-headed. The fact that he was right about how they'd been treating Genevieve rankled.

"I'm going for lunch with her today. I'll speak to her," Francine said.

"You do that," Colin said through tight lips. He pointed at the computer monitor. "Can we please stop talking about Jenny and start watching this video your dad recorded?"

"He didn't record it. I did." Francine rolled her eyes and finished with her best Nikki imitation. "I mean, like, duh."

That broke the tension and brought smiles to everyone's faces. Nikki was a nineteen-year-old student who had come into their lives two years ago. She had adopted Colin and Genevieve as her parents and had wormed her way into everyone's hearts with her youthful enthusiasm for life.

Colin and Genevieve lived in what used to be two large neighbouring apartments. The connecting wall in the living areas had been taken out, making it an enormous apartment. Colin and Genevieve lived in one side, Nikki and Vinnie in the other. A strange, but very happy family.

Francine didn't care that Vinnie chuckled at her bad impression and that Manny's lips twitched again. It was Colin's soft smile that put her at ease. She loved getting Manny riled up. Irritating Vinnie when he was cooking was the best part of her day. But she needed Colin to be that reliable, and annoyingly calm, pillar.

"Okay, smartarse. Can we please watch the video you recorded?" Colin asked.

"Immediately." With two clicks, Francine played the recording from the beginning. A few times Colin asked her to pause it while he studied the artwork her dad had stopped at. Apart from that, no one else said anything for the duration of the recording.

When it ended, Vinnie put his hand on her shoulder. "Did he promise he wasn't going to check these guys out?"

She looked over her shoulder at him. "He did."

"But you don't believe him."

"I should. He's a priest. He shouldn't be lying."

"He lied to his driver."

"And I'm going to give him a piece of my mind about that." As a matter of fact, she was building up quite a long lecture she planned to give her dad when she Skyped with him tonight. If she managed to catch him on Skype. She had a suspicion that he was going to block communication from her for a few days. It wasn't going to help her worry less about him. "Or I'm going to have to resort to plan B."

"Plan B?" Manny asked.

Francine's smile conveyed a warning. "My mom."

"Oh, yeah." Vinnie nodded. "That lady is scary. Wait until you meet her, old man. She can turn a computer into a block of cheese. By sheer will. I've never met anyone like her."

"No?" Manny looked from Vinnie to Francine and back. "Never?"

"Hah!" Vinnie laughed. "Like mother, like daughter."

This was the second time today someone had told her she took after her parents. Since she had the utmost respect for those two people, she didn't mind. But she did mind how funny the men found it. "At least my mother—and my father—know what spices to add when they're cooking."

Vinnie's laughter disappeared. "That's not even remotely funny, Franny."

"Could someone please tell me why these paintings are in this man's cellar?" Colin's frustrated question interrupted Francine's fun.

"Wait," Vinnie said. "Is this our case? Are we pursuing this?"

"We should." Colin pointed at the monitor. "If that is the real Léger, and I'm sure it is, the Paris Museum of Modern Art will be indebted to us forever."

"Of course we're looking into this." Francine turned to Manny. "At least I am."

"And if I don't agree, you're just going to go ahead and follow in your daddy's stubborn footsteps, aren't you?" Manny grumbled something under his breath when Francine blew him a kiss, red spots appearing on his cheeks. Her flirtation never embarrassed him, so Francine smiled happily. Once again she'd succeeded in annoying him. He turned his back on her. "We're going to need to establish whether those paintings are real or not."

"I'll fly over to Brazil tonight and have your answer by tomorrow." Colin looked like he was ready to leave this very moment.

"Ooh! Road trip!" Francine clapped her hands. "Let's all go. Mom and Daddy would love to see you two again and meet Mister Meany."

"No. No road trip." Manny used his final-answer tone. "Frey, don't you have some colleague over there who could go have a look at those paintings?"

Colin thought about it. "Nobody I trust enough. The best person to authenticate paintings in Brazil is notorious for making paintings disappear."

"A thief. Great. What about the universities? Museums?"

"Incompetent and all their best people left the country."

"Dammit, Frey. Don't you have any alternative?"

"It's either me there or the paintings here."

Francine recognised the look on Manny's face. She shook a finger at him. "No. I am not asking Daddy to bring those paintings here. No."

"Why not?"

"Because… because he doesn't have a passport." For the first time ever she was thrilled to say that. It was another argument she frequently had with her dad. She'd even offered to have one done for him on the sly, but that had elicited righteous outrage.

"Does your—"

"Don't drag my mom into this. What's with you today? Do you *want* me to kill you in your sleep?"

Colin and Vinnie laughed. Manny stared.

"What about the alleged murder?" Colin waved his hand between Manny and Francine to break their staring match. "Do we think that this Mateas Almeida was murdered?"

"How the hell do I know?" Manny shrugged. "I don't even know who this guy is… was."

"Give me a moment." Francine changed windows and entered a few keywords into the search engine she'd designed. As usual, it didn't disappoint her. "He was the owner of a real-estate development company in Rio de Janeiro. Hmm. This explains his rich friends. He was the seventeenth richest man in the country."

"Old money?" Colin asked.

"Nope." She scrolled down the biography from the company's website. "He grew up very poor. Doesn't say where. Hmm. I'll find out. Anyway, he was really good at school and got a scholarship to study engineering. After that, he worked for two years before he started his own business from his one-room flat. Three years later, he moved into a small office. Five years after that, he bought an office building. For the last fifteen-odd years he was expanding his business. But it says here he also did a lot of philanthropic work. I'll ask Daddy about it."

"We need to ask your dad a lot of questions about this man."

"If he'll speak to us," she mumbled.

"What was that?" Manny lowered his brow. "Supermodel?"

She sighed. "Daddy knows me as well as I know him. Which

means I know he's going to poke his nose where it doesn't belong and he knows I'm going to make him promise to not do it."

"And that's why you're going to get that amazing mother of yours involved," Vinnie said. "She'll keep him in line."

Francine laughed. Loudly. "Oh, Vinnie. I don't think the Pope or even Baby Jesus could keep my dad in line."

"But he's a priest," Manny said.

"And a wonderful one at that. He's known in the whole of Rio for the work he's done in the community, for his wisdom and his willingness to go to bat for his people. Rich and poor."

"But he's not popular with the authorities?" Manny's lips turned down.

"Don't you dare judge my dad, handsome. FYI, he's very popular with the authorities. He's helped them put away some of the worst gang leaders."

"I wonder if Daniel knows someone in Brazil." Vinnie's suggestion came out of the blue, but made perfect sense. Daniel Cassel was a GIPN team leader—France's equivalent of SWAT. Vinnie had become good friends with Daniel and his team.

"Phone him, criminal. Find out if he has contacts there." Manny turned to Colin when Vinnie walked to the far side of the cavernous room, his phone pressed against his ear. "Tell me about this painting and the heist."

"Five paintings were stolen by what the authorities believed to be one thief. The security cameras caught a man climbing through a window, entering the museum. He proceeded to take five paintings. In 2010, their combined worth was estimated at a hundred million euros."

"Bloody hell."

"That's around a hundred and fifteen million US dollars," Francine said. "It's been five years, so it might be worth more."

"Very likely." Colin nodded towards the computer. "Four of the five paintings stolen were hanging in that basement. Assuming they were the original paintings."

"Phone your father, supermodel. We need to get those paintings." When she didn't move, Manny pushed her smartphone closer. "Now."

Francine made sure Manny saw her displeasure. She knew her dad wasn't going to answer his phone. But since she also knew Manny would insist until she relented, she picked up her phone and dialled her dad's cell phone. He didn't answer. There was also no answer at his house nor at the church. After trying three more times, she sent her dad an SMS, asking him to contact her immediately. Then she turned to Manny. "I told you so."

"Hmph." Manny rubbed his stubbly chin. "The paintings, Frey."

Colin snorted. "I understand why Jenny gets pissed off with you for deviating so much from the topic. And don't look at me like that. I'm immune to your scowls."

"Daniel said he knows a buddy who might be able to help us out." Vinnie walked back to stand next to Colin. "He'll let me know what the dude says."

"It would help to see those paintings up close," Colin said. "The stolen works were paintings by Picasso, Matisse, Braque, Modigliani and Léger. The first painting your dad focussed on was the piece by Léger, the Still Life with Candlestick."

"Give me a sec." Francine had that painting on the monitor before Manny could get impatient.

"Ah, what a beauty." Colin tilted his head. "Léger painted this in 1922. He was right on a par with Picasso and Braque as an outstanding cubist artist. His technique was and still is widely studied and admired. But after some time, cubist artists' works became increasingly abstract and Léger hated that. During World War I, he moved away from the Picasso-like abstraction and returned to his cubist roots. As you can see in this painting, he loved bold colours and strong lines. This work specifically was a move towards modernism."

"It looks very flat to me." Manny leaned away from the monitor. "I didn't like Braque's work when we had that case and I don't like this."

"What? You prefer posters of cars on your walls?" Colin spat out the words.

"Be fair, Colin." Francine had witnessed an argument like this before. It had been ugly. "You've seen the art on handsome's walls."

"No, he hasn't." Manny's eyes widened when he saw Francine's guilty expression and straightened. He shook a finger at Colin. "You've broken into my house? Because I sure as hell have not invited you into my home."

"A fact that has not gone unnoticed, Millard." Colin shrugged. "So I decided to have a little look around your dump. I have to admit I was surprised when I didn't find car posters on your walls, but actual paintings. Although I doubt you chose any of them. Not with your sense of style."

Vinnie moved very fast when Manny got up. He pushed himself between Colin and Manny. "We really need Jen-girl.

She has much better control over our conversations. Old man, why don't you rest your weary body? Dude, take a few steps back. Hey, it's almost lunchtime. Why don't you all go eat in separate places?"

"Oh, shit!" Francine looked at her watch. "Genevieve is going to give me another lecture about punctuality and showing respect." She jumped up, grabbed her oversized handbag and rushed to the elevator. "I don't want any blood on my desk. Listen to Vinnie or take your fight to the other side of the room."

Chapter THREE

"I'm sorry, girlfriend. I'm really sorry." Francine fell into the seat across from Genevieve, her expression pleading. "I lost track of time. I really planned to be on time."

"No problem." Genevieve closed the cover of her e-reader and put it in her handbag. Like everything else, the e-reader had a designated place in Genevieve's handbag. Francine had never seen a woman's accessory that could pass a military inspection. "I was reading."

Francine froze in her seat. She stopped trying to get her handbag's wide strap to stay on the rounded back of the chair. Instead she dropped it by her feet. "You're not upset?"

"No. According to the book I'm reading, friends should accept each other as they are. You are…" Genevieve lifted one index finger and took a deep breath. She swallowed as if she had difficulty not finishing her sentence. "I accept you as you are, so I brought a book in preparation."

Francine's laugh caught the attention of a few other restaurant guests. When Genevieve reacted with a confused frown, Francine's laughter died down. "Are you serious? Oh, my God. You are serious."

"Why wouldn't I be serious about this?"

"Of course. My mistake." Francine pushed her fingers through her long hair, barely resisting the urge to pull. She lowered her arms and took a deep breath. "Thank you for accepting my tardiness. And for anticipating it."

"You're welcome." Genevieve's answer was so sincere that Francine didn't have the heart to tell her she had been sarcastic. Genevieve lifted her glass. "I've only ordered water. Should we call the waiter and place our order?"

"Good idea." Francine needed the distraction. She needed to flirt with the waiter so at least something about this lunch would feel normal. Henrique, their usual waiter, was watching them from the bar when she looked up. She waved him over.

"My two favourite ladies," he said when he reached them. Henrique was in his mid-twenties, a postgraduate student, majoring in parks and recreation. The first time he'd mentioned it, Genevieve had dismissed his degree and current studies as the worst choice for career ambitions. He had been amused. "What can I get for you, Francine?"

"I'm feeling wicked today." Her slow wink made him pout. He was far too young for her tastes, but it didn't mean she couldn't appreciate the young man's kissable mouth. She sighed happily. "Bring me Earl Grey tea, please. A whole pot."

Henrique clutched his chest. "Oh, be still, my beating heart. A whole pot?"

"And an extra almond cookie," she said in her huskiest voice.

Henrique shuddered as he wrote it down. He composed himself and turned to Genevieve. "Doctor Lenard?"

Genevieve looked at Francine. "Shall we order lunch as well?"

"Sure. You first."

"Okay." Genevieve folded her hands neatly on her lap,

addressing Henrique as professionally as always. "No starter, only the salmon with a salad, please."

"Are you sure you don't want a starter?" He tried, but couldn't keep the teasing from his eyes.

Genevieve's hands relaxed as she studied him. Then she pointed at his eyes. "You're teasing me. Why are you teasing me? We're not friends."

Henrique's smile was sweet. He leaned slightly forward, not crowding Genevieve. "I think of us as almost-friends. That qualifies you for teasing."

"Oh." Genevieve thought about this. "I still don't want a starter."

They finished placing their orders, Francine flirting with Henrique the whole time. He left and they sat in silence for a few seconds. Francine loved Genevieve. She loved everything about her friend, from her absolute honesty to her lack of interest in learning idioms. Two Christmases ago, as a lark Vinnie had bought Genevieve a huge book with idioms. Genevieve had appreciated the gesture and had tried to read through it, but had told Francine that it wasn't good for her to read that book. Each idiom would result in hours of self-debate about the merits of using those words to describe situations and how inaccurate they were. After a week, Colin had pleaded with her to give up on it.

Genevieve's purity when expressing herself could be jarring to most people. To Francine, who had grown up in a convent with her nun-mother and adopted nun-aunts, that kind of honesty was a breeze. Her best friend did, however, lack the gentleness her mom and aunts wrapped their honesty in. But Francine didn't mind. She loved that she always knew where she stood with Genevieve. That was why the beautiful woman sitting across from her was Francine's first real female friend.

"You are staring at me." Genevieve's tone seldom deviated. The neutrality in which Genevieve expressed an opinion about the taste of a meal was the same tone she used for expressing her extreme displeasure or excitement. It had been hard for Francine to adapt to in the beginning. "Why?"

"You look gorgeous today."

"I look no different than any other day. My hair is the same. I wore this exact outfit sixteen days ago. Does that mean I looked gorgeous sixteen days ago as well?"

Francine laughed. "I'm sure you did."

"Then why didn't you tell me that day I looked gorgeous?"

"Maybe something is different today." There was. Francine tilted her head and opened her senses. She didn't read people like Genevieve did. She felt people. "Ah, something is different. You are excited about something. Your eyes are sparkling."

"It's not possible for a person's eyes to sparkle. It is merely light reflecting off one's corneas."

"Well, then your corneas are reflecting light really well today." Francine leaned back when Henrique brought her tea and Genevieve's green tea. She gave him a flirtatious wink and waited until he left to lean forward. "Why are you excited?"

"You are flawe…" Genevieve stopped. She moved the tea pot, placing it in the exact centre of her table setting. Again it was obvious how hard it was for her not to finish her sentence. "You are mistaken. I'm not excited."

"Hmm." Francine bit the inside of her lip. She was so tired of this.

"You are angry. Why? Because I'm not excited?"

"No, it's not that. Ooh, that's our food." Francine thanked all the gods that the kitchen had been very fast with their order today. Again Henrique was coming to her rescue.

Genevieve moved the tea pot to make space for her plate and nodded after inspecting her food. Henrique gave her a quick frown when he placed Francine's salad in front of her. She shook her head once and looked at him, batting her eyelashes. "This looks scrumptious. Thank you, Henrique."

He puffed out his chest, his smile playful. "Made from young vegetables. The best."

She laughed as he bowed and left. He was a wonderful young man. And her salad did look delicious.

"How are you?" Genevieve pushed the vegetables around her plate.

"I'm well. Yesterday, I hacked into that client's unhackable system. He said to Phillip that he didn't need additional insurance because no one could ever hack his system. You should've seen his face, girlfriend. We were sitting in the conference room when he said this to Phillip. While he was shooting his mouth off—"

"He what?" Genevieve dropped her fork.

"He was boasting." Since they'd moved into their new team room and didn't discuss cases with Genevieve on a daily basis, Francine had been slipping up more often, using euphemisms. She really wanted things back to what they were—Genevieve in the viewing room next to them, the team debriefing several times a day. She wanted the whole team to work together on cases again.

"And?" Genevieve picked up her utensil, her facial expression carefully schooled into interest.

Francine didn't answer. Instead she stared at Genevieve. This wasn't normal. Genevieve was never interested in the minutiae of anyone's life. Why was she asking for even more detail about a client she had no interest in? Genevieve only ever spent mental energy on something productive, not office gossip. Francine put her knife and fork down and placed both hands flat on the table. "This is it."

"It is what?" Genevieve looked up from her plate and her eyes widened. She must have registered Francine's expression. "What's wrong?"

"You." That one word came out too loud and Francine lowered her voice. "You are… wrong. You're not your usual self. You're being nice. You're not nice. Don't be nice."

"I don't understand. I was showing interest in you. Isn't that what friends do?"

"That's just it." Francine kept her voice lowered, but didn't hide her emotions. "You don't show fake interest in me. Our friendship is based on your interest in me being honest, real. You see when something is wrong because you read my face. Then you ask intrusive, rude questions until I answer you. That is always followed by the most brutal assessment of my situation with equally brutal insights. All of which I have grown to love because it's real. It's you. This"—Francine waved her hands towards Genevieve—"is not real."

Genevieve didn't move. Her expression didn't change. But Francine did notice an increase in her blinking. Thanks to her friendship with one of the best nonverbal experts in the world, she knew that meant Genevieve was thinking. Hard.

"Genevieve." Francine reached over and put her hand on Genevieve's side of the table, careful not to touch her. "I want my friend back."

Genevieve put her knife and fork down, stretched out her fingers and pressed the tips of her thumbs against the tips of her ring fingers. She stared at her fingers. "I've read nine books on friendship and they all say one should show interest in one's friends. One should never dismiss or invalidate a friend's feelings."

"You've never done that." Francine rolled her eyes. "You insult me, sure. But that's you calling me on my bullshit. You've never told me my emotions weren't real. You've told me it was irrational and beneath my intellect, but you've never dismissed anything I've said."

Genevieve was quiet for a long while. "I think you might have a different definition than I have for 'dismiss' and 'invalidate'. Telling you that your feelings don't count when we're discussing an issue is invalidating them."

Francine snorted. "Yeah, when we're talking about alien invasion, my emotions are so very, very important."

"Are you being sarcastic?" Genevieve narrowed her eyes, studying Francine's expression more closely.

"Duh!" Using Nikki's expression broke the tension in Genevieve's eyes.

She smiled. "I hate that word."

"I know." Francine touched Genevieve's hand with the tip of her finger. She needed the connection, but still respected Genevieve's intense dislike for physical contact. "I miss you."

"You see me almost every… That is not what you meant. Could you be more specific?"

"I miss you being you. And I miss working with you." Francine pulled her hand back and straightened. "We all miss you. The men all want you to join us in the new team room. I want you to be there. I want you to use your new viewing room. It's really fabulous. And it's easier to pop in and chat with you when you're a few feet away."

Genevieve picked up her fork and carefully broke the salmon apart. Then she separated the vegetables until she had all the fresh spinach leaves, cherry tomatoes, olives and cranberries in neat piles. When there was nothing more to organise, she pushed her plate away, again doing the thing with her thumbs and ring fingers. "I appear to have failed."

"In what?"

"My attempt to be a better friend. I should've gone with my rationale, not the advice of those books. They said that one should not intrude, one should respect one's friends' emotional space. That's why I haven't asked anyone why they looked so uncomfortable around me."

"Want to ask me some questions now?"

"Yes." The relief on Genevieve's face would've been funny if Francine didn't feel so guilty. Genevieve leaned closer, her hands relaxing. "First question, why are you feeling guilty?"

Francine smiled. Nothing stayed hidden from Genevieve. "I should've said something earlier. I knew things weren't right between us. Not just you and me, but all of us. Actually, I'm pissed off with myself. I know you well enough to know that if there was an issue, it is most likely ours."

"What issue? Is this the reason the team has kept me at a distance?"

"Shit." Francine had now completely lost her appetite and pushed her plate away. "God, we really suck at communicating. No one intended to keep you at a distance. Everyone intended to give you space."

"Why?"

"Because you were so overwhelmed by the last case."

"I was." Genevieve first pressed her thumbs to her ring fingers, then made tight fists and pushed them against her stomach. "I spent a week analysing how I was dealing with cases and came up with a new strategy."

Francine glanced at Genevieve's fists. "Does it have anything to do with your fingers?"

Genevieve relaxed her fists, placed her hands on the table and stared at them. "Yes, but I'm still working on it."

"Is it effective?" Whatever this 'it' was. How did her fingers help her cope?

Genevieve looked up. "Yes."

"Oh, come on, girlfriend. Give me more info on this finger-thing."

Genevieve lifted one hand, touched the tip of her thumb to the tip of her ring finger and took a deep breath. "For the last few months, I've been training my brain to respond to this physical action. Every time I felt safe, calm, relaxed or focussed, I would touch these fingers. I'm trying to recreate those feelings so I can handle this situation better."

"I don't need you to handle me better." Francine lifted her hand when Genevieve inhaled. "I know it's not what you said, but I need you to know that I've always been cool with our friendship."

Genevieve blinked a few times. "Thank you."

It was quiet for a few seconds and it was clear to Francine how much her friend was struggling. "Just say it. If I don't understand, I'll ask."

"I despise being constantly afraid." The words burst from Genevieve's lips. "I'm terrified something will happen to Colin when he goes on an assignment. That sends my thoughts to Vinnie's safety, then yours, Manny's, Phillip's and Nikki's. My mind goes into a loop, obsessing over ways I can ensure your physical safety, which is irrational and impossible. Then I agonise over your emotional wellbeing and the role I played in hurti—"

"Stop." Francine's sharp order halted her best friend's heartbreaking confession. "Does your finger-thing work?"

"Yes."

"Do it. Now." Francine watched as Genevieve touched the tips of her thumbs to her ring fingers. It took a few seconds, but the panic that had tightened Genevieve's features receded and her breathing slowed. "Wow. That's so cool."

"It works." Genevieve gave a shaky smile. "For now."

"Does this mean you can cope? That you can work with us again?"

Genevieve swallowed. "I've found a way to regain calm and focus, but I still fret over everyone. Sometimes the concern about your safety, your emotional wellbeing, everything consumes me. Working on cases that put our lives in danger exacerbated that to an unmanageable level. That's personally. Professionally, I was fine two weeks after the case, but no one else seemed fine. Except for Colin, everyone seemed uncomfortable around me. As if they were scared to say something."

"We were. We are all idiots. We thought the case really got to you and that you needed more time."

Genevieve shook her head. "You are not an idiot. None of

us are. You assumed I was psychologically damaged by the case. I assumed you no longer wanted me to work on cases. We all erred."

"Didn't Colin tell you what we were saying about you?"

"No." Genevieve thought about this for a moment. "He did tell me the books were not a good approach to my friendships and that I should be myself. That was what everyone needed."

"I hate it!"

"What? That I should be myself?"

"No." Francine rolled her eyes. "That a man can be so right."

"Why can't men be right?" Genevieve asked with sincere interest. It brought lightness and happiness to Francine's heart.

"No reason. I was just being flippant."

"I didn't think it was funny."

"I know. And it makes me so happy."

Genevieve frowned. "That is a very odd reaction."

"No, it's not. I'm happy that you are you." Francine clasped her hands together. "Please, please, please promise me that you'll burn those stupid friendship books."

"I can't burn them. They're all e-books." A small smile tugged at Genevieve's mouth. "But I have deleted most of them."

Genevieve seldom looked directly at anyone. Eye contact was a privilege she bestowed on very few. Francine's joy increased when Genevieve looked into her eyes for a few long seconds until they both smiled.

"I have to ask this for my peace of mind," Francine said.

"Are you really okay after the last case?"

"Yes." She grunted when she noticed Francine's expression. "You want me to expand, but I have nothing else to say. Maybe… I've been working very hard on separating my professional concerns from my personal worries."

Francine snorted. "Good luck with that."

"You're sarcastic again. Why?"

"Girlfriend, we worry about each other all the time. It's human. And don't give me that neurotypical crap. Give yourself permission to be human."

"I don't know how else to deal with this." Genevieve's soft admission punched Francine in the gut.

"Aw, honey. I think we're all just searching for a path in uncharted territory." Again she stretched her hand towards Genevieve. "You do what's right for you. We'll do what works for us and we'll all remember to talk. How's that for a solution?"

Genevieve nodded tightly. Her eyes were brighter and Francine wondered if Genevieve would ever allow herself to cry over something as silly as the love of a friend. But Francine knew her friend well enough to recognise the signs of severe discomfort. Francine straightened in her chair and flipped her hair over her shoulder. "Fabulous! Now you just need to come to the new team room. Your viewing room is an exact replica of the one you're still in."

Genevieve bit down on her lips for a few seconds, but couldn't hold it back. "Replica implies that it is exact. It's redundant to say 'exact replica'."

"I'll give you redundant." Francine couldn't let this opportunity go by untapped. "The new viewing room is an exact copied replicated duplication of your old room. There! Beat that!"

Genevieve stared at her with wide eyes. "You're being hyperbolic again. But you're happy."

"Yes, I am." Francine's smile was wide.

"Oh. Good." Genevieve cleared her throat. "I know the new viewing room looks similar and is even better in some ways. The cameras you've installed in the new rooms have very high-quality visuals."

"You've been watching us on the security cameras?" It shouldn't surprise Francine. Genevieve was at her best when she was observing others.

"Yes. Not often, but"—Genevieve blinked a few times, then pulled her shoulders back—"I've missed the companionship. A few times I watched you work."

"Not that we've been doing much. We've only had two small cases in the last four months. And I had that IT security thing for Phillip's client. Manny's been turning cases away."

"Except for this morning."

"Aha! I knew you were excited about something. You overheard our conversation, didn't you? You know that Manny agreed that we're going to look into my dad's case."

"I know of no such thing." A small frown pulled Genevieve's brows together. "What case do you have that involves your father? Is he well?"

"My dad is fine." Francine had told Genevieve a lot about her unorthodox childhood. Genevieve had found it fascinating that Francine's father was a priest, her mother a nun, and soon after her birth, they had agreed they weren't meant to be together. Both of them had always felt a calling to do God's work and had gone into their separate vocations. Francine still sometimes thought they'd tried to escape the reality of raising a child in a mouldy room in some favela while working a job with slave-labour wages. But she'd never regretted her upbringing. Few children were as loved and cared for as she'd been.

"Tell me about the case." Genevieve pulled her plate back and started eating the cherry tomatoes.

"No. You must first tell me why you are so excited. It's killing me not knowing what has your eyes sparkling."

"My eyes don't sparkle and I'm not excited." Genevieve dabbed at her mouth with the linen napkin. "But I know you won't stop, so I'll tell you why I appear to be more animated than usual."

"Animated. Really? Just call it excited and be done with it, girlfriend."

Genevieve ignored her. "I bought Nikki a spa voucher."

"Ooh, she's going to be so happy." Francine was surprised. Genevieve had nearly succeeded in putting Francine off spas for life when she'd recited the numerous germs growing in places like that. She'd also made a point of emphasising what a waste of time such frivolousness was—frivolousness both Nikki and Francine relished. "What does Colin say about it?"

Genevieve looked down. "He told me that it was a good idea. And he suggested for which spa I should get the voucher."

"Well, Nikki's going to love it."

"I hope so. It's to celebrate her exam results," Genevieve said with pride. "Nikki received her final results yesterday and did exceptionally well."

Francine leaned forward and pointed her manicured nail at Genevieve. "You are such a mommy."

"Buying a spa voucher has no maternal value."

"Of course it does. You and Colin treat that girl like my mom and dad treated me."

Genevieve froze. She blinked a few times and Francine wondered if she'd said something hurtful when Genevieve's eyes filled with tears. A few deep breaths later, Genevieve took a tissue from her handbag and carefully dabbed the corners of her eyes. "It was a spontaneous statement and your expression showed no deception markers. Do you really believe that?"

"Yes." Francine didn't even have to think about it. Genevieve and Colin gave Nikki the same unconditional acceptance and emotional safety Francine's parents had always given her.

"Thank you." Genevieve put her used tissue in a small plastic bag that also went to a designated place in her handbag. She swallowed twice. "I will treasure that compliment."

Genevieve had always expressed her approval of the relationship Francine had with her parents. Neither of them had pressured Francine into Christianity, into their lifestyles, and they'd always been proud of her. And she'd always had their unconditional support. It was the complete opposite to Genevieve's upbringing. Her parents had seen her autism as a blot on their perfect lives. They were the most pretentious people Francine had ever had the misfortune to meet. And Francine had met her fair share of pretentious people.

She hadn't realised how highly Genevieve regarded her parents until this moment. "My parents will love you. I wish you could meet them."

"I would like that."

"So, when are you going to give Nikki the voucher?"

"Tonight. Tell me about the case."

Francine knew that tone. Genevieve didn't want to talk more about the spa voucher. Leaving all that for later, Francine told Genevieve about her dad's call this morning, the cellar, the paintings, the recording. By the time she finished, Genevieve had cleared her plate and Francine was halfway through hers.

"What searches have you run on Mateas Almeida?"

"Only a basic bio. Then I came to lunch."

Genevieve folded her napkin and placed it on her plate. "We need to get back. We need to—"

"Have dessert," Francine interrupted. "The case can wait another five minutes. I want chocolate."

"You have plenty of chocolate in the top drawer of your desk."

"Not the same. I want chocolate dessert on a fancy plate and I want to eat it with heavy silverware."

Genevieve stared at her for a moment and sighed heavily. "Very well. But you shouldn't say it's going to take five minutes. Experience shows you will need at the very least twenty minutes to rhapsodise over your dessert."

Chapter FOUR

It was just after four when the ping of the elevator doors stopped the conversation in the new team room. As one, Francine and the men turned towards the elevator. Phillip, Nikki and Daniel had been the only other people who'd been to their new quarters since they'd moved here. It wasn't accessible to anyone else. Except Genevieve.

She stepped out of the elevator and Vinnie inhaled sharply. Of all of them, Francine thought Vinnie had missed working with Genevieve the most. He took a step towards Genevieve, beaming. "Jen-girl! You're here."

Genevieve walked into the new space, looked around and stopped a few feet from them. "I can't work here. Come to the old team room."

Without another word, she turned around and walked back to the elevator. The doors opened immediately and she left them in different degrees of shock.

"What the bleeding hell was that?" Manny got up from behind his desk.

"She wants us to meet her in the old team room." Colin walked to the elevator. "Didn't you hear her?"

"Frey, stop." Manny looked at Francine. "I thought you said she was working with us again, supermodel."

"She is. Maybe she saw something in here she didn't like and prefers the old rooms."

"But she's back." Vinnie joined Colin at the elevator. "It doesn't matter where we work, I'm just glad she's back."

"It does matter where we work, criminal." Manny's sombre tone reminded everyone why they'd needed to move their quarters.

Vinnie's shoulders dropped. "We have to get Jen-girl to come here. If we're dealing with violent bastards, she needs to be safe."

"We all need to be safe." Francine took her tablet and got up. "Let's go see what it would take to convince her to get her sexy butt in her newer, shinier, larger viewing room."

Manny grunted and followed her to join the other two. The elevator was too small for all four of them. They had done that as a security measure to ensure they would never again be ambushed by a team of bad guys fitting into one elevator. Francine waved Colin and Vinnie on when the elevator doors opened. She knew Colin wanted to be with Genevieve. As did Vinnie.

"You sure she's okay, supermodel?" Manny asked when the other two left.

"Yes." She'd told them about the conversation she'd had with Genevieve. Only the part pertaining to work. Genevieve's coping mechanism was hers to share. The whole time Francine had relayed her lunch chat, Colin had looked smug. Until Manny had reminded him they all had played a role in bringing trouble to Genevieve's door.

Manny's concern was on a different level than theirs though. He felt responsible for their safety as his team. The heavy weight he carried was visible in the dark rings under his eyes and his downturned mouth. Francine stepped into him, only a few millimetres preventing full-body contact. Ignoring his scowl, she played with his jacket's lapel. "Are you worried about me too?"

"I worry about everyone's safety."

She pouted. "Not even a teensy-weensy little bit more worried about me?"

"I'm a lot more worried about you." Manny grabbed her hand and pulled her flush against him. "With this kind of ridiculous behaviour, God knows what kind of trouble you will land yourself in. And I don't know if I'll be there to bail you out. You're not as big and ugly as the criminal or as wily as Frey."

Francine was stunned. Manny had always pushed her away. She ignored the feeling of being cocooned in safety and searched for a way to take back control. Manny wasn't that much taller than her when she was wearing her ten-centimetre boots. She only needed to stretch her neck a little to have her lips a breath away from his. "You have no idea just how wily I can be, handsome."

The elevator door pinged behind them, breaking the moment. For a second Francine thought Manny would kiss her just to make a point, but he dropped her hand and stepped into the elevator. He waited until she joined him and they were descending before he looked at her. "Never underestimate my wiliness, supermodel. You're still a babe."

"Ooh, handsome." Francine pressed her hand against her chest, fluttering her eyelids, her voice breathless. "You think I'm a babe?"

Manny glowered at her and turned to watch the digital numbers tracking their descent. Francine allowed herself a triumphant smile aimed at the back of his head. "And you can wipe that smile off your face, supermodel. You know exactly what I meant."

Francine didn't lose a beat. "I do. But when I say you're a babe, I mean you're a *babe*."

The doors opened and she pushed past Manny, her head high. She was itching to look around and see the expression on his face, but wanted to keep the upper hand. She hoped he was blushing. Or that the sexy vein on his forehead was throbbing with irritation. Oh, how she loved riling him.

Two security doors and another tense elevator ride later, they walked into Rousseau & Rousseau's main foyer. Francine felt like skipping to the old team room. In the elevator, she'd glanced at Manny. Not only had the vein on his forehead been prominent, but his face also had a red hue. It was a good day.

After the shooting incident, Phillip had had the interior completely redone. If possible, it looked even more affluent than before. Phillip and Colin had worked together with an interior designer to create an atmosphere of understated elegance. Francine loved the heavy wooden reception desk placed in front of bookshelves filled with leather-bound and antique books. The lush carpet under her feet brought more intimacy to the rooms and made her want to pull off her boots and walk around barefoot.

Phillip had unquestioningly accepted each of Colin's artwork recommendations. The interior decorator had been enthusiastic about each acquisition and had suggested darker walls with carefully placed lighting. The result was spectacular.

It was not Francine's style, but every time she came here, she wanted to grab an antique book and curl up on the leather sofa with a cup of hot chocolate. A pity Phillip wasn't open to the idea of having a hot chocolate fountain or at the very least a hot chocolate machine.

They walked into the old team room and Francine felt a pang of nostalgia. Compared to their new space, this room was cramped. But they'd had good times here. Genevieve, Colin and Vinnie were already seated in their usual places at the round table. Genevieve had her laptop open in front of her.

"Okay, Doc." Manny sat down heavily. "Tell us why you can't work in the new rooms."

"I don't know where everything is. Not yet. And none of my things are there." She clicked on her laptop's touchpad and looked up when Vinnie chuckled. "Why is that funny? Oh. Oh, my. Did you assume that I couldn't work there at all?"

"Yup."

"That was my miscommunication. I apologise. I'm a bit distracted by what I've found."

"What did you find, Doc?"

"Hello, everyone." Timothée Renaud, Phillip's personal assistant for the last eighteen months, walked in with a tray. "I thought you would like some snacks while you're working."

He put the tray down and started unloading steaming beverages and two large plates with cookies. Francine liked the fashion-conscious young man. He had proven himself not only trustworthy, but also reliable, even if he sometimes appeared frightened by his own shadow. He sneered as he put Manny's milky tea on the table. "Your poison, sir."

Manny's glare no longer had the same intimidating effect on Tim as it had had in the beginning. But Tim did take a step back.

Francine took a sip of her coffee and tilted her head. "Have you been working out, Tim?"

Manny's scowl intensified when Tim pushed his shoulders back, his defined pectoral muscles straining against his tailored light-blue shirt. "Can you see the difference?"

"You're looking very buff." And no longer as if a strong wind could pick him up and drop him a few streets away.

His chest puffed. "I've been working really—"

"How did you know we would be here?" Manny's clipped question deflated some of Tim's posture.

"I know everything." He turned his back on Manny and looked at Francine. "I saw you come in on the security monitors and hoped you would be here. I miss having you guys here. Most of you."

Manny muttered a rude reply. Tim froze for a second before scratching his smoothly shaven cheek with his middle finger. Francine laughed.

"Thank you, Tim." Colin took two cookies. "This is very welcome."

"Just holler if you need anything else." He took the tray, walked to the door and turned around. "I really miss having you around."

It had been a security decision to limit Tim's access to their new quarters. Francine had to admit also missing Tim's snappy outfits and fantastic pastries. As a compromise, there was an open video conferencing feed from Tim's computer to Francine's. Any time he needed to make contact, all he had to do was click on an icon on his computer.

"Doc? Your discovery?" Manny stirred a spoonful of sugar into his tea.

"I watched Francine's recording of her father three times. A few observations first. If you suspect Almeida's wife of killing her husband, you're wrong. Her grief was genuine and strong. I picked up no cues that would lead me to think she'd wished her husband ill. The sister showed great distress, but not because of Almeida's death. She hates seeing Milena in such emotional pain. I'm certain she would not do anything to cause her sister any harm, including killing Mateas Almeida."

"Did you get anything from the audio of the three men?"

"I'm much stronger in analysing body language. Words are meaningless to me without the context of non-verbal cues. Just going by the tone of their voices, I have observations, but none of it is concrete."

"Okay, now that you've given yourself a disclaimer." Manny leaned forward. "What did you hear, Doc?"

"Listen to the men when they noticed Father Tomás." Genevieve tapped on the laptop's touchpad and the recording came through the sound system.

"Quiet. The priest is coming," the deep voice from the recording said.

"Nah, it's just the local yokel. He only speaks Portuguese." It was the whiny voice Francine had taken an immediate dislike to.

"Are you sure?" Deep Voice asked.

"Yeah. He's been here for the last thirty-something years and I've never heard him speak anything but Portuguese. The old man doesn't even travel."

"I don't know about his linguistic skills, but I do know that he's never even taken a holiday." The third voice held an authority the others didn't. "The locals all talk about it. He's always at the church and available to his parishioners. He's harmless."

Genevieve stopped the recording. "The third man has a different accent than the others."

"So?" Manny asked.

"I found a recorded interview Mateas Almeida gave to a news channel three years ago. It took a long time, but I found one where he gave an interview in French. He had a similar accent to the first two men. We know that Almeida was born and grew up in Brazil. He never resided in another country, but has travelled extensively. He was a highly respected man in Brazil. Few people ever found a way out of the socioeconomic class they were born into. Because of this, he was interviewed by many Brazilian magazines, newspapers and other media outlets. In one of them, he talked about education and mentioned how important it is to know different languages. He said to succeed in the business world, he realised the importance of speaking English. Since the Chinese population—"

"His French accent, Doc?"

"Oh. I'm giving too much detail again. Okay. According to the article, he and three of his childhood friends took French lessons when they went to university." She bit down on her lips, but then the words burst out. "They are also fluent in English, Mandarin and Spanish."

"So you are assuming that these three men are his childhood friends?" Francine asked.

"No. But I'm considering it a possibility. I listened to Almeida's interview. His French pronunciation is the same as the first two men. The man who spoke last has different enunciation."

"Play him again," Colin said. He tilted his head and listened when Genevieve replayed the few sentences. Francine paid attention, but didn't have much hope. She'd never been good with recognising accents. Colin nodded when Genevieve stopped the recording. "He sounds local. As if he lived in France for a long time, probably Paris."

"I don't know." Genevieve leaned back in her chair. "There's something more."

Francine recognised the look on Genevieve's face. She was already gone. Francine called it the moments Genevieve disappeared into her head. Now was one of those times.

Genevieve was staring at the glass doors separating the team room from her viewing room. But Francine knew she wasn't seeing anything. She was most likely writing some Mozart concerto or symphony in her head. For some reason, that calmed her, helped her focus and apparently also helped form the neural paths needed to bring important connections from her secret brain to her public brain. At least that was how Francine translated Genevieve's very complicated and exhaustive explanation.

Manny lifted one eyebrow when Genevieve started rocking in her chair. "This is going to take a while."

"Be patient, Millard." Colin shifted, his body moving slightly in front of Genevieve.

"Of course I'm patient, you irritating thief."

"I got it." Genevieve glanced at the two men. "Thank you."

Manny raised his eyebrows and Colin shrugged. They didn't know what they'd said or done to help. For a few seconds, the only sound in the team room was Genevieve working on her laptop. Francine was curious how the usual bickering between Manny and Colin could've led to identifying a voice.

"Talk to us, Doc."

"Your arguing reminded me of when you arrested Colin." That had happened many years ago, after Manny had investigated Colin for a lengthy period. "I have the interview footage here."

"You have that recording?" Colin's surprise mirrored Manny's. "Why on earth did you look at that?"

"I watched it when I first met you," she said as if it should've been obvious. "I didn't trust you and needed as much information on you as possible before I allowed you in my apartment."

"You didn't allow me in, love."

"Because you persisted in breaking into my place for the first six months." She shook her head. "You're not pulling me into another silly debate about your recollection of our history."

Colin smiled and reached for her, but Genevieve moved away. He chuckled.

"Back off, Frey. Doc, for the love of all that is holy, please focus."

Genevieve looked up from her laptop and stared at Manny until his scowl lifted and he sighed again. She nodded once. "When you took Colin to the police station, an Interpol officer came to take him away."

"It was a sweet, sweet moment." Colin used that event often to irritate Manny. The moment Interpol had heard that Manny had arrested one of the most wanted international thieves, they had swooped in, using every legal trick they could to get their hands on Colin. They had been following Colin's thefts and had seen that he'd only stolen property that had already been stolen. He'd returned many paintings, sculptures and confidential documents to their original owners. Interpol had wanted him to work with them. To this day, only three people at Interpol knew Colin was still stealing back property. Now it was not only looted artwork and top-secret documents, but also data and other information that had landed in the wrong hands.

"Listen." Genevieve tapped her laptop's touchpad. She didn't turn the screen for them to watch.

A man's voice sounded in the room. "My apologies, Colonel Millard. I'm just here on orders. This is far above my pay grade. It doesn't help to shoot this messenger."

"It will make me feel much better." Even then Manny became surly when he was being crossed.

The other man laughed. "Please don't shoot me."

"No. Please, do shoot him." Colin's disdain was unmistakeable. It had taken a long time before he'd trusted Manny. "Then we can be roommates in prison. Oh, how I would love to room with you, Millard."

"Shut up, Frey." A shuffle of paper sounded. "Bloody hell. Come on. We're going to speak to the bosses."

Genevieve stopped the recording and Francine made a mental note to watch it later. She wanted to see what Manny looked like fifteen years ago.

"Play it again." Colin had the same intent focus he'd had earlier. Genevieve complied and again they listened to the short clip. When Genevieve stopped the recording, Colin's eyes were wide. "How did you know?"

She lifted one shoulder. "I remembered."

"When was the last time you listened to this?"

"A few seconds ago. Ah, you mean before that? Two years and seven months."

"And you remember his voice?" Colin looked at the rest of them. "Because this is the same man. It's the same voice."

"I heard it too," Vinnie said. "It's that little click sound he makes after he pauses a bit. Right, Jen-girl?"

"That is the most prominent similarity between the two voices. But it's also in the melody of his speech and the rhythm he uses."

"I'm feeling very blonde." Francine was in awe. "Seriously? You guys heard all of that. Handsome, did you also hear rhythms and melodies and clicks?"

"I was too busy reliving the worst day of my life." Manny ignored Colin and Vinnie's chuckles. "Doc, I don't like what you're implying here."

"I don't know what you think I'm implying. I'm saying that there are unmistakable similarities between these two voices. You don't have to like it, but it is true."

"What he means is he doesn't like that a law enforcement officer has gone to the dark side, love." Colin lifted his hand. "Is working with possible criminal elements."

"Murderers, if Almeida's wife is to be believed." Francine picked up her tablet and opened the Interpol network. It tickled her pink that she no longer had to hack into this agency's system. Her whole adult life, she'd been a white-hat hacker. For a short while in the beginning she'd veered into the black-hat scene, but then Colin and Vinnie had come into her life.

By then, Colin had already been working with Interpol. He'd been given an assignment to retrieve documents stolen from a safe in the American embassy in Paris. His initial search had revealed that an American lobbyist was behind the theft. He'd never received any support from Interpol in his work. They'd wanted to remain as far removed from his activities as possible. And that was when he'd contacted her. She was the only one who could get into the US State Department's system.

Francine had loved that challenge and had given him the name of the lobbyist within twenty minutes. It had thrilled and disgusted her that the lobbyist was the American ambassador's cousin, who had visited the ambassador the same week the document disappeared. The thrill came from the confirmation of her belief that everyone involved in politics was crooked. But she was truly disgusted that one family member could do this to another.

Two days after she'd helped Colin, a man reminding her of the mafia enforcers in the old movies appeared on her doorstep. He'd brought her payment from Colin, since she'd insisted on cash. The large, muscular man had pushed his way into her basement apartment, taken one look around and said his Auntie Helen would have a heart attack if she walked into such a sty. His insult was tempered by a wink and Francine had immediately liked him. Vinnie still called her apartment a sty every time he visited. Even when she'd cleaned and all her clothes were in her wardrobe.

"Aha!" Francine lifted her tablet. "Got him!"

"Haden Cardoso?" Genevieve asked.

"The one and only." She wasn't surprised that Genevieve had also identified the man. "What have you got on him?"

"Only his name. I remember it from Colin's arrest file."

"Well, this is strange." Francine tried again to get into Haden Cardoso's personnel file, but couldn't. She reached for Genevieve's computer and waited until she received a reluctant nod before she pulled it closer and tried again. "Give me a moment."

"What's wrong, supermodel?" Manny moved his chair closer to look at the laptop monitor. "Aw, hell. You're doing your hacking thing again."

Francine loved this challenge. For some reason, the Interpol system didn't want to give her access to this man's file. And Francine had clearance to go into all personnel files. Her conspiracy theory alarms were screaming at her, adding to her happiness.

In a complete anticlimax, she managed to bypass a few flimsy firewalls and protocols and opened the file. She pointed at the monitor. "There you go. Now we can see why Interpol didn't want us to see what Cardoso has been up to."

Manny pushed closer. "Haden Cardoso, born 14 March 1968 in Rio de Janeiro, Brazil."

"You were right, Jen-girl," Vinnie said. "He is the third voice."

"We don't know that yet. A birthplace is hardly concrete evidence."

"Oh, come on. Even you have to agree that with all of this—what do you always call it?—circumstantial evidence stacking up against the dude, we're getting to concrete very fast."

"Well, our Haden is"—Francine paused dramatically—"Lieutenant Haden Cardoso, who works for the DRPJ."

"The *Direction Régionale de Police Judiciaire de Paris*?" Manny's head jerked back. The DRPJ, or DPJ, was a unit of France's national police. They investigated all kinds of crimes, with central brigades taking the most complex cases in their areas of expertise. "When did Cardoso join them?"

Francine checked. "Hmm. He has an interesting history. He got his PhD in finance when he was twenty-five."

"That's young. Really young." Genevieve tilted her head to the side. "How did he end up with the DPJ?"

Francine scrolled down. "He was recruited by a French pharmaceutical company after he graduated. He worked in their headquarters in Rio for two years before they relocated him to their Paris office."

Colin slapped his thigh. "I was right. That's where he got his accent from."

"He worked there for six months when he approached the DPJ with irregularities he'd noticed in the company's books." Francine bounced in her chair. "A whistleblower. The man is a whistleblower."

"What crime?" Manny asked.

"Price-fixing across the Eurozone." She pointed at her laptop. "See! All these huge pharmaceutical companies are corrupt, stealing from the little peo—"

"Supermodel!"

"What? It's true. It proves everything I always say."

"Stop blathering and tell us when he joined the DPJ."

"Right after that case. He's been working in the… Ooh, Vin. You're going to love this." She took a deep breath. "The SDLCODF department."

"I hate frigging acronyms." Vinnie crossed his arms.

Everyone laughed. Except Genevieve. "What does it stand for?"

"In short? Organised and financial crime unit."

"And what? He's working undercover in Brazil?" Manny asked in disbelief. "He didn't strike me as the type."

"It looks as if he's been quite active as an undercover operative in the last twelve years. Before that he worked as a consultant for the DPJ as well as Interpol." She scrolled further down his file. "He goes into a company as a mid-level financial manager and soon that company is buried under indictments."

"Why is he in Brazil?" Vinnie asked.

"A joint operation with the white-collar crime division over at the Brazilian Federal Police Department." She smiled at Vinnie. "Or the DPF."

Genevieve sighed and reached for her computer. "It might be more prudent for me to read this information. It will be much faster."

She aligned the corners of her laptop to be the same exact distance from the edge of the round table. Only then did she focus on the laptop monitor. As usual, Francine marvelled at the speed Genevieve was reading. She scrolled through the pages, frowning or narrowing her eyes every now and then. "He's played an instrumental role in seven very large cases. In three of those, including his first case, he was the whistleblower who brought the cases to the DPJ. He appears to be a very good asset to the DPJ."

"Who's his handler?" Manny asked.

Genevieve scrolled back a few pages. "Brigadier Clarisse Rossi."

"Bloody, friggin' hell." Manny rubbed his hands hard over his face. "I talked to her this afternoon."

"You spoke to her?" Francine was surprised. "How did you know to phone her?"

"That's just it. I didn't. My first call was to a buddy of mine in Interpol who has contacts in Brazil. He made a few calls over there and was told that Almeida has been investigated a few times in the last twenty years. Each time it was for tax fraud and each time the authorities didn't find anything to nail him."

Colin leaned towards Genevieve. "He means they didn't have concrete evidence they could use in court."

Genevieve nodded.

"My buddy told me his contact in Brazil told him there was another investigation into Almeida at the moment," Manny continued. "A huge investigation and that he was surprised Interpol didn't know about this. Apparently, it's a joint operation between the DPJ and the DPF."

"I really hate acronyms," Vinnie grumbled.

"The Brazilian guy told my buddy I should contact Brigadier Rossi. When I did, she talked a lot, but gave me very little. When I put the phone down, all I knew was there was an open investigation into Mateas Almeida."

"You don't trust her." Genevieve narrowed her eyes. "There's more. What did she say?"

"She didn't say anything, but my gut is telling me something is off here."

Genevieve no longer berated them when they mentioned their gut feelings. After years of witnessing Vinnie, Manny and Colin's gut feelings proving valuable, she'd accepted it.

"Want me to check her out?" Francine reached for her tablet.

"No, supermodel. We can do this tomorrow. It's time we finish for the day."

Genevieve straightened. "Is it five o'clock already?"

"What are you so excited about?" Manny asked.

"I'm not excited." Genevieve glanced at Francine.

"It's all over your face, girlfriend." Francine smiled when Genevieve touched her face, then quickly dropped her hand.

"I bought Nikki a spa voucher and want to give it to her."

Vinnie laughed. "The little punk is going to love it. Can't wait to see her face."

"That's settled then." Manny got up. "I can't believe I'm going to be home before six. I might even watch a movie tonight."

Francine was also glad to leave early. She wanted to get to her work station at home and look further into this Haden person. Even though she had a similar system set up in the new team room, she still loved working from home. It made her feel sneaky and not like she was doing a legitimate investigation. She had no shame in admitting there was much more excitement in going places where you weren't supposed to.

Chapter FIVE

Francine shot up in her bed, looking around for whatever had woken her. After a heartbeat, the sound of church organs filled her bedroom again. She pushed her hand under her pillow and pulled out her smartphone. The screen was dark. No one was phoning her on this phone.

She shook her head to wake up and pushed her hand under her pillow again. The moment she touched her second phone, it vibrated against her hand, the organ music reaching a crescendo. A quick swipe over the screen and she brought it to her ear. "Mom, what's wrong?"

"Hello to you too, Fifi." Sister Agnes, Mother Superior at a convent twenty kilometres north of Rio de Janeiro—and Francine's mom—never raised her voice. But today her voice had a tremor in it. One Francine hadn't heard before.

"Mom." Francine searched her bedcovers for her other smartphone. She didn't remember dropping it. Just how far could it have gone? "Don't teach me manners now. It's three o'clock in the morning. You never phone me at this hour. What is wrong?"

"Your dad."

Francine froze. It felt like someone had put a vice around her chest and was busy squeezing the life out of her. "What happened?"

"He's in the hospital. He got mugged."

The pressure on her chest lifted and Francine exhaled a breath she hadn't realised she was holding. "Is he okay?"

Her mom and dad had a wonderful friendship. Rebelling against the impossible expectations of her wealthy French family, her mom had gone to Rio for the Mardi Gras during her first year at university. There she'd met Francine's dad and they immediately became friends. Caught up in the craziness that was the Mardi Gras, they quickly took their friendship to the next level.

That, and the outrage from Agnes' family for having the audacity to defy them and make a public spectacle of their long-standing good name, was all Agnes had needed to tear up her return ticket. Two months later, the whirlwind part of the romance had cooled down to a sweet friendship. By which time Francine had already been conceived.

Somewhere during the pregnancy and all the family fights, her mom and dad realised that neither were ready for getting married, working full-time at dead-end jobs and looking after a little baby.

It was Francine's eccentric, rich great-aunt who had jokingly suggested her mom go to a convent. Francine's mom had considered it and a week later walked into a convent. Her dad had seen how content Agnes was and soon joined the seminary. When Francine was born, her father was advised not to make contact with her.

But when Francine turned seven, she'd hacked into the birth registry to find the identity of the man her mother always described as the most wonderful man she'd ever met. Her mother had been horrified that Francine would think she'd deliberately kept this information from Francine. She hadn't. She'd been strongly advised by the Mother Superior of her convent to only give out this information if Francine asked.

Because Francine'd had such a great childhood with many nuns clucking over her, she'd never thought to ask. Until the day she was bored with her maths homework and tried to find something interesting to do.

By then her dad had moved to a parish closer to them. The priest he assisted had encouraged him to take his parental duties seriously. He'd visited the next day and every other day until she graduated.

In her whole life, she'd only seen her mom and dad argue about poetry, music and history. Never about her. One thing Francine had always known was how loved she was. She'd also learned the foundations of true friendship from her parents. That was why she wasn't surprised that her mother was with her dad at the hospital.

"He's a silly old man, Fifi. I can't believe he's excited about being mugged."

Francine found her first smartphone at her feet and swiped the screen. She had a bad feeling about this. "What did Daddy do?"

"He played Sherlock Holmes. He's been babbling so much that the nurses asked me to leave so they could patch him up."

"Patch him up? How bad is it, Mom?" Francine found the number she was looking for and sent Manny a three-word SMS that her dad had been mugged. It surprised her to see her hand trembling.

"He was punched a few times, so it's nothing too bad. They did manage to give him a black eye and a cut above his eyebrow."

"Nothing too bad? Mom, he was beaten. Did he tell you who did it?"

"He said you would know. Apparently he sent you photos."

Francine looked at the phone in her hand. Manny had replied to her SMS with a curt *5 min*, but she couldn't pay attention to that now. The icon blinked in the top bar and she tapped on it. Those eight photos must have been sent in the last two hours. When she'd gone to bed just after one, there had been no messages from her dad.

The first photo was badly zoomed, but she could clearly make out three men. Their postures were aggressive and they seemed really large. "I'm looking at the photos now, Mom. Was he beaten up by three men?"

"He said so. The nurses didn't believe him. Only a few bruises, a black eye and a small cut? That's not the work of three men."

Francine flipped through the photos until she found one that had better detail. Her stomach dropped. She was looking at a familiar face. "Mommy? I need your help."

"Anything, Fifi. What do you need?"

"Get Daddy away from the hospital and out of town. Please do it. These are dangerous people."

"This is a dangerous country, honey."

"Mom." Francine froze when she heard a single beep downstairs in her loft apartment. Wondering if her mind was playing tricks with her, she tilted her head, listening for any other invasive sounds.

"Fine. I'll talk to your dad." The hesitance in her mother's voice pulled her full attention back to the conversation. "But where are we supposed to go? And for how long?"

Francine thought for a moment. "Why don't you go visit Uncle Hugo?"

"That's seven hours by train!"

"I know." And that was why she wanted them there. "Please, Mom."

"I'll do it. And I'll also deal with your dad putting his nose where it doesn't belong."

"Thank you, Mom." Francine stiffened when she heard noises in the corridor outside her apartment. She opened her bedside drawer and grabbed the stun gun from all the other junk stuffed in there. "And please tell Dad to phone me. He's been ignoring my calls and I need to speak to him."

Francine got up and moved to the side of her bedroom door. Someone was at her front door and hadn't set off any of her many alarms.

"I'll get your dad to phone you. Ooh, the nurse is calling me. I'll speak to you soon, Fifi."

"Please be careful, Mom."

"Love you too, honey."

"Love you, Mom." Francine ended the call and ran back to her bed. In the messy bedside table, she found her taser and took that as well. The taser was great for getting an intruder from a distance. But if he needed any reminding that he wasn't welcome, she would get up real close with her stun gun and make sure he got the message.

Without turning on a light, she navigated down the stairs. She wanted to get that bastard before he got into her apartment. The front door opened and Francine dropped all efforts to remain quiet. She wasn't going to allow any trespasser to reach her downstairs living area. As she ran to the front door, she lifted both weapons, her left index finger ready to pull the trigger and taser the arsehole who dared break into her home.

The man had his back to her, closing her front door. Perfect. She ran another metre closer and pulled the trigger. Two small projectiles shot from the taser and entered the soft flesh of the man's buttocks just as he turned around.

"Oh, shit!" Francine took her finger off the trigger, but it was too late. "Oh, shit, shit, shit, shit!"

Manny fell to his knees, his hands stopping him from falling flat on his face. His breathing was heavy, his head hanging. Francine dropped both weapons and ran to him. When she'd bought the taser, she'd wondered if it was wise that she had control over how long the currents would enter someone's body. Now she was glad for it. It had been two seconds at most, but it had sent Manny to his knees. He was never going to forgive her for this.

"Manny, are you okay?" At forty-something, Manny was in great physical shape, but it didn't exclude him from experiencing heart problems after such a shock. She sat down on her haunches and touched his shoulder. "Talk to me."

Manny lifted his head, glaring at her. "What… the… holy… fucking… hell, supermodel?"

"You broke into my apartment."

He looked like it pained him to breathe. He took a few deep breaths and straightened, but remained on his knees. "I didn't break in, female. You gave me all the security codes. You gave me a bloody key!"

"It was for emergencies only." Even to her ears, this explanation came out with a complete lack of confidence.

Manny twisted and winced. He sucked a deep breath in through his teeth and jerked when he pulled out the first probe. For a second he didn't move. When he pulled out the second probe, Francine wished she'd never bought the stupid things. "Fuck, supermodel!"

"I'm sorry, Manny. I really thought you were breaking in."

"I told you I was going to be here in five minutes." Manny got up, favouring his left side, and held out his hand to Francine. As furious as he was, he still remained a gentleman. Francine took his hand and stood up.

"You didn't say you were going to be here. You only said 'five minutes'."

Manny glared at her for what felt like an eternity. With an irate grunt, he pushed past her and walked into her apartment. Limping slightly, he went straight to the coffee table next to her oversized sofa and turned on the lamp. Soft light bathed her apartment, but didn't soften the expression on Manny's face.

"You are not Doc. You should know that if you SMS me that your dad got mugged, I'm going to come around."

Francine walked to him, slightly miffed. "I should know no such thing. When did you ever do something like this?"

"Bloody hell, supermodel." Manny's glare intensified. "What are you wearing?"

Francine looked down at the t-shirt barely touching her thighs. "A t-shirt."

"A t-shirt? Your t-shirt? The t-shirt you got on the last ever holiday you took? When you went to Greece and bought an ugly t-shirt because the seventy-year-old shop owner wouldn't take no for an answer? That t-shirt?"

"I always wondered what the story was behind this shirt."

"It's my shirt!" he bellowed, his face red. He shook both hands at her and turned away.

Francine's eyes were drawn to the two red dots on his left butt. Renewed guilt ate at her. "You're going to need to look at that."

"At what?" He turned and when he saw where she was looking he shook his head emphatically. "No, you're not getting near my arse."

There was no way Francine was going to let that go. No amount of guilt was powerful enough to stop her. She took a step closer and lowered her eyelashes. "You know you want me near your arse, handsome. Don't be shy now."

"Go put on some clothes, woman." Manny took a step back, his mouth twisting when he rested his weight on his left leg.

"I'm covered."

"Barely." He looked even angrier. "No makeup, wearing a t-shirt that you stole from me God knows when, in possession of illegal weapons and you're still bloody beautiful."

Francine's mouth dropped open. Of all the things Manny could've said, this was completely unexpected. She closed her mouth, tried to think of a quick retort and came up empty.

"Cat got your tongue? Good. Now get upstairs, put on clothes that you paid for. I'm making tea." He didn't wait for her to respond. A good thing, Francine thought as she watched him limping to the kitchen. She still didn't have anything to say.

A few minutes later, she walked into the kitchen wearing yoga pants and his t-shirt. When she'd swiped it from a pile of clean laundry in his house one day, she'd never thought it would become her favourite sleep-shirt. The material was soft and the bright flowers were so unlike Manny that she smiled every time she imagined him wearing it. She wasn't going to take it off just because Grumpy said so.

He was standing with his back to her, lifting the teabag out of a cup.

"There's boxed milk in the top left cupboard."

He looked up and frowned when he saw her outfit. "I want my shirt back."

"And I want a pony." She sat by the restored wooden kitchen table. "Or a unicorn."

Manny brought two mugs to the table and carefully sat down across from her. There was already milk in his tea. Clearly, he'd found the milk while she had been in her room. The first time he'd visited her, he complained so much about having to drink black tea that she made sure she always had long-life milk in her cupboards. Manny was one of the few people ever to come into her apartment. He was the only one who drank milk in his tea.

"Supermodel, you can't have that taser. It's illegal."

"Illegal, schmegal."

"Have you declared it? Is it registered to your name?"

"Of course not. I'm not going to invite police inspection into my life." Francine took her tea. "But a girl's gotta protect herself, handsome. And in case you didn't notice, I have a taser *and* a stun gun."

"Bloody hell." He picked up his mug, put it down and picked it up again. "You… you're…"

"What? A pain in your arse?" She waited for it and wasn't

disappointed. Manny's lips twitched. "I saw it! You smiled! You're so strong and powerful, you won't even remember those little stings tomorrow."

Manny leaned forward. "Oh, I'll remember, supermodel. Don't think I will ever forget this."

"I would expect nothing less. Just please stop nagging about my self-defence system."

"System? What else have you got?" He lifted one hand, his palm towards her. "No, I don't want to know. You will brag about other illegalities in your apartment. I will want to arrest you and you'll beg me again to get my handcuffs out. My arse hurts. I can't handle that right now."

They smiled at each other. Moments like these were rare. Manny wasn't a man who smiled often. But when he did, it touched Francine's soul. His smile removed from his face a lifetime of chasing criminals, seeing the worst side of humanity and the cynicism that came with it. Instead, he looked younger, more carefree. And more attractive. When his smile came from genuine pleasure, the dimple in his right cheek was more pronounced. Like now.

"You—"

"I know that look, supermodel. You're going to say something to piss me off."

"I'm not!" She was. She was going to tell him he was handsome. It always pissed him off. Even when it was the truth.

Manny grunted and took a sip of his tea. "Tell me about your dad. Is he okay?"

Maybe it wasn't a good idea to piss him off even more. As it was, she was going to pay dearly for the taser incident. She played with her mug while telling him everything her mom had said. "I tried phoning my dad just now, but he didn't answer. He's most likely still being treated."

"Are you sure your mom will get him away?"

Francine snorted. "My dad and I have nothing on my mom in the stubborn department. She'll get him out of Dodge."

"Show me those photos your dad sent."

Francine found the photos on her phone and handed the device to Manny. He flipped through it, squinting to see past the bad quality of the photos. His eyes widened, then narrowed. With his thumb and forefinger, he stretched the image and Francine knew he'd found the one that had caught her attention as well.

"Are you looking at Lieutenant Cardoso?"

"That bloody bastard." Manny tapped on the screen and flipped through the other photos. "Your dad is not the best photographer."

"Or the best at listening to his daughter." She was going to give her dad a huge piece of her mind. "I can't believe he went after Lieutenant Cardoso. What was he thinking? I told him to stay out of this. And look at what happened. He got beaten up."

"But not killed." Manny put the phone down. "Like you said, he wasn't even badly injured."

"So you also think that is suspicious." She pushed her fingers through her hair. "I can't believe I just said that. My God, I'm thinking something isn't right because my dad came off lightly. This is screwing with my mind."

"Take a deep breath, supermodel." Manny took her mug from her trembling hands and put it next to his.

"I don't want to take a deep breath. I want my dad to listen to me. I want my mom and dad to be safe. I don't want to pull them into my world."

"Hey, you're not doing anything. Your dad is a big boy. He made the decision to go looking for Lieutenant Cardoso."

Francine frowned. "I don't even know if that's what he did. I wish he would call me back."

"Try again. Maybe he'll answer now." Manny waited while she dialled her dad again. The call went to voicemail. She closed her eyes against the frustration building up in her and left an angry message. When she looked up, Manny's eyebrows were raised. "Glad to see I'm not the only victim of that sharp tongue."

"Don't test me, handsome."

"Or what? You'll taser me again?"

"God." She dropped her head in both hands. "I'm never going to hear the end of this."

"Nope."

They sat in silence for a while. Francine was really worried about her dad. He was an intelligent man and was no stranger to violence. He worked in a country rife with it and with people who were victims of the standard crimes plaguing the lower-income classes as well as crimes related to the more affluent.

Her dad's congregation was an interesting mix of rich and poor, both classes sharing certain types of suffering. She was saddened every time her dad told her he'd lost another parishioner to domestic violence, alcoholism or something in that line. But she didn't know if her dad was prepared to deal with whatever situation Mateas Almeida's death had unleashed. Gang violence touched the poor while drive-by shootings were just as common amongst the rich. Murder was an effective way of eliminating competition.

"You're shaking."

Francine stretched out her fingers and stared at their uncontrollable trembling. She made tight fists and tucked her hands under her arms. "I'm angry."

"No, you're worried. And that makes you angry." Manny chewed the inside of his lip. He did that when he was looking for solutions. "I can bring your parents here."

"What?"

"You heard me. I can make a few calls and have your folks here this time tomorrow."

A telling sensation burned behind her eyes. She blinked a few times. "Legally?"

"It won't be exactly protocol, but I could make this work."

"You'd do that for me?" Francine was surprised Manny would suggest any action outside of the rules he lived by. He and Genevieve were the only people she'd met in her adult life who lived so strictly by the book. Even within their very unorthodox team, Manny constantly pushed them to find ways to work within the law as much as possible.

"I would."

She shook her head. "I can't let you violate your integrity, handsome. I'll find a way to get my parents to a safe place."

"And break how many laws in the process? No." He leaned towards her. "Let me do this, supermodel. I'll do it right. No one will later be arrested for fake passports, fake visas, credit card fraud and whatever else you have planned."

She smiled. "You think you know me so well."

"I do. I know your parents don't travel, so I don't know if their travel documents are up to date. I also know your paranoia about airport security will most likely have you phone one of Frey's forger friends to whip up a couple of passports. Am I right or am I right?"

"I'm going to charge my taser again."

He lowered his brow and looked at her. No glare. No annoyance. Just a penetrating look. "Let me do this, supermodel."

"I won't let you use this against me when I do something to annoy you."

"Agreed." He took his mug and took a long sip. "But I'll use the taser incident against you for a long time still."

"Whatever." She did her best Nikki imitation and teased another small smile from Manny.

The shock of her mom's phone call and the taser incident were slowly dissipating. Enough to allow Francine to notice things. Firstly, her tea. Manny had made her favourite orange-cinnamon tea. She'd once told him it was her comfort beverage. For himself he'd made average black tea and put his disgusting milk in it. She also took note of his outfit. He was wearing the tan trousers they'd bought three weeks ago, the tailored black shirt she'd given him for Christmas and the suede jacket she hated with the passion of a million suns. Many a day, she dreamed about shredding that eighties throwback with a blunt knife.

"Why are you dressed?" She leaned to the side to peek under the table. "You're wearing polished shoes. Why?"

"Because I don't like walking around barefoot when I'm not on a beach somewhere."

She put both hands flat on the table and narrowed her eyes. "You live a ten-minute drive from me. Why did it take you five minutes?"

"I drove fast. And I was on my way to work."

"It's three am, handsome. Why were you going to work?"

"Did you get your nosiness from your mother or father?" She leaned forward. "Answer me."

"I got a call from a pal of mine. Someone in the DPJ is panicking because we looked up Lieutenant Cardoso."

"Did your pal say who?" Francine wasn't going to ask the pal's name. She also had confidential informants whose identity she would protect with her life.

"No. Only that he'd heard through the grapevine that my call to Brazil and the DPJ rattled some cages."

"And what did you plan to do? Log into Interpol's database with your ID and rattle some more cages?"

"No need to be a smartarse. I was going to log in using your ID."

"Hah. Funny." She liked seeing Manny's lighter side. "Seriously, what was your plan?"

"Getting on the horn with a few trusted contacts and catching up on old times."

"Can I suggest a better plan?"

"Hacking into the DPJ's database is never going to trump speaking to people and getting human opinions, supermodel." He put his empty mug down. "But it will be a good addition to my plan. Maybe we could get a better picture of who this Cardoso bastard is and why this Rossi woman lied to me."

"Want to wait for me or meet me at the office? It will take me ten minutes to get ready."

"I'll wait. It will give me time to search for and seize more illegal weapons you hold on this premises."

Francine got up. "Careful where you search, handsome. You might not be ready for what you find."

He shook his head, took her half-empty cup and walked to the sink. "Ten minutes, supermodel. Ten minutes and I start searching under the clothes draped over your furniture."

She laughed and went up to her room. There would be time tomorrow or next week to catch up on her beauty sleep. Her curiosity had been triggered and she needed to sate it. She also needed to make sure her parents were safe.

Chapter SIX

It was a great feeling to have everyone back together. Vinnie was sitting at the round table for a change, not on the large sofa he'd bought and declared his work station. It was ugly. A bulky piece of furniture covered in dark blue fabric, it had space enough for Vinnie to stretch out and read his magazines. Francine had seen him hide two handguns and one assault rifle in and under the sofa. He'd pushed it in front of the windows, giving him a full view of the team room and the elevator. It wasn't a work station. It was a guard post.

Manny was paging through a small eighties-style black phonebook and Colin was at his desk, working on his computer. Francine glanced at Genevieve for the umpteenth time this morning. She was staring at her bank of monitors, engrossed in Lieutenant Cardoso's case files.

Vinnie, Colin and Genevieve had arrived shortly before seven this morning. Apparently they'd also had difficulty sleeping and had decided to come in early to look further into the case. But the main reason for coming in so early had been to move Genevieve's stuff from her old viewing room to the new one.

It had taken Manny, Vinnie and Colin less than an hour to move the three antique-looking cabinets into their new space.

But it had taken them another twenty minutes to move everything to the exact places Genevieve had insisted on. Francine had been highly entertained by it all. Especially when they'd moved the centre cabinet five millimetres to the left when Genevieve had explicitly asked them to move it only three millimetres.

Once the men had managed to move the bulky piece of furniture two millimetres back, Genevieve had slowly turned around the room a few times, inspecting everything. Even Francine had sighed in relief when Genevieve had nodded and sat down on her chair. While the men had been moving the furniture, Genevieve had admitted that the new viewing room was a vast improvement on the old one. The larger space made her feel less constricted. She might even allow the whole team to join her in her space. The old viewing room had been too small.

What had pleased Genevieve in particular had been Colin's new workspace. Previously, he had insisted in joining her in the viewing room because he couldn't share space with Manny for long periods. But he'd worked on a small desk pressed against the wall not to steal too much of Genevieve's room. Now, he had a beautiful oak desk, positioned similarly as before, but it was part of the arrangement instead of an intrusive addition.

Church bells broke the silence in the team room. Francine grabbed her second smartphone and looked at Manny. "It's my dad."

"Well, answer it." He got up and walked to her desk. For the last three hours, he had been chatting and laughing with old friends over the phone. So far, it hadn't been fruitful.

"It's not a call. It's an SMS." Francine opened the message and uttered a frustrated sound. She closed her fist around the phone and shook it towards Manny. "Why doesn't he phone me? What am I supposed to do with this?"

Manny grabbed her hand a second before she flung the phone against the wall. "Slow down, tiger. Let me see." He pried her fingers open and took the phone. "What the hell does this mean?"

"See? This man is driving me insane." She flicked her hair over her shoulder. "I have phoned him every twenty minutes since three o'clock this morning. Has he answered any of my calls? No. Has he reassured me he is fine? No. Has he sent me a cryptic message? Yes!"

"What cryptic message?" Genevieve stood in the doorway separating the team room from hers. The heavy glass doors made her viewing room soundproof when closed. Colin was standing next to her, frowning.

"'They're planning a heist in Strasbourg. Soon.'" Francine flicked her hair again. She didn't care that Genevieve might see this as a nervous gesture. She was beyond nervous. She was outraged. "That is what my dad sends me. Not who is planning this heist, what kind of heist or when. Just this."

"See if you can reach him." Manny nodded at her other phone. "Try your mom too."

"I've been phoning my mom, but her phone is turned off." Francine picked up her phone and pressed the last dialled number. She hadn't phoned anyone except her dad. Every twenty minutes. After the third ring, it went to voice mail. She swiped angrily at the screen to end the call. "Not answering. He might not want to speak to me, but he cannot hide from me. I'm tracking him."

"You're tracking your own dad?" Vinnie snorted. "Cold, man. Cold."

"Not cold. Worried sick." She hated feeling so powerless. "He's done this before. And every time we have huge arguments about this."

Genevieve walked closer. "When did he do this before?"

"When he… Oh, my God." Why had she not thought about this? "A few times, my dad helped the federal police with their investigations. He has a reputation in the area for being trustworthy, someone people can go to when they are too scared to report a crime at a police station. Many times he's been the go-between with the public and the police. So much so that the police trust him. A lot. I know of three cases he helped with that involved serious crimes. Those were the times my dad ignored my calls like he does now."

"What does that mean?" Genevieve asked. "Why did he ignore your calls in the past?"

Francine swallowed. "He was scared I would figure out how dangerous the situation was and he didn't want me poking around. He was trying to protect me."

"He's not ignoring you now." Vinnie put the magazine he was reading on the round table. "He sent you an SMS."

"That I don't understand!"

"You're being very melodramatic. More than usual." Genevieve stepped even closer, studying Francine's face. "Is it only the concern about your parents causing you to act out of character? Oh. Hmm. You're feeling guilty about something."

Francine lifted her hand to stop her best friend. For some crazy reason, she felt like confessing all her sins whenever Genevieve analysed her nonverbal cues. Needless to say, the first confession she wanted to make today was about this morning's unfortunate incident. "I'm not feeling guilty."

Manny's snort drew Genevieve's attention and she turned towards him. She stared at his face, back at Francine, again at Manny and finally settled on Francine. "What happened?"

There was no point trying to hide her feelings from the human lie detector. Francine pulled her shoulders back. "I accidentally tasered Manny."

The shocked silence that followed didn't last long. Vinnie was the first to react. It started with a chuckle, then another and soon developed into roaring laughter. "You… old man… taser… you…"

Colin's amusement was more directed at Manny's undisguised disgust when he saw the tears streaming down Vinnie's face. Francine tried to feel guilty, but couldn't. The men's mirth was too contagious. And an indignant Manny was too much fun. Unable to stop herself, she pointed at Manny's backside. "I shot him in the butt."

Vinnie fell forward onto the table, slapping his hand on the wood, laughing so hard that he was no longer making any sound. Only wheezing came from his heaving chest as he wiped the tears from his eyes. Colin walked to the closest chair and sat down, laughing more than Francine had seen in a long time. Even Genevieve was smiling, even though she looked questioningly from one friend to the next. If it took forever to gain Manny's forgiveness, it would be completely worth watching her friends sharing a moment like this.

Manny tried, but he couldn't hide the lightness that crept into his eyes. His usual frown was no longer evident and his tight lips twitched nonstop. Eventually all the chuckles died down to occasional sniggers. Vinnie cleared his throat and sighed happily. "Name it and I'll buy it for you, Francine. You've earned whatever spa treatment or high-heeled shoes or sparkly jewellery you want."

"No need to enjoy it so much, criminal."

"Aw, old man. I can't remember the last time anything gave me such deep, deep joy." Vinnie nodded towards Manny's backside. "Hurt like a son of bitch, didn't it?"

Manny's grunt sent Vinnie into another bout of laughter. He wiped more tears from his cheeks and looked at Francine. "Whatever you want, I'll get you two."

"Will you explain this later?" Genevieve's soft question made Francine giggle. Genevieve was standing next to Colin, looking down at him. "I don't understand why it's funny that Francine hurt Manny."

Colin grinned. "Yes, love. I'll explain later."

"Great. Then maybe we could get back to work." Manny returned to his desk.

Vinnie leaned towards Francine. "I want all the details. Everything."

"Put a sock in it, criminal. We have work to do." Manny was all business. "Doc, have you found something in those files?"

By the time Genevieve had approved the arrangement of her furniture, Francine had forwarded to her all Lieutenant Cardoso's files she'd found on the DPJ's system. Francine had made sure no one would know they were looking into

Lieutenant Cardoso. She had tiptoed in, copied those files and got out without leaving a single trace.

"Lieutenant Haden Cardoso has had impressive success since he started working for the DPJ. They've been very smart sending him undercover to all these different companies. He's been working two jobs for the last twelve years."

"What exactly is his role in the DPJ?" Manny asked.

"From what I gleaned in his files, his main focus has been his employment in the companies. The DPJ placed him in companies that had connections to illegal trades of some sort. One company he worked for was a front for a large organised crime syndicate. In every job, he went in as mid-management, never a position high enough to be remembered. After a few months, sometimes years, he had all the information needed for the DPJ to stop all the company's operations without compromising Lieutenant Cardoso's identity."

"Have you found a connection between Lieutenant Cardoso and Almeida?" Manny asked.

"There was nothing in his case files that indicated he'd had contact with Mateas Almeida. I have not yet had time to look for more." Genevieve leaned against the round table. "There appears to be circumstantial evidence linking the paintings in Almeida's cellar and Lieutenant Cardoso."

"Explain."

"In 2010, Lieutenant Cardoso was working on a case in Paris. At first, he was employed as the assistant to the accounting manager in an investment firm. After six months, he was given his own office and was put in charge of three accounts. The company had over three hundred clients, so dealing with only three accounts was significant. Lieutenant

Cardoso had gained the trust of one of the board members. These three accounts—"

"Doc, is this relevant to the case?"

Genevieve thought about it. "No. I apologise."

"Tell us the relevant stuff then."

She didn't answer immediately, appearing to consider what would be relevant.

"The relevant stuff is that Lieutenant Cardoso was in Paris when the paintings hanging in Almeida's cellar were stolen from the Paris Museum of Modern Art." Colin winked at Genevieve. "It is a weak link on its own, but putting him at the house where these paintings have most probably been for the last five years makes for a stronger connection. Add to that the photos Francine's dad sent... well, that connects him directly to those paintings, if you ask me."

"Doc?" Manny raised his eyebrows and waited for Genevieve.

"I don't like making connections without factual evidence." She nodded once. "But this circumstantial evidence is suspicious."

"Why did your dad send you those photos with Lieutenant Asshat in them?" Vinnie asked.

"I would ask him if I could get him to answer his phone." Francine took a moment to push down the frustration and intense concern for her parents. "This is guesswork, but I'm thinking that it might have been Lieutenant Cardoso who beat my dad up. I have no idea why he would do that. It's very possible that my dad had been asking questions. Or maybe my dad followed him somewhere. Hmm. No, he wouldn't have done that. But he would've asked too many questions."

"What are we thinking about Lieutenant Asshat?" Vinnie asked. "Is he undercover? Has he gone to the dark side? Did he beat up your dad to protect his cover?"

"That is pointless speculation." Genevieve gave Vinnie a reproving look.

"Show them the photos, supermodel."

"I managed to enhance the photos quite a lot." With one click, a large screen rolled down the wall opposite her. The men turned to look at it. Francine put four of the best photos on the screen. "The one top-left is definitely the best. My dad sent me eight photos, but the others are badly out of focus."

"That is unmistakeably Lieutenant Cardoso." Genevieve walked closer to the screen. "Do any of the other photos give us better visuals of these two men's faces?"

Francine brought the remaining photos up, three at the top and two at the bottom. The bottom two were mere blurs. If she hadn't seen the other photos, she would never have guessed those were people. The top three showed three men, but the phone had been too low when the photos were taken. These were headless photos.

"Hmm. Very interesting."

"What's interesting, Doctor Face-reader?" Manny narrowed his eyes at the screen. "What are you seeing?"

"Insufficient aggression. See here?" She pointed at Lieutenant Cardoso's body. "His hands are open, his arms are not very far away from his torso and his forearms aren't on full display. This is not the body language of an aggressive male."

"What does this mean, Doc?"

"I don't know. I don't have context."

"What can you tell from their facial expressions?" Francine brought back the four photos she had spent an hour enhancing.

Genevieve studied the photos for a few moments. "This doesn't make sense. See how the corners of Lieutenant Cardoso's mouth are turned down and his brows are pulled together? That's remorse. He's not displaying anger, aggression or any markers that would be normally associated with this event. The other men look more aggressive, but not angry."

"I was right." Vinnie gave a slow, superior nod. "Lieutenant Asshat beat your dad up as a warning."

Genevieve bit the insides of her lips for a second, then turned towards Vinnie. "His surname isn't Asshat. And you cannot possibly know what his motivation was for beating up Francine's dad or that he even did beat up Francine's dad. Speculation is a waste of time, Vinnie. You should know this by now. We would use our time more prudently if we looked at possible heist opportunities."

"So you think my dad's SMS is for real?"

"Is it in his character to build fantastical theories about conspiracies that have no basis?"

"Well, ouch." Francine smiled. "No, girlfriend. I got my conspiracy theory passion from my great-aunt. My dad is level-headed. Not like you. Rather like… like Colin."

"Um. Thank you?" Colin said.

"Oh, it was totally a compliment." In Francine's life, Colin played a huge stabilising role. She looked back at Genevieve. "My dad wouldn't send a message like this as a prank."

"Let's assume that your dad has info he couldn't share over the phone for some reason." Manny winced as soon as the words left his mouth. He got up and walked to Francine's desk, leaned against it and made sure she was looking at him before he continued. "I'm not saying your dad is in danger or anything like that. Don't go looking for ghosts. What I'm saying is that we should work on the assumption that his warning about a heist has credence. What do we do now, supermodel?"

She stared at him, drawing strength from his scowl. Worrying about her parents was a time and energy suck. Working would take her mind away from creating a million worst-case scenarios. She turned her chair to face her computer. "We find out what is worth stealing in Strasbourg."

"Wouldn't that list be a bit long?" Vinnie asked.

"Not if we look into any special exhibitions. Maybe something that's either opening or closing this week." Her fingers flew over her keyboard while she spoke. A few clicks with her mouse and her search pushed all her worries to the background.

"Eliminate exhibitions with large artwork," Colin said. "That's one of the few perks of making life-size statues. Those are seldom stolen."

The others discussed different art heists and the easiest way to escape with the most valuable artworks. Francine wasn't paying full attention, but did catch a few things that might help her eliminate more exhibitions. A few minutes later, Manny walked to the round table to join the men. Genevieve brought a chair closer and sat down next to Francine. Together they worked through every exhibition in the city. It was a tedious process, especially with Genevieve insisting on more details than Francine considered necessary. It took them an hour, but in the end Francine was glad Genevieve had been so nitpicky. It had made her see things she wouldn't have usually.

"We have a shortlist," Francine said over her shoulder. She leaned back in her chair, pleased that they were on the right track. Two clicks of her mouse later, she had the list on the large screen against the wall.

"Four possibilities," Manny said.

"Yes. The one you're looking at now is a personal collection of artwork. Monsieur Sauveterre has been collecting impressionist art for the last thirty years. His collection's estimated worth is ninety million euros." She changed windows to the next website. "The next option is this coin collection. There are Krugerrands, 1804 silver dollars worth around three million euros, fourteenth- and seventeenth-century coins, all valued in the millions. An easy collection to grab and run."

"Those are easy to take and even easier to transport," Colin said.

"What else do you have?" Manny asked.

"I have another private collection. It's antique knives and swords from the times before Christ until now. We're talking the low millions of euros, but something to consider."

"No." Colin shook his head. "I don't think so. Those things are clunky and hard to transport without damaging the blades or hilts. Paintings might be larger, but they are easier to transport safely. What's next?"

"I left my favourite for last." Francine smiled. "Antique jewellery."

"Can you be any more female?" Manny squinted at the large screen. "What are we looking at?"

"The Voclain Jewellery Museum's having a special Victorian exhibition."

"It's one of my favourite museums," Colin said. "It's spacious, well designed and their exhibits are always tasteful and worth seeing. This Victorian exhibition has necklaces, pendants, brooches, earrings, rings and everything else from that era. Many of these pieces are on loan from the Victoria and Albert Museum in London."

"What prices are we talking about, Frey?" Manny asked.

"Earrings worth thirty thousand euros, necklaces worth a hundred thousand. All in all, I think this exhibition has around eight hundred different pieces." Colin paused for a moment. "A rough estimate would put this exhibition at around three million euros. Then there is the permanent exhibition with another two thousand or so pieces of antique jewellery."

"Do you think it's worth stealing rather than, say, the coins?"

"If it were me?" Colin smiled when Manny nodded tightly. "I'd go for the coins. But… the jewellery exhibition is closing this week and they're transporting it. That always makes it easier to grab and run. It is hard to guess which they would go for. It would be helpful if I knew more about the thieves or who's hiring them. That would make it easier to know what they were targeting."

"I suggest we look into all four of these as possibilities," Genevieve said. "I will look for any connections between Lieutenant Cardoso and these exhibitions."

"I'll look into the owners of these collections, the museums, staff and any other dirt I can dig up." Francine loved opening closets and watching the skeletons tumble out.

"Try not to break too many laws, supermodel." Manny was silent for a few seconds, scratching his stubbled jaw. "Doc, what else can you tell me about Lieutenant Cardoso?"

"He's a very factual writer. His reports are detailed, with information and impressions of the people involved. The reports also have a pattern. When he starts a new job, he doesn't report frequently. It varies, but with each new job he sent reports once every seven to ten days. The more access he has to information, the more frequent his reports become. Up to a daily report in some cases."

"What's he working on at the moment?" Manny asked.

"There is very little mention of the investigation into Almeida, but there is a second investigation. Lieutenant Cardoso is also looking into a French electronics company that has a global reach. This is the company he's working for at present."

"It's a young company." Francine had recognised the name. "I reckon Cardoso's investigation into this company is only a reason for him to be in Brazil and his real beef is with Almeida."

"That is a gross supposition." Genevieve sounded outraged.

"Not that gross." Francine winked at her friend. "Cardoso's file states that his first priority in Brazil is to make contact with Almeida. His second is the company he's working for."

"Is Cardoso also mid-level management in this company?" Manny asked.

"Yes," Genevieve said. "He holds the third highest position in their small financial department in Rio."

"Ooh, Rio." Francine loved that city. "I miss the nightlife, the food, the music."

"Please, tell us more about his current case, Doc."

"He started seven months ago. In his second report, he mentions that he got the position because he is Brazilian." Genevieve stopped and bit down on the inside of her lips. Francine knew the gesture and wondered what astute observation Genevieve was reluctant to share because of a lack of evidence or facts or whatever reasons were holding her back.

"Doc." Manny drummed his fingers on the arm of his chair. "You might as well just say what you think."

"It's just an oddity. It doesn't mean anything."

"You saw it, love." Colin took her hand. "That means it goes against pattern and might be very important."

She thought about it, then nodded. "The last three months, his reports have been different. It started very subtly, but the change is much clearer in the last three reports. The first four months he sent his reports to Clarisse Rossi once a week. He reported his findings on the company as well as time he spent with Almeida. Then he didn't submit his usual weekly report on time. His next report seemed... censored. I don't know how else to put it. It doesn't have the same detailed information as all his previous reports. There is still a lot of information, but... I don't know. From then on, it seems as if he's withholding information."

"In what way, Doc?"

"His sentences have become terser. Where previously, he would share his opinions of the people they were looking into, now he only shares facts about them. He's not been sharing less information, just fewer personal observations."

"Maybe he was told to do that," Francine said.

"That is a possibility, but after almost twelve years of reports that were so similar in style, this caught my attention."

"Then I say we look into what happened three months ago." Manny rubbed his chin. "Did Brigadier Clarisse Rossi mention anything in her reports at the time?"

"No." Genevieve shook her head. "As before, she attached Lieutenant Cardoso's report to her weekly report when she sent it to her supervisor."

"What are your thoughts about Rossi, Doc?"

"That was going to be my next point. Her reports are also showing changes going back three months. Have you read her personnel file?"

"Yes." Manny frowned. "That's why I can't understand why she lied to me."

"Why?" Vinnie asked. "What's in her personnel file?"

"Clarisse Rossi has one of the highest closing rates for investigations. She's highly respected and has a pile of letters of commendation in her file. Her peer reviews describe her as someone with honour and integrity."

"What's changed in her reports?" Francine asked.

"Her language changed," Genevieve said. "She used to use a lot more positive adjectives describing the progress in the cases she was working on. I double-checked to make sure, but it was eighty-four days ago that the tone of her reports changed dramatically. That day, her reports were negative, the vocabulary sombre. She's not sent another positive report since."

"Curiouser and curiouser." Francine rubbed her hands. "So? What happened eighty-four days ago in the lives of Haden Cardoso and Clarisse Rossi?"

"I think it's time we bring her in and find out." Manny reached for his phone. "I'm sure she'll come in if we ask for her help on a case that involves her investigation."

Genevieve got up. "I'll look for recordings of Brigadier Rossi interviewing suspects. I might learn something more about her from it."

"Okay, people. We all have our work cut out for us. Let's get to it." Manny swiped his phone's screen, tapped on it a few times and held it to his ear. "Let's see if we can get this woman in our den."

Chapter SEVEN

"Lunch!" Vinnie's loud announcement jerked Francine out of her research. She glanced at the time. They'd been working five hours without a break. Often Genevieve became hyper-focussed and forgot about everything except what she was working on. Francine related well to that. It might not come from the same neurological function, but she'd been having so much fun slipping in and out of systems that she hadn't been paying attention to the time.

Vinnie and Nikki walked to the round table, both carrying large picnic baskets. The smell of home cooking had Francine out of her chair in a heartbeat. "Please tell me you made lasagne. I could do with some comfort food stuffed with carbs for energy."

"Sorry, Franny. I made ravioli."

"And I helped. This is a late lunch, so it's not huge. The big punk is baking something in the oven for dinner." Nikki took plates from Vinnie's basket and started setting the table. "I made the potato salad."

"Vinnie's recipe?" Francine loved the creamy potato salad. And she planned to make Vinnie pay for not sharing the recipe with her.

Nikki smiled sweetly. "I'm his favourite. He gave me the recipe."

Vinnie bumped Nikki out of the way with his hip and she punched him on his arm, most likely hurting her hand more than his hard biceps. When Nikki had landed in their lives, Francine hadn't foreseen liking the young girl this much. Her emotional openness and guilelessness gave the very wrong impression that she was naïve. Being raised by a father who'd controlled most of the weapons trafficked through France, Nikki had been exposed to a side of life most people didn't even know existed. Instead of making her suspicious and cynical, it had made her compassionate, astute and street-smart.

"Don't you dare share my Auntie Teresa's recipe with this philistine." Vinnie had a very low tolerance of Francine's attempts to improve his cooking. Not that she ever could. It was just so much fun suggesting spices or herbs she knew would never work. Without fail Vinnie tried to ignore her until he eventually chased her out of his kitchen with threats of violence. "She'll butcher it until it tastes like it comes out of a twenty-year-old tin forgotten in someone's scullery."

"Scullery?" Manny walked to the table. "I haven't heard that word in a long time. Seems too sophisticated for you, criminal."

"Up yours, old man." Vinnie placed two large serving dishes on thick placemats and stood back. "Lunch is served."

"Where's Doc G?" Nikki looked towards Genevieve's viewing room. "Is she coming?"

"Why don't you call her? She sealed the doors to watch some footage, so she didn't hear the Neanderthal shout." Francine looked down her nose at Vinnie.

Nikki smiled and walked to the glass doors. She was as part of the team as any of them, even if she didn't help them investigate cases. In the beginning, Francine had felt protective towards her, wanting to keep the dark side of humanity from her. But she'd soon learned that Nikki had seen her fair share of ugliness and had somehow found a way of not allowing it to taint her. They never shared cases with her, but also didn't censor anything when she was around. All of them knew no information would ever pass Nikki's lips.

Genevieve didn't take notice when Nikki entered the viewing room. Nikki gave Colin a sideways hug and walked over to where Genevieve sat unmoving, watching Clarisse Rossi interviewing a smartly dressed man. Nikki sat down on the chair next to Genevieve and said something so quietly, Francine couldn't hear. Genevieve looked away from the twelve monitors in front of her and smiled.

Francine wondered if Genevieve knew how expressive her face became whenever she was with Nikki. With any of them, Genevieve seldom expressed her emotions. When with Colin, she was more relaxed. But when she was with Nikki, she softened, the affection she had for Nikki showing.

In the viewing room, Genevieve's eyes widened at something Nikki whispered. Her expression sobered and as she opened her mouth, Nikki giggled. "Gotcha! Come on, the others are waiting for us. Vinnie and I brought food."

Colin got up, smiling and shaking his head at Nikki. "That was cruel."

"And funny." She leaned towards Genevieve, but didn't touch her. "Doc G's reaction was so serious."

"Getting a tattoo is a serious decision, Nikki." Genevieve got up and looked down at Nikki. "Especially getting one above your pubic bone."

"What the bloody hell?" Manny froze in his chair, panic creeping over his face.

"Punk?" Vinnie stood next to the table, his arms crossed, muscles bulging. "Talk."

Nikki walked right up to Vinnie, stopping only when she was toe to toe with him. She copied his posture, folding her arms and staring up at him. Facing Vinnie like this, she was eye level with his chest and half his width. It was comical to watch the standoff between them.

"Well?" Vinnie lowered his head, glaring at her. "What's this about getting a tattoo?"

"Oh, my God. You're like totally going to tell me I can't get one." She leaned closer to Vinnie until their noses touched. "I was pulling Doc G's leg, but now I'm thinking that I will get a huge arrow pointing down."

"Bloody hell!" Manny rubbed his hands hard over his face. "Doc, stop that girl before I have a coronary."

"You already have coronary arteries." Genevieve blinked a few times, her head tilted. "Why would you get extra blood vessels around your heart because Nikki's talking about a tattoo on her pubi—"

"Don't say that." Manny pressed his fists against his eyes. "Just don't."

Francine laughed and pulled Nikki away from Vinnie. "Way to go, chickadee. You've just scared ten years off Manny and given Vinnie a mild panic attack. From my heart, I thank you. You're the best."

"I know. Right?" Nikki giggled and went to stand next to Genevieve. "I was just kidding with Doc G. Last night, she gave me this totally awesome voucher for a spa. I didn't know what I was going to use it for and when I checked their website and saw they did tattoos… well, I thought it was funny."

"Not funny, little punk." Vinnie was still glaring at her. "Those things are permanent. If you're doing it, you'd better be sure you want it forever."

"You're not getting a tattoo." Manny stabbed the large spoon into the ravioli. "Not if I have a say in it."

Had Manny said this to Francine, she would've gotten two tattoos. The moment someone told her not to do something, it riled her up so much she immediately did the opposite. Not Nikki. She smiled sweetly at Manny. "I love you too, Manny."

Manny grunted as redness crept up his neck. He spooned more onto his plate, not looking away from the food. "Sit. Eat."

"I'm not staying." Nikki rubbed her hands together. "I'm meeting some friends for coffee. They're paying for my death by chocolate cake."

"Why?" Francine asked.

"I like totally kicked their butts in art history." She glanced at Genevieve and rolled her eyes. "Okay, I beat them by like two percent, but they're buying my cake."

"I do wish you'd stop using 'like' in every sentence." Genevieve's lips thinned. "It serves no other purpose in the sentence but to make you sound incapable of expressing yourself."

"Love you too, Doc G." She kissed the air next to Genevieve's cheek. "I'll see you at home. I'm off to choose like the biggest piece of cake."

Nikki waved at everyone and left with a bounce in her step. Francine sat down next to Manny and put a generous helping of potato salad on her plate. "You do know that she speaks like that because you ask her not to."

Genevieve sighed as she sat down. "I know. I try hard not to mention it, but sometimes it's too much. I can see the triumph in her expression every time I correct her."

"She's a little punk." The affection in Vinnie's voice softened his words.

For a short while no one spoke, the only sounds in the team room the cutlery against the plates. Vinnie's home cooking would beat any gourmet chef's creations. He had an amazing ability to bring out natural flavours with the perfect amount of whatever spices or herbs he used. Which was one of the reasons Francine enjoyed suggesting something that would be a disaster in the dish.

"Rossi is coming in tomorrow or the day after at the latest." Manny dished another helping onto his plate. "I got her boss on the phone and he promised she'll help us whatever way she can with the case."

Genevieve glanced at Manny, but didn't say anything. So Francine did. "You used the we-work-for-the-president card, didn't you?"

Manny shrugged. "She was avoiding my calls, so I did what I had to do."

"A man after my own heart."

"At least I didn't break any laws, supermodel." Manny glared at her. "Was it necessary to hack every single museum?"

"None of their websites gave me the info I needed. And I was not going to waste hours going through articles and back-page gossip columns to get information Genevieve would decimate in a nanosecond." Francine narrowed her eyes when

Genevieve didn't comment on her hyperbolic language. "Anyway. Want to hear what I found out or do you want to prance around on your high horse some more?"

This time Francine frowned when Genevieve didn't react. Genevieve didn't process verbal communication the same way Francine and the others around the table did. Non-neurotypicals took what they heard at face value. Wordplay held no amusement for them—only confusion.

Francine had had to eliminate as many metaphors and cultural references from her speech as possible. It had taught her how many euphemisms she used and she'd had to learn to express her thoughts clearly if she didn't want to spend an hour explaining herself. It had been illuminating, to say the least.

"What did you find out, supermodel?" Manny leaned back in his chair. He narrowed his eyes at Francine, glanced at Genevieve and looked back at Francine. She wasn't surprised that he'd also noticed Genevieve's lack of attention.

"I checked out the museums and that one gallery. It was a quick look, but I didn't find anything suspicious. Their finances look healthy, the staff's finances show no strange increase or alarming debts. No one is driving cars that are above their means and their accommodation fits their income. I'm sure I could find something if I spent more time on each place, but I don't think this is an inside job."

"Did you check out the husbands and wives?" Vinnie asked. "Sometimes it's not the person working there, but someone close to them who is the insider."

"I've had four places and only five hours, so no." Francine shook her head. "I didn't check out the spouses. My reasoning was that if the spouse had come into money or had money problems, it would show in some way in the staff member's life. All of them had a few extra euros in their bank accounts."

"Their bank accounts, supermodel?" Manny gave a resigned sigh. "Are you sure there are no irregularities?"

"Not where I looked."

"What do you think we should be looking at?"

"Which of those four options are the most attractive to steal."

Manny pushed his empty plate away. "Frey?"

"The coins or the jewellery." Colin put his knife and fork down. "I'd still rather go for the coins, but after looking at the antique jewellery in that exhibit, I think most thieves would go for the jewellery."

"I knew it!" Francine did a seated victory dance, ignoring Manny's annoyed look.

Colin smiled at Francine. "The jewellery might not be as quick to take as one painting, but they're much easier to get abroad without damage."

"Hmm. Doc? Do you have something for us? Did you find any link between Lieutenant Cardoso and any of the galleries?"

Everyone's attention turned to Genevieve, but she didn't notice. She was staring at the opposite wall, her hand moving slightly as if she was conducting a concerto. Francine knew the signs. This wasn't a shutdown, where Genevieve had no awareness of what was happening around her. She was merely lost in thought, most likely mentally playing one of Mozart's compositions to help her filter through all the information rushing through her mind.

Colin put his hand on Genevieve's forearm. "Jenny."

She inhaled sharply, her eyes jerking down to Colin's hand. She closed her eyes briefly and looked up. "My apologies. I was thinking."

"We know." Manny lifted both eyebrows. "Did you find a link between Lieutenant Cardoso and any of the museums or galleries?"

"No." Genevieve shifted in her chair. "Apart from the change in his communication, I have not found anything that appears suspicious."

"You've been watching footage of Clarisse Rossi." Francine knew Genevieve would never waste her time watching something that didn't warrant attention. "Is there something about her that's suspicious?"

"Yes, but it might not be suspicious in a criminal way." Genevieve paused. She did that before she tried to explain something in a way Francine and the others would understand. "Brigadier Rossi is an accomplished interrogator. She employs numerous techniques to gain the other person's trust and does it in a manner that is natural. That tells me she has an innate ability or that she's proficient at applying these techniques. I've watched her get confessions without people being aware they were implicating themselves or contradicting their previous account of whatever incident they were talking about. Even when she confronts them with their crime, she treats them with respect and it is returned."

"Okay, she's good. We get that." Manny was impatient as usual. "Now tell us what's wrong with her."

"I don't know. I think it might be personal, since there is no mention in her personnel file or any incident reports of a traumatic event three months ago." Genevieve looked towards her viewing room. "I watched eleven interviews she's had in the last year. Until three months ago, her conduct was as I described before. In the last three months, she loses attention while interviewing and she takes much longer to build rapport with the suspect. Her personal appearance also seems to have regressed. She's lost considerable weight, her hair is no longer as neatly styled and in the last interview, her shirt was un-ironed."

"What did you see on her face, Doc?"

"When she managed to put her full attention on the interview, her expressions were relevant to that. But when she lost focus, I saw fear, deep concern, sadness, confusion and anger."

"What do you make of that?" Francine asked. "It sounds like someone close to her died."

"I checked. There have been no deaths in her family. Colin checked her husband and children's social media pages and they appear to be upbeat, going about life as usual."

"I looked into her finances when we first talked about her." Francine raised her hand towards Manny without even looking at him. "Don't. Just don't, handsome. I believe that we learn the most from people by looking at their spending habits. Brigadier Rossi has the spending habits of a working mom. She buys clothes fit for teenagers, pays school fees and buys a lot of food. Her husband is an architect and earns a healthy salary. He pays the kids' tuition fees, including a very expensive university course for the oldest. There was nothing that raised red flags."

"Doc, I want you to sit in when we talk to her. We need to find out what happened three months ago that changed

Lieutenant Cardoso's writing and made Rossi lose weight." Manny turned towards Francine. "I want more info on her and her family."

Francine couldn't help herself. "Say it. I dare you. Say it."

"Bugger off, supermodel." Manny's lips thinned. "Just do what you're good at and report back."

"Sir! Yes, sir," she said in her huskiest voice. And smiled when Manny glowered at her. "We'll know her favourite ice-cream before she walks into the conference room."

Manny grunted, then frowned when he caught Genevieve staring at him. "What now, Doctor Face-reader?"

Genevieve inhaled, but shook her head as if she'd reconsidered what she was saying. She continued studying Manny, then looked at Francine, a small frown pulling her eyebrows together. Her eyes narrowed and she faced Manny. "Why are you worried about Francine? Is it because she shot you?"

"She did not shoot me." Manny slumped deeper into his chair and pushed his hands into his pockets. "She electrocuted me."

A quick comeback was on the tip of Francine's tongue, but she didn't say anything. If Genevieve saw concern in Manny's expression, there had to be something behind that. Francine leaned into his personal space. "Are you worried about me, handsome?"

"Of course I worry about you." He leaned away. "About how you would survive prison if you get convicted for all your cyber-trespassing."

"You're deflecting." Genevieve was really interested now. "Your concern has nothing to do with Francine being incarcerated. Do you have knowledge of something endangering her? No. Her family?"

"Doc." Manny sat up. "Bloody hell. Stop digging for trouble."

Cold fear gripped Francine's heart. She grabbed Manny's arm. "Is it my parents? What happened? Did your guys find them at Uncle Hugo's house?"

Manny closed his eyes briefly and took a deep breath. On the exhale, he shifted in his chair to face Francine. He put his hand over hers. "They weren't there."

"What do you mean they weren't there?" Francine didn't care that her voice was a bit louder and higher than usual. Guilt was eating at her. She'd been so busy having fun hacking and snooping, she'd not been checking her dad's GPS co-ordinates.

"When my guys got there, your uncle said they never arrived. They phoned him to tell him they'd made other plans."

"Why didn't they phone me?" Francine grabbed her phone next to her empty plate and swiped the screen. "Nothing. Not one phone call or SMS. I have to go there. I have to find them."

"Francine." Manny almost never called her by her name. The urgency he infused in it made her take a shuddering breath and look at him. He took both her hands and lowered his brow, his stare honest. "We'll find them. But you can't go rushing off God knows where. We don't even know if their lives are in danger."

"I forgot about them," she whispered. "I've been too busy working."

"You didn't forget about them. You were working to help them." He leaned closer to her. "We *will* find them. You know we are stronger when we do things together. You're not alone."

"You should've told me earlier."

"I wanted to give my contacts time to give a more complete report. I don't go off half-cocked."

Francine half-registered the opening Manny had given her to use the double entendre. She couldn't. The concern for her parents' wellbeing overwhelmed her senses. She squeezed Manny's hands, picked up her tablet and considered her next step.

"We'll find them." Vinnie got up. "I've got some contacts in Brazil. I'll get them on it immediately."

"Should I apologise?" Genevieve's soft question drew Francine's attention away from her tablet. Genevieve was looking at Colin.

"No," Francine said before Colin could answer. Her voice was strong. "Never apologise for being you, for asking questions, for keeping us honest."

"I wasn't lying, supermodel."

"I know, handsome. You were just being protective and cocky." She winked at him, but her attempt at humour didn't work. Her heart wasn't in it.

"I do feel regret for causing you such distress." Genevieve got up. "I will do what I can to help you find your parents."

"Thanks, girlfriend." Francine started tapping on her tablet. It didn't take her long to find what she was looking for. Her heart skipped a beat, then drummed against her breastbone. "This can't be right."

"What's that, supermodel?" Manny leaned over to look at her tablet, but she pulled it away from him.

"No. There must be a mistake." She checked the settings, double-checked everything else and stared wide-eyed at the device in her hands. "This is not possible."

"Supermodel!" Manny grabbed the tablet from her lax fingers. "What's this? GPS?"

"Yes. I stopped checking my dad's location when I got into the museum and gallery stuff."

"This is not Brazil."

"I know!" She sucked in air through her clenched teeth. "It's Strasbourg."

"The airport, to be exact." Manny looked up from the tablet. "Why is your father's phone at the Strasbourg International Airport?"

"That wily, conniving, sneaky priest." Francine rushed to her computer, ignoring Manny's demands to speak to him and Genevieve, Colin and Vinnie moving closer to see what she was doing. It wasn't the first time she'd gone where she didn't belong, but this time there was an urgency that helped her access the airport's security feeds in record time. One by one, she flicked through the different cameras, looking for the man she was going to throttle. Then hug.

"There." Genevieve stepped closer and pointed at the top left-hand corner of the computer monitor. "That couple looks out of place."

"Everyone looks out of place, Doc." Manny put his hand on Francine's shoulder. "Zoom in on them."

Francine did and shook her head. How on earth had Genevieve seen her mother and father in that sea of people? "It's them, all right."

"They're not wearing their clothes," Vinnie said.

"They don't only wear cassocks and habits, doofus." Francine stared at her mother, pointing at a few open chairs. She was wearing a blue floral skirt, a white blouse and a dark blue jacket. If it weren't for the unsightly sneakers, her mother would've passed for an elegant, middle-aged lady. Her dad looked like a professor with his brown trousers, flannel shirt and tweed jacket. Francine wanted to groan loudly when she saw the elbow patches as her dad walked to the chairs and sat down next to her mom. Like the vast majority of travellers moving in and out of the screen, her dad had his smartphone in his hand. Without looking anywhere specific, he lifted it slightly and waved it as if he was looking for a signal.

"They are waiting," Genevieve said.

Francine got up, glaring at the monitor. "Yes. He knows I would be looking. That's him waving at me."

"Well then, supermodel. Let's not keep them waiting." Manny gestured towards the elevator. "I'll drive."

Chapter EIGHT

Francine loved and hated airports. The thrill of pulling your luggage behind you, knowing that you were going to discover new places, meet new people and experience a new culture always got her heart pumping. She glanced up at the cameras she'd hacked less than an hour ago. That was what she hated. Being watched, checked, double-checked, inspected, recorded, remembered. It didn't sit well with her paranoid, conspiracy-theorising self.

She barely noticed the heads turning to look at her and Manny walking purposefully to the public area of the airport. Her tight designer jeans, white silk shirt and faux-leather jacket did not particularly make her stand out in the sea of well-dressed and not so well-dressed travellers. Neither was it her high-heeled red boots or her jewellery. It was their expressions.

They'd had an epic argument on the way here. Manny had been driving like a scared teenager and she'd told him so. Repeatedly. She'd wanted to get to the airport, to her parents, as soon as possible. Manny had wanted to observe the road rules. All of them. Now the scowl on his face was more severe than usual, his posture more upright. She made sure to have an irritating smile on her face and winked at him as much as she could. She wished she had her taser with her. Then her smile would be genuine.

She glanced at her tablet and saw her parents on the same bench they'd been on since she'd first tracked them there. Her mom was chatting to a lady on the bench next to her, smiling at the woman's two toddlers. Some of Francine's anger melted. She didn't really care how her parents had got here. In a few minutes she was going to hug them.

A tour group came through the doors, cutting off her view to the waiting area. Manny took her elbow and steered her through the excited tourists. The moment she saw her dad reading his book and her mom laughing at something one of the kids had said, what was left of her anger disappeared. She lengthened her strides. Manny let go of her arm, but didn't leave her side. Her mom looked up and saw them coming, her eyes and her smile widening.

"Fifi!" Francine's mother jumped up and ran to her. Francine got her height from her lanky dad, her mom a few centimetres shorter, but with enough personality to always appear seven feet tall. Her mom wrapped her arms around Francine, hugging her tight. These were the moments Francine was reminded how privileged she was. Her mom's arms tightened briefly before she leaned back to look into Francine's face. "Are those tears? Why on earth are you sad, Fifi?"

"Not sad, Mom. Happy to see you and Dad safe." And touched that her mom was speaking English, being considerate of Manny standing next to her.

Her mom leaned a bit closer. "You have to talk to him, Fifi. It took everything I had to get him to mind his own business."

"I can hear you, Sister Agnes." Francine's dad nudged her mom. "Let me hug my daughter."

"I'm so angry with you, Daddy." Francine threw her arms around her dad's neck and held him close. "I hope you're ready for a long lecture."

"I've had twelve hours of it on the plane, Fifi."

Francine pushed away from her dad to inspect his face. His left eyebrow was swollen, the three stitches above his bushy brow looking tender, but not red and infected. The bruising around his eye was only slightly visible against his olive skin. "You scared me, Daddy."

"Oh, pumpkin." Her dad pulled her into another hug. After a few seconds, he put his mouth close to her ear and whispered, "Is that your Manny? Why does he look so angry?"

Francine stepped back. Manny was standing next to her, his customary frown pulling his brow low. She took Manny's arm and pulled him closer. "This is Colonel Manfred Millard, Daddy. Manny, my mom and dad, Sister Agnes and Father Tomás."

Her dad was the same height as Manny, a few centimetres taller than Francine. Manny frequently used bad posture to create an image of absentmindedness and incompetence. She wanted to punch him in the arm when he slumped as he held out his hand to greet her mom. "Pleased to meet you, Sister Agnes."

"Oh, please." Francine's mom took Manny's hand in both hers and shook it warmly. "Call me Aggie. All my friends do."

"And you must call me Tomás." Francine's dad stood closer. Francine groaned, knowing what was coming. The argument in the car and her excitement to see her parents had made her forget to warn Manny. Her dad took Manny's right hand in his and pulled Manny a bit closer. He put his left hand on Manny's chest and bowed his head.

"What the…?" Manny looked at Francine. "What the bleeding… blazes is your dad doing?"

"Oh, don't mind him." Francine's mom waved her hand. "He's just feeling your heart."

"My what?" It was clear that Manny wanted to move as far away from her dad as he could. Yet he stood there, allowing the older man to rest his open hand on Manny's chest. He was still looking at Francine. "I see where you get it from."

"Get what from?"

Manny just snorted and looked pointedly first at her dad, then at her mom. He lifted one eyebrow and glowered at Francine while her dad stood with his head bowed. A few seconds later, her dad looked up, into Manny's eyes and nodded. "Good."

Francine knew this process too well. Her dad believed when he had his hand so close to someone's heart, he felt what kind of person he or she was. As her dad stepped away, it was clear that he'd made up his mind about Manny.

"Are you done, Daddy? Can we go?"

"All done, Fifi. He's a good man. You chose well."

Francine didn't know where her dad got the idea that Manny was hers. Even though she talked a lot about her friends, she knew she'd never given that impression. She glanced at her mom, who widened her eyes and lifted her shoulders. Francine rolled her eyes. "Come on, then. Manny parked fifty thousand miles away. It's going to take us forever to get to the car."

"Why don't I take your parents to the car and you can walk back, supermodel?" Manny stepped to her other side, putting her between him and her parents.

She smiled sweetly at him. "Sure. You can be alone in the car with them for the next half an hour going back into the city."

Her mother laughed. "I'm sure Colonel Millard can handle us."

"Manny, please." Manny looked around Francine to make eye contact with her mom. "Thanks for having faith in me, Aggie."

Francine's mom winked at Manny and started telling them about the people they'd seen and spoken to while waiting for Francine. This conversation continued until they reached Manny's car. Francine was intrigued that her parents didn't say a single thing about the flight, the people sitting next to them or even the food.

Her phone pinged and she took it from her red Furla handbag. As soon as she saw the message, she smiled. "Ooh! Vinnie said he's making dinner and that we should go to Genevieve's. Nikki's finished early with her friends and will be joining us."

"That would be lovely." Francine's dad got in the back of the car as soon as Manny put their small bags in the boot.

"Yes, I can't wait to meet Genevieve and little Nikki." Her mom joined her dad and closed the door, leaving Manny and Francine standing outside the car.

"We haven't talked about where your parents are going to stay." Manny leaned against the back of the car. "Want to take them to a hotel?"

"I haven't thought about it at all." She'd been too excited to have her parents here. The reason they were here pressed down on her, removing the happiness she had felt when she'd seen them in the terminal. "We need to keep them safe."

"They can stay in my place. No, don't argue. You can't put them up in your lah-di-dah loft. It's all open space and you don't have extra bedrooms. I have two bedrooms. I'll bunk down at Doc's and give your parents my place."

"Has anyone else seen your place?" A few months ago, Manny had asked Francine if she liked interior decorating. One look at his discomfort and Francine had clapped her hands in glee, agreeing to redecorate his entire house before he even had the chance to ask. It had been fun working around a strict budget and an even stricter owner. She'd had weeks of fun torturing Manny with suggestions of ruffles and lace. The end result had been simplicity, warm colours and no floral motifs.

"Apart from Frey breaking and entering, no one else has seen—"

"My masterful skills displayed? Ooh, my parents will love your place."

"Then it's settled."

"My dad was right, you know. You really are a good man." She leaned in. "And handsome to boot."

"Just get in the car, supermodel." He walked past her and opened the driver's door. "And warn me next time one of your family members is going to feel my heart."

She laughed and got in the passenger seat. Immediately, her mom asked about the weather prediction, worried her jacket wouldn't be warm enough. All the way to Genevieve's apartment in the city centre, they discussed the many different activities around the city. Sightseeing, visiting the many parks and going to the numerous historical churches were on her parents' list.

Traffic wasn't too bad until they reached the city centre. It was close to five o'clock, the roads filled with workers desperate to get away from their day jobs. Manny patiently manoeuvred his old sedan through the streets, listening to her mom and dad chatting about what they wanted to see first.

Francine knew Manny was leaving the real questions about her parents' presence in Strasbourg until they were with Genevieve. She didn't like the idea that her parents would be studied while answering Manny's intrusive questions. Her desire for them to be safe overrode that dislike and she became impatient to learn how and why they came to Strasbourg.

They were lucky to find parking close enough to Genevieve's building and got out. Her mom looked wide-eyed around her. "What a beautiful street. So quaint."

"Genevieve likes it here." Even though Francine was sure her friend hadn't bought the apartment because of the high-class eclecticist buildings and the old lampposts lining the street. When Francine had come here the first time, the street had reminded her of the way American movies always depicted French cities—romantic and atmospheric.

"Well, I can't wait to meet her." Her mom fell into step next to Manny. She chatted about innocuous things, her light manner putting Manny at ease and even eliciting a chuckle from him.

Her mom was like that. She brought smiles to everyone she crossed paths with. Her light-heartedness had caused a few negative situations in the convent. A few of her colleagues had been of the mindset that women of God had no place laughing or making light of life. Their calling was a serious one, to be treated with the utmost solemnity. Francine had been proud of her mom for persevering, even if her mom's smile had been sad sometimes. Eventually, those nuns had left for other, more serious convents and her mom had taken leadership. Theirs was a convent that promoted happiness in a society that frequently didn't experience much of it.

Soon they were in front of Genevieve's building. The moment Manny rang Genevieve's apartment number, the door was buzzed open. Francine was first out of the elevator, but didn't even get the chance to ring the doorbell.

The door flew open and Nikki ran into the hallway. "You're here!"

"Get back inside, punk," Vinnie called from inside the apartment. "And bring the guests with you."

"Hi! I'm Nikki." She grabbed Francine's mom and dad by the hand. "We'd better get inside."

Francine stood to the side to allow Nikki to pull her amused parents into the apartment. Manny shook his head and gestured for Francine to follow her parents. He locked the door as soon as everyone was inside the apartment.

Nikki was hugging Francine's mom. "I've heard so much about you. You're like the coolest nun in the history of nunnery."

Francine's mom laughed and hugged Nikki back. "I'm so happy to finally meet you."

"Fifi didn't tell us you were such a beautiful young woman." Francine's dad opened his arms and hugged Nikki tightly.

"Who's Fifi?" Genevieve stood next to Colin in the sitting area, watching the exchange with interest.

"Oh, you must be Genevieve." Francine's mom walked towards them. "Such a pleasure to meet you."

Genevieve leaned slightly back as if worried that Francine's mom might touch her. Colin took half a step forward, putting himself between the two women. "Aggie. It's so good to see you again."

"As gallant as always." Francine's mom hugged Colin and stepped back, looking at Genevieve. "Thank you for being such a wonderful friend to Fifi."

"I don't know a Fifi."

"Oh." Francine's mom laughed. "Francine. We call her Fifi. Thank goodness she stopped telling me I shouldn't call her that."

"As if you would." Francine put her arm around her mom's shoulders. "Genevieve, this is my mom, Aggie."

"I can see the resemblance." Genevieve looked between them. "The jawline, eyes and mouth are similar. You also share a lot of gestures, especially the hand gestures."

"I'm Tomás." Francine's dad joined them in the sitting area, holding out his hand to Colin. "Good to see you again, son."

"I wish it was under happier circumstances, but I'm glad you're here." Colin shook his hand warmly. "We must make time for chess while you're here."

"I would love that." Her dad looked at Genevieve. "A worthy opponent if ever I met one."

"You're not being entirely truthful." Genevieve tilted her head. "You consider him much better than you at chess."

Francine's dad chuckled. "It's like meeting God. Nothing but the truth will suffice."

Genevieve tensed for a second, studied Francine's dad's expression and relaxed. "I will try to minimise my observations."

"Oh, please don't." Francine's mom waved the suggestion away. "It's so refreshing to be expected to be truthful without all the euphemisms. I grow tired of constantly having to soften my honest opinions."

"You really didn't fall far from the tree." Manny sat down on one of the sofas and cleared his throat. "Francine, I mean Fifi here takes a lot after both her parents."

Francine stepped back, bringing her heel down on Manny's foot. He grunted loudly and she turned around, fake surprise on her face. "Oh, I'm sorry. Did I stand on your foot?"

"Don't start." Nikki pushed in between everyone. "I helped the big punk make dinner and it's almost ready. We're not going to argue around the table. Not when we have guests of honour."

"You must be tired after the long flight." Colin gestured at the sofa next to them, waiting until her parents were seated before he and Genevieve sat down next to Manny. "We'll have dinner, then you can settle in for the night."

"We haven't made arrangements for accommodation." Francine's mom turned to her. "We didn't even think to ask if we could stay with you."

"Of course you can stay with me, mom." She sat next to her mom and took her hand. "Always."

"Supermodel." Manny gave her an exasperated look before turning to her parents. "You will stay in my house for as long as you need to. Your daughter's place is not set up for guests."

"And half her wardrobe is draped over chairs, tables and doors. Right?" Francine's mom sighed happily. "She never understood the concept of a cupboard with doors."

"Where are you going to stay?" Francine's dad asked Manny.

"He'll have my room," Nikki said. "I was planning to go away for the weekend with a friend, so I'll just stay with her a few days before."

Genevieve inhaled sharply, with one hand she pressed her thumb to her ring finger and with the other she reached for Colin's hand. The last case had put Nikki in hospital, her life in grave danger. Francine often caught Genevieve controlling her responses to something Nikki said or did. Since she also felt overprotective of the young woman, she completely understood Genevieve's instinct to ban Nikki from ever leaving the house. Francine admired Genevieve's restraint and that she even encouraged Nikki to socialise.

"Dinner!" Vinnie's announcement brought Nikki out of her chair, hurrying to the dining room table and fussing with the setting. She showed Francine's mom and dad to their chairs and everyone else took their usual places at the table.

Manny didn't even wait until her parents had finished the main course before he put his knife and fork on his plate. "So? Did you two get here by legal means or did you take a page out of your daughter's book?"

"Hey!" Francine wanted to stab Manny with her fork. "That is uncalled for."

"It's all right, honey." Her mom didn't flinch under Manny's scrutiny. "I'm not surprised at the suspicion. I am surprised you waited so long to ask us about it."

"You didn't answer my question." Manny slumped in his chair. This time Francine wanted to stab him in the same place she'd tasered him this morning. How dare he use his bad-posture technique on her mom? Her mom!

"Yes, I didn't. Tomás?"

"We used forged passports." He reached into his jacket pocket and put two passports on the table.

Colin picked it up and paged through them. "Exceptional craftsmanship. Unless you are on a watch list, you would not get flagged for these."

"Give me those." Manny held out his hand and grabbed them as soon as Colin handed the two booklets to him. "Bloody hell. I knew this was going to bring us trouble."

"They were being smart, handsome." Francine leaned over to look at the passports. "British passports? Your accents will never sound British."

"Not all British people speak like Millard and you know it." Colin leaned forward. "Did you come here with a commercial airline?"

"No. They didn't." Genevieve pointed at her dad's face. "He's more nervous than Aggie."

"Nervous? Why?" Manny narrowed his eyes.

"Because you are treating them like criminals." Francine leaned over to put herself between Manny and her parents. "Daddy, how did you get here?"

"Francine, now—"

"Daddy!" She slapped her hand over her mouth. "What have you done?"

"You shouldn't have called her Francine." It looked like her mom was having fun. "And we will never get away with any deception here, Tomás. Tell them."

"Tell us what?" Francine's heart was racing. "Did they follow you here? Who knows you came here? Who else knows about your passport? You should turn your phones off. They could be tracking you as we speak."

Manny put his hand on her shoulder and pulled her back. "Take a breath, supermodel. Give them a chance to explain themselves."

"Tell them, Tomás." Francine's mom smiled at Genevieve. "She's going to see the truth in any case."

Her dad put his cutlery on his half-emptied plate. He dabbed at his mouth with the linen napkin and carefully placed it back on his lap. "Haden organised a private jet to bring us here."

"Haden Cardoso?" Manny straightened. "We understood he was the man who beat you up."

Francine's dad cleared his throat. "Not exactly. I was beaten up by thugs."

"And what, Daddy? You're best friends with this Cardoso man? I saw him on the photos you sent me. He was there when you were beaten up." Francine was livid. "Not everybody has good somewhere in their hearts, Daddy. You have to learn that."

Manny put his hand on her shoulder again and squeezed. His voice was much calmer when he said, "Tell us everything that happened."

Her dad looked at her. "I'm sorry, Fifi. I know you told me I shouldn't ask any questions, but… I thought a few wouldn't do any harm. I knew that Mateas had been in the area for the last eleven years, but I didn't know much about his life before that. So I asked Maria. She's the wife of the Almeidas' groundskeeper, Alex. Poorer people like to talk about the lives of the rich. In our community, those wealthy families' lives are more entertaining than the Brazilian soap operas.

"Anyway, Maria told me that Mateas Almeida met with three friends every month. They spent a lot of time in the garden and sometimes Alex overheard their conversations. What he'd been able to put together is that these men have been friends since childhood. They grew up in Favela da Rocinha, one of the slums in Rio. Alex didn't know how they got rich, but he'd drawn conclusions that they'd helped each other. Then one day, a few months ago, another man joined them. He was also a childhood friend, but not as well off as them."

Everyone was captivated by her dad's story. No one was eating or moving. Especially Genevieve. She studied Francine's dad with an intensity bordering on rudeness.

"This new man brought new energy to the group," her dad continued. "They laughed more and started planning a new trip. The new man owns property in France and that's why these men decided to plan a trip here. Apparently they hadn't been to France in five years. When I asked her if her husband knew any names, she could only remember the new man's. She said they called each other by nicknames, except for him. They called him Haden."

"Bloody hell." Manny nodded once. "What else did she tell you?"

"She said Alex told her Haden was different to the others. He seemed kinder, even when they made fun of his old car. I asked about the men, but Maria didn't know anything else, so I left. I went to the bakery and on my way home, I was mugged."

"Oh, Daddy." Francine hugged herself tightly. She didn't want to think that the outcome could've been so much different.

"I know you want me to listen to you, Fifi. But this might have been a blessing in disguise. Haden wasn't the one who got those thugs to try to scare me away from asking questions. He stopped them."

"He what?" Manny's question verbalised everyone's disbelieving expressions.

"As you can see, they didn't hurt Tomás badly." Francine's mom pointed at his face. "I saw the pictures of those men. Tomás could've looked much worse if they'd been serious."

"I think it was the collar. Even the worst of the worst generally don't touch priests." Francine's dad shrugged. "Well, they were just getting warmed up when a voice told them to stop."

"Haden." Francine thought about the photo her dad had taken. She reluctantly admired his presence of mind.

"He told them they'd better leave before he spread the word they were attacking men of God. He knew them by name and said he would tell their mothers." Francine's dad chuckled. "That got their attention and they ran. He told me to mind my own business and forget everything I'd heard and seen. I told him I wasn't going to."

"Daddy!"

He raised one hand. "I told him I wasn't going to and that I knew people who could help him. Fifi, he was the man who told the others to leave me alone when I was waiting for Enrico to pick me up. I knew then there was something special about him. When he was standing there in that alley, I knew I was right. I told him I knew he was in over his head and that I knew very powerful people."

"Why do you think Manny is powerful?" Genevieve asked.

"Excuse me?" Her dad frowned.

"You looked at Manny when you said you knew powerful people. Manny is not that powerful."

"Thanks, Doc." Manny huffed. "Don't mind her, Tomás. What happened next?"

"He walked away. I phoned Enrico, who took me to the hospital."

"Only after Enrico phoned me." Francine's mom picked up her knife and fork. "Enrico knows no one else can talk sense into your father's head."

"And using forged passports is sensible?" Manny asked. "How did you get from Cardoso walking away to him organising a private jet for you?"

"And where did you get these passports?" Francine tapped on the booklets with a manicured nail.

"After I spoke to you, just before I was released, Haden came to the hospital. He said that he'd looked into me and heard that I had a reputation for helping people. He wanted to know what I meant about knowing very powerful people. I told him I have contacts with people who work directly for one of the European heads of state. I didn't give him any information to compromise you or your team, Fifi."

"He's telling the truth." Genevieve nodded, not taking her eyes off Francine's dad.

"Thank you." Her dad smiled warmly at Genevieve. "It wasn't this easy to convince Haden I was being sincere though. Eventually your mom stepped in and that's when he caved. He asked if we could help him. He said he was working undercover and didn't know who he could trust anymore."

"Did he say who he's working for?" Colin asked.

"He refused. He said it would put our lives in bigger danger." Her dad made a dismissive sound. "That was his main reason for not accepting our help in the first place. He was trying to protect us. I told him God was all the protection I needed. God and my daughter."

"And her tasers." Vinnie looked at Manny and chuckled. "Priceless."

Francine's dad looked at the two men with a slight frown before he continued. "We asked him how we could help. He said he needed to be in France, that he needed to stop a heist. He was scared all his aliases had been compromised and couldn't travel with the passports he had."

"Oh, hell." Manny rubbed his hands over his eyes. "You commissioned *three* forged passports? Do you know that I should arrest you right now?"

"But you won't." Her dad winked at Manny. "Fifi told me you threaten to arrest her all the time."

"One of these days I will." Manny mumbled something about apples falling from trees.

"You got these and organised a private jet in under"—Vinnie glanced at his watch—"two hours? Impressive."

"The jet is all Haden's doing. I don't know whose it is, but he made one phone call and we were on our way to the airport as soon as we picked up our passports."

"Where is he now?"

Her dad hesitated.

"Daddy?"

"He doesn't know any of you. He doesn't know if you can be trusted."

"I don't give a bloody damn what he wants. We need to make sure he's safe."

"Can't we just give him this one evening to rest? He was so tired when we arrived."

"I don't plan to question him now." It was clear Manny intended to interrogate Haden soon. "But I want to get a protective detail on him."

"You're not being truthful." Genevieve frowned at Manny. "What do you plan to do with Haden?"

"Doc." Manny exhaled angrily. "For once…"

"He's a good man, Manny." Francine's dad looked straight at Manny, his eyes pleading. "Don't do anything to him."

"I'm not going to do anything to him." Manny pushed his hands deep into his pockets. "I plan to get Daniel to watch over him tonight. I don't want him disappearing on us."

"The leader of the GIPN team," Francine said softly, hoping her parents would remember the stories she'd told them about working with Daniel and his team.

"Very well then." Some of the concern left her dad's eyes. "Haden is staying in a guesthouse close to the Orangery, under the name Laurent Poulain."

"The alias I created for you?" Francine was surprised her dad would give something so important to a virtual stranger. "You really trust him, don't you?"

Her dad nodded. "I wish you would too. You'll see when you meet him—he's an honest man. And he's a very scared man."

Francine looked at her mom. "Daddy felt this man's heart, didn't he?"

Her mom smiled. "You know how he is, Fi."

"Have I been wrong yet?" Her dad's expression was serious. He truly had some special insight into people.

Francine sighed. "Not that I know of, Daddy."

"Then please be kind to this man."

"We'll make sure nothing happens to him, Tomás." Manny got up from the table, taking his smartphone from his pocket. "Tomorrow, we'll start working on finding out why he is such a scared man."

Chapter NINE

"What took you so long?" Manny stood in front of the elevator, his arms folded, his foot tapping. "I phoned you thirty minutes ago."

Francine stepped out of the elevator into Rousseau & Rousseau's reception area. "It's half past five in the morning, handsome. I needed to have a shower first."

"Not when I tell you to get your arse down here ASAP." Something had made Manny angry and he was taking it out on her. When he'd phoned her, it had felt like she had just fallen asleep. She'd been up until three this morning, looking for any and all information on Mateas Almeida, the school he went to and friends from those times. She'd found very little and had gone to bed exhausted, frustrated and worried about her parents.

"Not this morning, handsome. I'm not in the mood for your little hissy fit."

"My what?" He took a step closer to her, their noses almost touching. "I'm having a 'little hissy fit' because Lieutenant Cardoso slipped out in the early hours this morning. Daniel saw him just as he disappeared down the street of his guest house and couldn't catch up with him. I've been chasing that idiot since four this morning."

Francine hadn't had enough coffee for this. "It must be so hard doing your job at all hours of the morning. Poor baby."

"Don't push me, supermodel." Manny was standing too close. The temptation to reach up just a little and lick his nose was almost too much to resist. But the outrage that would follow stopped her.

She lifted one eyebrow. "Or what? You're going to huff and puff and blow my house down? Pah! You're no wolf. You're a cuddly bear. You're my cuddly-wuddly bear."

Manny's face turned red, the artery on his forehead becoming more prominent. His nostrils flared and he shook a finger at her. "You. You and your family. You're all trouble."

"Look at you talking sexy to me." She blew him a kiss. "So tell me. Where is Lieutenant Cardoso and what did my dad do to piss you off?"

"How do you…" Manny took a step back and breathed a few times deeply. "Security downstairs—"

"Downstairs where?"

"In this bloody building." Manny took another calming breath. "They phoned me an hour ago to tell me Lieutenant Cardoso was ringing the doorbell, insisting on speaking to Fifi."

"Seriously? How did he know to find me here?"

"Oh, you should really ask him." Something in his tone warned her.

"Okay, what did my dad do?"

"Daniel went to my place to check on your parents when Lieutenant Cardoso disappeared. He was there when I phoned him with the news that Cardoso was here. Your mom and dad then insisted on being here as well. As soon as they saw

Cardoso, they advised him to not answer any of my questions until you and Doc were here." He walked towards the reception desk, turned around and walked back, shaking his finger at her again. "You've got to get your parents under control."

Francine snorted. "Not happening. Been trying my whole life."

The elevator pinged behind her and the doors opened. Genevieve, Colin and Vinnie froze mid-step when they saw Manny and Francine. They stared at each other for a few moments before Colin tugged Genevieve's hand lightly and walked into the foyer. "Having a lovers' tiff, are we?"

"Fuck off, Frey."

Vinnie chuckled and walked to Francine. "Where's Lieutenant Asshat?"

Genevieve looked down the hallway. "Is he in the conference room?"

"With this one's parents." Manny glared at Francine. "Let's go find out what the hell he was doing here."

"He didn't tell you?" Genevieve asked.

Manny relayed the past two hours' events to the others. They stopped in front of the closed conference door. "Doc, I want you to read the blazes out of this guy."

"I have never done such a thing."

Manny's lips thinned. "I want you to do your face-reader thing, missy. And I want you to do it well."

"I always do it well."

Colin smirked. "You're really having a bad morning, aren't you, Millard? Why don't we just go in and do what each of us do best?"

Manny made a sound deep in his throat and opened the door. His shoulders dropped and his back hunched in the familiar slump. He put his hands in his trouser pockets and sauntered into the room. "Your friends have arrived."

"This is our daughter, Francine Bianchi." Francine's dad got up and pulled Francine closer to the man sitting on the far side of the table. "Fifi, this is Haden Cardoso."

Lieutenant Cardoso got up and held out his hand. "Pleased to meet you."

Francine shook her dad's hand from her elbow and calmly walked to Lieutenant Cardoso. She stopped in front of him and assessed him for a second. Then she pulled back her fist and punched him as hard as she could in the face.

The room exploded.

Francine's mom uttered a weird squeak, her dad gasped, Manny swore and Vinnie burst out laughing. Lieutenant Cardoso held the side of his face, his eyes blazing. That triggered more anger in Francine. How dare he be pissed off at her when he was the one who'd allowed her dad to be beaten up?

She pulled her fist back again, but strong arms grabbed her from behind and pulled her back. She struggled to get out of the firm hold clamping her arms against her body, not once taking her eyes off Haden Cardoso.

"Holy hell, supermodel. Calm down." Manny took a step back, taking her with him. She pushed her heel into his foot, wanting to unleash all her fury onto the man who was now beginning to look worried. Manny's hold tightened even more. "Calm down!"

Manny's order right next to her ear broke through her rare bout of aggression. She slumped against his chest and after a few deep breaths patted his thigh. "I'm calm."

"Good." He brought his mouth close to her ear. "You got him good, supermodel. That's my girl."

His approval removed some of the regret she felt for what her parents had just witnessed. She pulled her shoulders back and stood straight when Manny dropped his arms and stepped around to stand next to her. Keeping her eyes on Lieutenant Cardoso, she flicked her hair over her shoulder. "I'm not sorry."

"Fifi."

"No, Father Tomás." Lieutenant Cardoso took a tentative step towards Francine. "I understand your anger. I'm truly sorry for what happened to your father."

Francine didn't respond. She just stared at his face, wishing she had Genevieve's powers of observation.

"Remorse," Genevieve said softly. "It's genuine."

"She's right." He glanced at Genevieve, but quickly returned to Francine.

When she stepped closer, Manny's hand closed over her shoulder. Not holding her back, supporting her. She looked Lieutenant Cardoso straight in the eye. "If you ever do something like that to me or mine again, I will wipe you off this planet. And I don't mean physically. I mean digitally. You will not exist anywhere."

"Bloody hell, supermodel," Manny said and gently pulled her away from Lieutenant Cardoso. "You can't make those threats when there's law enforcement listening."

She jerked her shoulder from his hold. "Just saying it like it is."

"Got it." Lieutenant Cardoso nodded once and turned his attention towards Genevieve. "You look familiar."

"This is Doctor Genevieve Lenard," Francine's mom said. "She's Fifi's best friend."

"*The* Doctor Lenard? Wow. Such an honour." Lieutenant Cardoso stepped forward and held his hand out. He dropped his hand when Genevieve glared at it, leaning away from him. "I've attended three of your lectures. The first one really got me interested in nonverbal communication. Since then I've read up a lot about it and it's saved my life many times."

"How nice." There was no warmth in Manny's tone. He pointed at the table. "Let's sit down. It's time to talk."

"Yes." Lieutenant Cardoso sat down, some of the tension leaving his face. "Your team has an amazing reputation."

"How did you find us?" Francine crossed her arms, tucking her throbbing hand away. She didn't care that he might see it as defensive. It wasn't. It was to control the urge she had to punch him again. But her hand was hurting like a son of a hussy.

Manny took her by the elbow and pushed her into a chair. Everyone else sat down as well, Genevieve putting the most distance between her and Lieutenant Cardoso. She also chose a place that gave her the best observation point. Francine leaned forward. "Huh? How did you find us?"

"Your parents told me what a whiz you are with computers and that you have friends who are very powerful." Lieutenant Cardoso looked apologetically at Francine's dad. "When we landed here, you saw the poster advertising the Van Gogh exhibition and said your daughter would most likely take you there. That was when I put two and two together. The grapevine has it that you guys work art cases, that you have one of the best hackers in the world on your team. All I had to do was research where your headquarters are."

Lieutenant Cardoso moved his jaw and pressed his fingertips against the bruise starting to form. Francine felt like beating her chest. Bastard. A small voice in the back of her head tried to tell her Lieutenant Cardoso hadn't been the one punching her dad. He'd stopped the beating. Francine cursed the little voice into silence and glared at the lieutenant.

He was wearing well-worn jeans, a plain white t-shirt and a dark brown jacket. Francine couldn't help feeling smug that his drawn features took away from his fresh and relaxed appearance. Lieutenant Cardoso was one of those men who aged so well that the women at his school reunion would sigh wistfully and the men would stare daggers at him. He looked as if he hadn't slept well in months, yet he was able to figure out where to find Francine. Good-looking and smart. Son of a Brazilian strumpet.

"Well, aren't you just clever." Francine didn't like that it had been this easy to find them, but there was nothing she could do to stop their reputation from spreading. The information was freely available on the web. Once again, she was glad they had extensive security in place.

"You're all here." Daniel walked into the room and put a tray on the table, the smell of coffee filling the air. "I don't know how anyone takes their poison, so there's milk, sugar and spoons for everyone."

"We don't take poison." Genevieve looked suspiciously at the mug Daniel placed in front of her. A few times, Francine and Genevieve had discussed Daniel over lunch. Despite Francine having hacked into his life and knowing all his personal details, he was still an enigma. Always friendly, controlled, empathetic and one hell of a team leader. But he never gave any indication of his personal thoughts, of how he felt about any situation.

"Sorry, Genevieve." Laughter lines crinkled the corners of his eyes. "Bad, bad expression. I promise this coffee comes straight from your machine."

Francine wasn't surprised when Genevieve gently pushed the mug away. Almost two years ago, the coffee had indeed been poisoned, drugging Genevieve and Colin. They'd been abducted and it had been traumatic in many ways.

Lieutenant Cardoso didn't have any qualms about the coffee. He gratefully took a mug and sipped. "Thank you."

"Don't thank me yet." Daniel sat down next to Francine's dad. "You have a lot of questions to answer. First one. Why did you feel the need to sneak out in the small hours of the morning?"

"I wanted to see if you guys were as good as the rumours say you are." A small smile played around his lips. "Seems like I must've gotten lucky."

"Was Mateas Almeida murdered, Lieutenant Cardoso?" Manny's question wiped the smile off Lieutenant Cardoso's face. Clearly, Manny wasn't going to play games with their guest.

"I don't know." Lieutenant Cardoso put his mug on the table. "A heart attack at forty-seven is not unheard of. And please call me Haden."

"Will there be an autopsy?" Francine asked, her tone cold.

"I think Milena Almeida will insist on it," Francine's dad said. "They have a lot of power in the area and she is well-respected. I think her wishes will be granted."

"Not that we can believe the results." Francine had seen far too many cases that were covered up because someone had thrown enough money at the right official.

"Fifi, have faith. We'll get to the truth."

"Of course!" She slapped her hand to her forehead. "You are friends with the medical examiner."

"Why would anyone want to kill Almeida?" Manny asked.

For a few seconds Lieutenant Cardoso didn't say anything. He took another sip of his coffee, gathering his thoughts. He looked at Francine. "You checked out my history?"

"Of course."

"So you know that I grew up in Favela da Rocinha." He took another sip of coffee, not noticing her surprise. That information hadn't been in his file. "It was a difficult time, but it was easier with friends. There were six of us. Alex Santos, Marcos Gallo, Vitor Ribeiro, Raul Fernandez, Mateas and me. We constantly competed against each other. At first it was little-boy stuff—who could jump into the river in winter, who could run the fastest. By the time we reached puberty, we all wanted out of the life we had been born into. Our options were crime or education. So we started competing academically. I was third smartest. I could never even think to compete against Mateas and Marcos. They were too smart for all of us, for that life. A very long story short, we all got our degrees, got into business and became successful in our own rights."

"Except you didn't stay only in business," Manny said.

He lifted one shoulder. "I know it sounds stupid, but I knew working with the DPJ was what I was supposed to do."

"Still doesn't tell us why anyone wants Almeida dead." Manny slid down a bit lower in his chair.

"I lost the close contact I had with Marcos, Alex, Vitor, Raul and Mateas when I moved to Europe. We still stayed in touch, but nothing like before. I was here for eleven years when the bosses called me in. Apparently, my childhood friend, Mateas Almeida had been getting himself into all kinds of shady business deals. The Federal Police in Brazil couldn't get enough evidence against him. So they reached out to the DPJ because Mateas had branched out to international real-estate development, including projects in France. He'd partnered up with a French company that so far we only know to be a shell corporation.

"The Brazilian white-collar crime guys were sure Mateas was securing properties for Brazil's criminal elite in countries that don't extradite. When they approached the DPJ, I was the first who came to mind. They knew my history and asked if I'd be willing to exploit childhood contacts to infiltrate and find out what I could. I had just finished an assignment and didn't mind going back to Brazil. You know, home cooking and all that.

"I went in as a financial manager in a medium-sized Brazilian company. It was easy to secure the job and within a month I had an apartment and was back in Rio." He took a sip of his coffee. "I'd always been closer to Mateas than to the others, so it was easy to reconnect with him. Soon, I was back in the inner circle, but something was off. Marcos, Alex and Vitor didn't trust me and I didn't know why."

"Could they have known you're working for the DPJ?"

"No way." He looked at Francine. "How good is my cover?"

"Good." It was one of the reasons she suspected him of changing loyalties.

"The DPJ made sure I never made a name for myself in the corporate sector. Always lower on the totem pole, I was easy to forget." He gave a half-hearted laugh.

"Almeida?" Manny was becoming impatient.

Lieutenant Cardoso nodded. "The five of us got together twice a month. It was always at Mateas' estate, for privacy, they said. They often gave me hell for my small sedan and my mid-level job. After two months, they offered me a job working for them. I didn't want to seem too eager and delayed accepting."

"What happened?" Genevieve was staring at his mouth. "It made you sad."

"You're as good as I thought." He swallowed. "We were at Mateas' estate one day when Marcos asked me if I wanted to make some extra money. Of course, I said. Who wouldn't? That's when I knew I was in. They told me they had something huge planned, but they needed my help. They never gave me any specifics and I didn't want to push too much."

"Why did that make you sad?" Francine's mom asked.

"I didn't want the DPJ to be right about the only people who supported me throughout my childhood. God, I was so angry that all of them were getting their hands dirty."

"Did they tell you what they'd done before?" Colin asked.

"Two heists. One art heist in 2010 and a diamond heist in 2013."

"Knew it," Colin said softly.

"And you know that they're planning another heist? Here in Strasbourg?" Manny was watching Lieutenant Cardoso through narrowed eyes.

"Not one hundred percent. They haven't told me what exactly they were planning. All I know is that it involves drones, electronics and getting something out in a crate."

"Wait. What?" Francine sat up. "Drones? No one said anything about drones."

"As far as I gathered from hints in our conversations, they were going to use the drones to get into the building and disable the entire security system."

"What building? Where?" Daniel took his smartphone from one of the side pockets in his cargo pants.

"I don't know."

"What do you know?" Manny asked.

"Not much. Because of my history in France, they wanted me to organise the transport."

"I want all that detail." Francine picked up her tablet. "What, where, when. Everything."

"It's a crate that will go into the cargo hold of a commercial flight." He closed his eyes and gave the flight number. When he opened his eyes, he shrugged. "I think it's a decoy."

"Do you now." Manny's lips were pressed tightly together. "You're doing a pretty good job derailing this conversation, taking the attention away from Almeida's murder."

"Not intentionally." Lieutenant Cardoso raised both hands. "There is just so much to tell."

"Then tell."

Francine swiped her tablet screen and started working. She divided her attention between running searches and making sure she didn't miss any nuances in the conversation. Anything Lieutenant Cardoso said could help narrow down her search.

"Five months ago, Mateas' cousin died. For some reason it shook him."

"I remember that," Francine's dad said. "Before that, he came to confession once every three months or so. After that sad event, he started coming weekly."

"Did he confess something we need to know?" Manny asked.

"Nothing criminal. Only the regrets he had about decisions he made in his personal life, lies he told his wife, lies he told his friends. He was never specific." Her dad frowned at Francine. "What? I'm not breaking any laws or vows or ethics here."

"I didn't say anything."

"You did." Genevieve waved her index finger around Francine's face. "Your widened eyes indicated shock, then your smile indicated pride."

"Doc. Not now." Manny turned back to Lieutenant Cardoso. "What happened after this cousin's death?"

"He wanted out. He said he had enough money, he didn't need to do this and that everyone had what they deserved. From the conversations, these guys planned and executed the heists because they thought they were smarter than even the best law enforcement agencies in the world. They did it because they could."

"But?" Manny prompted when he paused.

"I didn't understand what he meant about everyone having what they deserved. Marcos, Alex and Vitor's reactions to that were far too strong. They were furious when he said that. That was when I knew there was a story behind that statement—a story I didn't know."

"They were angry enough about it to kill him?" Daniel asked.

"Not about what he'd said, no. I think it was because he wanted to pull out. He only mentioned it once more when I was with them and they quickly shot him down, saying they were not going to have that discussion again."

"Which means they talked about it when you weren't there."

"That's what I assumed." Lieutenant Cardoso chewed his lip for a while. "You guys don't know any of this?"

"No." Manny went still. "Should we?"

Lieutenant Cardoso nodded. "This was all in my reports."

"What reports?" Francine lifted her tablet. "I read the reports you sent to Brigadier Clarisse Rossi and there's no mention of heists or drones or any of the stuff you just told us about."

"Fuck." This was the first time Lieutenant Cardoso lost his composure. "I knew it! I knew this wasn't getting back to the DPJ."

"Speak." Manny didn't move, his quiet order menacing.

"I waited with this intel. I wanted to make sure I wasn't being emotional about it, so I only sent in a report with this information about three months ago. By then, Marcos, Alex and Vitor had become more authoritative, listening less to Mateas. The dynamics had shifted and I knew they didn't trust Mateas as much anymore."

"Did they trust you?"

"In hindsight, not as much as I thought."

"Now do you think you could've been made?"

"No." He shook his head with certainty. "My cover was... is... good. They didn't trust me because they thought

I wasn't smart enough or didn't have big enough balls."

"What does the size of your testicles have to do with their trust?" Genevieve's frown intensified when everyone except Lieutenant Cardoso laughed.

Colin kissed her on her cheek. "An expression, love."

"I know that. Vinnie uses it often, so I researched it. My question to Lieutenant Cardoso is why his apparent lack of testosterone-induced courage would negatively affect their trust."

"Um… I think they thought I would back out when the pressure became too much. When they brought me in on their scheme, Marcos Gallo said that my lack of career advancement showed I was weak. Too weak to deal with their secrets. He was the one insisting that I wasn't given all the details. I pretended that it didn't matter to me. That I was just there for the friendship and this adventure."

"What happened three months ago?" Genevieve asked.

"Nothing specific. No, wait. That was when I sent this intel in. Yes, it was about three months ago. And that's when Clarisse got all weird on me."

"What do you mean weird?" Manny asked.

"She's been my handler for the last six years. We were a strong team and I always knew she had my back. She also has been very quick with her communication. I would send in a report and at the most an hour later would get confirmation of receipt. It didn't matter whether it was afternoon, evening or two o'clock in the morning. She would always respond with a quick thank you." He briefly closed his eyes and shook his head. "That was the first time I had to wait twenty-four hours before she responded."

"What did she say?"

"The usual. She got it and thank you. But it didn't sit right with me, you know? It made me pay attention. It was like that day was a turning point. After that, she didn't contact me as often. When we spoke on the phone, she was evasive and rushed to finish the call. There was none of that before." He took another sip of coffee. "At first, I thought she might have a situation at work or at home. I asked a trusted contact and he checked her out, came back to me and said there was nothing out of the ordinary in her life. Not personally or professionally. So I left it at that."

"You suspect something," Genevieve said.

"Hell, yes. When no one asked any questions about a possible heist or the use of drones, you bet I got suspicious. I asked her once about it and her reaction was so evasive that I immediately backed off. I knew something was wrong and wasn't about to poke a sleeping bear."

"Expression," Colin said softly to Genevieve. She nodded, not looking away from Lieutenant Cardoso's face.

"Whatever is going down this week, you can be sure Clarisse is involved in it."

Manny's phone pinged. A second later, Daniel's phone rang. He didn't get up when he answered with a terse greeting. Francine was watching his face become expressionless when her tablet vibrated with an update. "Oh, my God!"

"What's happening?" Lieutenant Cardoso had a white-knuckle grip on the armrests of his chair, his jaw tight.

"There's been a heist." Francine was reading the real-time transcript of the Voclain Jewellery Museum's security call to the police.

"Holy hell." Manny pressed his fist against his temple, staring at the screen of his smartphone. "Two million euros' worth of antique jewellery has been stolen from the Voclain Jewellery Museum."

"You totally called it, dude." Vinnie nodded at Colin.

"Did you know about this?" Manny got up, rested his fists on the table and leaned towards Lieutenant Cardoso. "So help me, if you knew about this—"

"I didn't. I swear! The container is booked for the end of the week. I thought they were planning this for Friday."

"I'm off." Daniel's phone rang again. He answered it with a quick order to hold. He lowered the phone. "I'm securing the scene and then I want you there."

Manny acknowledged Daniel with a single nod, not taking his black look off Lieutenant Cardoso. "I'm not done with you. Not by a long shot."

Chapter TEN

"Doc, are you sure?" Manny stared at Lieutenant Cardoso, who was talking to Colin at the entrance to the largest room of the Voclain Museum. Colin was disguised as an elderly man in a three-piece suit, slip-on shoes and a cane. This was one of the seventeenth-century poet aliases he used. Manny's lip curled. "You need to be sure Cardoso is telling the truth."

"I can accept it if you don't trust yourself or if you don't trust Lieutenant Cardoso. But have I ever been mistaken in my analysis?" Genevieve's tone was clipped.

Manny pushed his fists in his pockets. "No offence, Doc, but that man has been undercover in some capacity for the last twelve years. His whole life is a lie. How do you know he even believes he's telling the truth?"

Francine looked up from her tablet to see how Genevieve would answer a question she hadn't thought about. After Daniel had left, Manny had grilled Lieutenant Cardoso, trying to trip him up. He hadn't. Lieutenant Cardoso's story had stayed consistent with his initial account. Genevieve had studied his every expression and had declared he had been truthful in all his answers.

Manny had been reluctant to believe it, but had had to shelve his questioning when Daniel had called to say the building had been cleared and they'd better get to the Voclain

Museum as soon as possible. That had been three hours ago and Francine was ready to implode with frustration.

When they'd arrived, Daniel had immediately taken them through the deceptively large building to a vault in the back. The heavy steel door had been left open, making millions of euros in other artworks easy pickings.

Monsieur Poirier, the curator, had constantly dabbed at his face with a silk handkerchief while talking about the great loss to the art world and to his good standing with his insurance company. He'd been appalled at the suggestion that any of his staff might have been involved in such a heinous crime, but had given his full co-operation to let them interview everyone on the Voclain Museum's payroll.

All nineteen employees had been present and it had been a tedious process interviewing them. Especially since Manny had insisted Francine sit in as they interviewed the employees so she could check if their online history contradicted anything they said. A red-blooded woman could look at only so many cat videos and baby photos on social media and go through only so many financials that epitomised middle-class before wanting to hack the NSA or some Chinese agency.

While Manny had interrogated everyone and Genevieve observed them with a hawk eye, Francine had been multitasking, running all kinds of searches. Just as she had seriously considered hacking the Chinese government website, the head of security had walked in to be interviewed. A retired cop, he took his position seriously and even Francine could see his distress written all over his face. He'd been particularly baffled about the security system showing no breach.

When he'd arrived at seven this morning, all systems had shown there'd been no activity during the night. It was only when Monsieur Poirier had arrived a few minutes later and gone to the vault that they'd discovered the heist.

Francine had done a quick check and had confirmed her suspicions that their system had been hacked. Without any video footage of the heist, the investigation would be much more challenging. That was why she was looking for cameras in the vicinity that might have caught something.

"Lieutenant Cardoso displayed no deception cues when he said he had worked his whole life, his whole career to end crime and corruption in the corporate sector." Genevieve looked over when Colin and Lieutenant Cardoso walked deeper into the room, chatting softly. Lieutenant Cardoso said something that brought Colin to a complete halt. The glance Colin shot at Manny was filled with fury. He stepped in front of Cardoso and turned his back on them, keeping their hushed conversation secret. Francine couldn't wait to hear what Manny had done this time to piss Colin off.

Genevieve frowned at Colin's strange behaviour, but turned back to Manny. "When Lieutenant Cardoso talked about his childhood friends possibly killing Mateas Almeida and definitely being involved in crime, there was sadness, shame and a lot of anger."

"Do *you* trust him, Doc?"

"No. I don't know him, therefore I don't trust him. But I do trust what he said to be the truth."

"Splitting hairs again." Manny grunted. "Never mind. Frey! Bring Lieutenant Cardoso here."

"With pleasure." The false friendliness in Colin's tone made Francine cringe. She took a step back as he and Cardoso walked towards them.

"Please call me Haden." There was no humour in Lieutenant Cardoso's smile as he stopped a few feet from them. "I don't think I will be a lieutenant after this fiasco is over."

"And why is that?" Manny pushed his hands in his pockets, slouching.

"I was supposed to prevent this from happening." He chewed the inside of his lip. "If they pulled this off today without contacting me, it means I'm no longer part of this."

"Or you've been made," Manny said.

"I really don't want to believe that, but it's becoming a more obvious possibility."

"They got away with three steel briefcases." Colin's lips were tight.

"Why are you so angry?" Genevieve asked, looking at Colin's mouth.

"I'm not angry, love. I'm livid." Again he looked at Manny as if he wanted to peel his skin off with a blunt knife.

"What did you do, handsome?" Ooh, this was fun.

"No." Colin took a step closer to Manny. "Ask Millard what he *didn't* do."

"I was going to tell you, Frey." Manny shrugged. "But we first had to interview Cardoso. Priorities."

Colin took another step and Francine stupidly pushed between the two men. She put her hand on Colin's chest and pushed hard enough to make him step back. "What are you two chest-beating teddy bears talking about?"

"I brought the art from Mateas' cellar with me." Haden leaned back when everyone turned to stare at him. "I gave it to Colonel Millard this morning and he put it in another conference room."

Colin leaned forward. "And Millard decided that authenticating the paintings is not as important as getting answers to his questions."

Francine didn't care that Colin had his dander up because he could already have inspected those masterpieces and have been on an art high. She counted to three before she could push the words through her teeth. "My parents knew about this?"

"It was Father Tomás who convinced Milena to let us take the paintings. Her sister wasn't as keen on it, but Milena didn't want stolen goods in her home."

Manny squeezed her elbow before pushing his hands back in his pockets. "The paintings are ready for you to inspect when we get back, Frey. Stop getting your knickers in a knot and focus on the now. You too, supermodel. You can shout at your dad later. Take a deep breath and tell me who hacked the museum's system."

"Someone who is quite good," a familiar voice said behind Francine.

She swung around, her smile happy and wide. "Pink! You're here."

"And armed." He lifted his tablet. "Like you."

Pink was the technology expert on Daniel's team. More than once, he'd impressed Francine with his IT skills as well as exceptional knowledge of technology.

"Have you been able to track the hacker?" Francine pushed her annoyance at her dad, and her worry, to the background.

"Nope. But as soon as I get behind my computers, he's toast."

"Who says it's a he?" She lifted one eyebrow.

"Touché, oh queen of all hackers."

"If you two jokers are finished." Manny's nostrils flared. "The museum's system?"

"The curator is furious," Pink said. "He paid in the five figures for a pretty sophisticated system. He kept saying he should've chosen the other company who'd tendered at the same time, but this company claimed to have the best system on the market."

"Pah!" Francine rolled her eyes. "They always say that, but it is seldom so sophisticated."

Pink shrugged. "The Pegasus system is one of the better ones on the market."

"Is this the system the museum used?" Colin asked.

"Yes." She lifted her tablet. "It's a good system, but it's not unhackable. A good hacker would only have to try a tiny bit harder to get in."

"A smart programmer would then be able to get the system to do anything he"—Pink looked at her—"or she wanted."

Manny looked at the cameras in the corners of the room. "Including making it look as if nothing happened."

"Yup."

"Okay, then tell me how they got in. None of the doors show any signs of forced entry." Manny pointed his chin at Francine's tablet. "Can you do your thing and check if they overrode those keypad locks at any of the doors?"

This was a modern building, but designed to fit in with the nineteenth-century-style buildings in Strasbourg. It looked like an old castle, square with an open-air courtyard in the centre. The courtyards of castles from that time would have had access from the outside, but the courtyard in this building was an enclosed space, frequently used for small concerts, cheese and wine events and outdoor exhibitions. The four-story building was constructed with modern material, but exquisitely designed and decorated to create an old-world atmosphere. Not Francine's taste, but her old-moneyed family would appreciate its stateliness.

"I'll need my computer for that." Francine wanted to get back to the team room. And she wanted to speak to her parents.

"I can get started on that." Pink nodded towards the front door. "The truck is here."

The GIPN team had a state-of-the-art truck kitted out with technology that most hackers dreamed about. Francine wished she could join Pink in the truck, but Manny wanted her on hand. "Gotta stay here. You go ahead. Let me know as soon as you get anything."

"Will do." Pink nodded towards the others. "Later."

"Have you spoken to the curator again, Frey?" Manny had been extremely annoyed when the curator had recognised Colin. Or rather, had recognised the disguise Colin was currently wearing. The curator was under the impression the grey-haired man wearing designer glasses and an eccentric bow tie was an art historian, not an art thief. Manny had reluctantly agreed to let Colin speak to the curator.

"He said three doors to the outside can only be opened from the inside of the building. There are only two doors that can be opened from the outside. One is in the courtyard and one is the back entrance."

"The very secure back entrance." Haden looked towards the right of the museum. "He said there was no way anyone could get in from the courtyard unless they got onto the roof and rappelled down."

Genevieve looked at Colin and he winked at her. That was how Colin had gained access to Genevieve's loft apartment when they'd first met—through the roof.

"All the other doors open from the inside, no locks outside to even pick," Colin said. "That makes it quite easy to determine the point of entry since we have only two choices."

"What about windows?" Manny asked.

"All the windows are too small to get through."

"Could drones get through them?" Francine was looking at a video on her tablet Pink had just sent her. She turned the tablet for Manny to see. "Drones like these?"

"Bloody hell." Manny leaned in. "How many of those bloody things are there?"

Colin stepped closer, his eyes widening when he saw five drones of different sizes flying down the street. "Which camera caught them?"

"The bank at the end of the street."

Manny sighed heavily. "See if you can find anything closer."

Colin straightened, his expression pensive. "The smallest one is small enough to fit through these windows. We need to check if any of them are open."

"Ask Daniel." Genevieve nodded towards the tall man walking towards them. "He's inspected the whole building."

Daniel's steps faltered when everyone turned to him. "What now?"

"Did you find any open windows?" Colin asked.

"Top floor washroom. There is no way anyone could've gotten through there." Daniel stopped next to Colin. "You might have scaled the wall to get there, but that space is too small for you."

"How about this?" Manny pulled Francine's tablet from her unwilling fingers with a grunt and showed Daniel. "Would this fit?"

"Huh." He leaned in. "Yup. That little one would fit."

Manny handed her tablet back, ignoring her glare. "Find the specs for that drone, supermodel. See what it can do."

"Sir, yes, sir." She half turned her back towards him in an exaggerated gesture, protecting her tablet from him, and got to work.

"Who opened that window?" Manny asked Daniel.

"The curator said that window is always open. Since it's on the top floor and facing the closed courtyard, they never closed it. He said it provides extra ventilation, which is always a good thing in public washrooms."

"What happened to Raul Fernandez?" Genevieve abruptly asked the question that had been bugging Francine since Haden had told them about his childhood friends.

"Who?" Manny rocked back on his heels. "Hmm. Cardoso, you haven't mentioned your other friend being part of this plan. Where is he in all this?"

"I don't know." Haden's shoulders rose almost to reach his ears when Manny lifted one eyebrow. "I don't! I asked them once where he was and they said gone. I asked where he'd gone and they said away. It was clear they didn't want to talk about him."

Francine made a mental note to search for Raul Fernandez.

"Did you look for him?" Daniel asked.

"Of course I did. Seven years ago, he had a successful software development company in Rio. He started travelling quite a lot in 2009, going to international trade shows with his software and apps. The last I saw of him was a trip he took to a Paris trade show in early 2010. We had a beer one evening and I didn't see him again. He disappeared. Gone."

"Hmm." Manny rubbed his jaw. "Early 2010, huh?"

"Same year as the Paris Museum of Modern Art heist," Colin said. "Too many coincidences here."

"They never mentioned him being part of that heist, they never mentioned him at all." Haden scratched his head. "The twice I asked about him, I was surprised by their reaction. The first time I was taken aback by their strong response, so I might've been mistaken then. But the second time, I was paying close attention. Going by what I learned about nonverbal communication, I saw guilt, anticipation, excitement and impatience."

"Any ideas why they would feel those things?" Colin asked.

"None." Haden shook his head.

"Ooh, lookee here." Francine clicked on her tablet, excited with the search results. "This drone is also called a dual-arm aerial manipulator."

"English, supermodel. Speak the Queen's English."

"Did you see it?" Pink called from the door as he ran to them. "Isn't it cool?"

"Got the specs here." She smiled at him. "It's a dual-arm aerial manipulator."

"Right, and it perfectly combines ground and aerial functions—"

"English!" Manny's voice echoed through the room, halting the crime scene investigators looking for physical evidence to log.

"This is a little robot that can fly." Francine opened the gallery on the manufacturer's website. "It was designed for bomb disposal units so they can operate from a safe distance. It flies in, lands gently where it's needed and stretches out its little arms. See there? Those clamps can twist the top off a bottle without moving the bottle a millimetre. It can pick a fine wire and cut it without setting off an unstable explosive device."

"I reckon they flew that baby through the upstairs window, straight downstairs and opened this door." Pink pointed to a map on his tablet screen. It was the blueprints for the museum, Pink's blunt index finger pointing to a door that opened into the small side street next to the large old building.

"Why that door?" Manny asked.

"It's one of the doors that only open from the inside," Colin said. "But most importantly, it's not covered by any museum security cameras. That street is darker than the main one. I would've chosen that door as well."

"Drones?" Manny shook his head. "Frey, have you heard of any heists done with drones?"

"No. This is a first." He looked impressed. "And unfortunately a very good idea."

Manny scowled. "Give me one good thing drones have brought us."

"Aerial sports photography, wildlife research, 3D mapping of landscapes, ooh, the list is long." Francine loved and hated the technology. "Sure, governments are using it to spy on us all the time, but there's so much good that can be done with it."

"Like delivering medicine or vaccines to hard-to-reach places. Or a drone that looks like a kid's toy, but is equipped with thermal-imaging technology that can be of great help during hostage situations, bomb threats and pursuits of armed suspects." Pink's eyes were bright with excitement. "I've requisitioned one for our team. It would rock if I could fly that over a building, a house, a shop and get a thermal image. We would know how many people were inside and where exactly they were. Some drones can fit in the palm of your hand. We could fly that right up to the suspects and they might not even see it. It could give real-time video footage of a hostage situation, an arms deal going down. I can't wait to get my hands on one."

The spying was cool, but made Francine even more paranoid. "I'm thinking rather how it could help delivering food to remote parts of the world where it is needed."

"Is any of this relevant to this heist?" Manny looked at her and Pink like they were the aliens Francine liked to fall back on when her conspiracy theories started to unravel.

Genevieve looked around. "Why would they mislead Lieutenant Cardoso about the day of the heist?"

"Haden, please."

Genevieve didn't acknowledge his request. Instead, she took a step closer to Colin. He took her hand and immediately her eyes got that faraway look she had when she was mentally writing Mozart, trying to find some elusive piece of the puzzle.

"I'm beginning to come to the realisation that they definitely fed me misinformation." Haden frowned at Genevieve, but looked away when Colin pinned him with a threatening stare. "I don't know why they would string me along."

Francine's tablet vibrated with a result on one of the many searches she was running. "Hmm. Huh."

"What, supermodel?"

She looked at Haden. "What's the name of Vitor Ribeiro's company?"

"Which one? He has two."

"Both."

He counted on his fingers. "Delta Rio is a small recruitment company he uses to hire out qualified workers in the construction industry. VR Shopping is his main commercial concern. It started as an internet store for designer wear, but now he has about fifty physical stores all over Brazil."

"Is this relevant?" Manny asked through his teeth.

"No," Francine said. "Not yet. I'm sure if I start digging…"

"Then do that." Manny looked towards the door. "We need to ask the curator more questions. Frey, call your friend over."

Colin glared at Manny for a few seconds before walking to where Monsieur Poirier was talking to a crime scene technician. "Monsieur Poirier, could you join us, please. We have a few questions that might help us find whoever committed this unforgivable crime."

Monsieur Poirier dabbed his face with his handkerchief and quickly walked to them, the corners of his mouth turned down. "This is utterly unacceptable. These jewels come from the Victorian era. They are priceless. If anyone worked on them, their value would be lost."

"I know." Colin shook his head in commiseration. If Francine hadn't known Colin for such a long time, she wouldn't have known it was all an act. "It must be so hard, but we're hoping you could answer a few questions for us."

Monsieur Poirier sighed deeply. "Anything to help."

"When did you install the new security system?"

"Eighteen months ago." His shoulders slumped. "We were promised it was state-of-the-art. No one would ever be able to breach it. And now look. I should've gone with GRAFS, the other security company. Oh, my. One cannot trust anyone these days. Do you have a suspect yet? Do you think the security company was involved?"

"We're just asking questions, Monsieur Poirier." Colin looked at Manny. "I think that's all for now, right?"

"For now." Manny watched as Monsieur Poirier walked away. "Is he in on this?"

"I don't think so," Colin said. "He's worked extremely hard to build this place to what it is today. I honestly don't believe he would jeopardise his work and his reputation for the jewellery."

"Not just jewellery, Frey. Two million euros' worth of jewellery."

Colin shook his head. "No. I've known him for eight years. It's not in his character. He's been consistent in his outrage every time there has been an art theft or a discovery of a forgery. No."

"I need to see the companies' details. And I need to see the maps." Genevieve stepped closer to Francine. "The maps."

This wasn't the first time Genevieve had made sudden demands after spending time in her head writing some Mozart concerto. Haden was the only one who looked at Genevieve as if she'd grown an extra head. Francine smiled gently. "Context?"

"Oh. Yes." Genevieve rubbed her arms. "We need to look at the companies owned by Lieutenant Cardoso's five friends. If they are as close as Lieutenant Cardoso suggests—"

"They are, and please call me Haden."

"—this is not their final plan."

"How do you know this, Doc?"

She turned to Colin. "How big a challenge was it for them to break in here?"

"On a scale from one to ten? I'd say a six. Nah, a five. They had the advantage of shutting down the security system. That means they had as much time as they needed to get in and out."

She looked at Haden. "You mentioned twice that they executed the previous heists because they saw them as a challenge. Can I trust your observation?"

"Completely." There was no hesitation in his answer. "They were treating the new heist like a game. For them it wasn't about the money or the gain, but rather the challenge."

"Then this doesn't make sense. Getting in here was relatively easy with the small drone. Getting out with the jewels held no challenge. So why did they do this if not for the value of their loot?" No one answered. "That's why we need to look into these men and their companies. We'll find the answers there."

"I'll work much faster with my computers." Francine loved her tablet, but it had limited capabilities. "We should go."

"There's not much else for us to do here in any case." Haden sighed. "We were too late. I was too late."

"Don't expect any sympathy from me. You screwed up. Stop feeling sorry for yourself and put on your big-girl panties." Francine had so much more she wanted to say to the man who'd watched her dad getting beaten up, but she would bide her time. "Which of your friends are hackers?"

"Why would he want to wear female underwear?" Genevieve asked.

"Because he's a girl." Francine knew Colin would explain the expression to Genevieve later. She raised her eyebrows and waited for Haden to answer her.

"Mateas and Marcos Gallo. They are great with IT stuff. Alex, Vitor and I have computer skills relevant to our professions, but those two are really good with programming and stuff. They often talked about things I had no knowledge of."

"We can safely scratch Mateas Almeida off the list." Francine turned towards the door. "I'm going to the team room to find out if Gallo hacked this system."

"And I need plans." Genevieve waved her hand around the room. "I need the floor plans for this building."

Before anyone had a chance to ask her about it, Genevieve spun around and marched to the door. Colin raised both shoulders and followed her, his steps measured, befitting an older man. Francine didn't care what Haden did, but since she'd come in Manny's car, she needed to organise transportation. "Coming or staying?"

"Com…" Manny's lips thinned when she lowered her lashes and gave him a seductive smile. "Just get in my bloody car, supermodel. I'll be there in five minutes."

Chapter ELEVEN

Francine was glad to see Vinnie had as always gone overboard with his lunch preparations. She was starving. In the centre of the round table was a large bowl of fruit salad, two different quiches and a Greek salad. She sat down and served healthy helpings onto her plate. The last five hours had been intense. Francine and Genevieve had spent the majority of that time sifting through data. The last hour, Francine had been unravelling a few online threads and had just broken through.

"Where are your parents?" Genevieve put another spoon of fruit salad on her plate.

"Um… I'm not sure." Francine had spoken with her mom twice and her dad once this morning, but those had been short conversations. She hadn't wanted to shout at her dad over the phone and was no longer as annoyed that he'd omitted telling her about smuggling those paintings into the country. To top it off, she felt guilty that she was caught up in this case when they were at last in Strasbourg. Both her parents had reassured her that they were in no rush to return to Brazil and would stay a bit longer to visit.

"The little punk took them sightseeing." Vinnie put another slice of the spinach quiche on his plate. "She doesn't have any classes this afternoon, so she decided to show them around."

Francine loved that girl. She was definitely going to buy Nikki the handbag she'd been gushing about.

"Haden is still in the conference room, looking through his email communication with Almeida, Gallo, Santos and Ribeiro for anything he might have missed."

Francine took another bite of Vinnie's exquisite quiche and nodded.

"Okay." Manny tapped with his knife on his plate. "Who's got what for me?"

"Oh, I have a Henri Matisse, an Amedeo Modigliani, a Pablo Picasso and a Fernand Léger. That's what I have." Colin's tone was backed up by his thin lips and flared nostrils.

"They're real?" Manny put a forkful of quiche in his mouth as if there was no animosity around the table. Francine was also curious. If those paintings were the real artworks stolen in 2010, it might take away the last of her annoyance at her dad risking himself and her mom being arrested on all kinds of charges. As much as she loved delicious scandals, she didn't want her parents to be headlines.

"You're an arse." Colin clenched his jaw and looked away for a few seconds, appearing to calm himself. "The Léger, Matisse and Modigliani are authentic. I'll give up one of my aliases if they're not the paintings that were stolen from the Paris Museum of Modern Art in 2010."

"And the Picasso?"

"I'm only ninety percent sure it's the real thing, but since it was found with the other three, I think it's safe to say it was also part of that heist."

"Weren't there five paintings stolen?" Francine asked.

"Yes. A Georges Braque painting was also taken, but Haden

said he and your dad looked for more paintings in the cellar and these four were the only ones there."

Francine changed her mind about no longer being annoyed with her dad. "Did you ask Haden how he managed to get those paintings into France?"

"Diplomatic pouch." Colin put his fork down and leaned back in his chair. "I swear, I couldn't make this stuff up. Apparently, some diplomat Haden didn't want to name owed him a favour. He organised the private plane that brought your parents and also put all four paintings in a diplomatic pouch."

"Which goes through customs without being checked." Francine couldn't believe her dad would be a party to something like this. No, wait. She could. He believed in right and wrong, but also believed that the laws weren't always right. Sharing this philosophy with a bishop had once landed him in hot water.

"Smart move." Colin picked up his fork again. "When those paintings were taken, their worth was just over one hundred million euros. We have eighty percent of that in the other conference room. Quite a thought, right? The 2010 heist was the biggest since the 1990 Boston heist."

"The one with the Flinck?" Vinnie asked.

"Yes. And this Paris heist was one of the big ones that has not been solved. Until now."

"We haven't solved all of it yet, Frey." Manny cut another slice of quiche and put it in his plate. "What else do we have?"

"Pink and Francine sent me all the video footage they were able to get in the area." Genevieve had watched every video over and over. "There were no people involved in the heist."

"What?" Manny's eyes widened.

"I said there were no people involved. At least not that I could see on the videos. The cameras Francine and Pink accessed covered all but half a metre of the main street and gave me a full view of the side street. One camera two buildings away is positioned on the top floor, which gave me an aerial view. In the time the heist took place, only one person walked in the street. He was drunk and appeared to be homeless."

"Frey?"

"I looked at it and agree with Jenny. If it were me disguised as a drunk bum, I would still have found a way to scope the area. This guy was looking at his feet the whole time, just shuffling along."

"His feet?" Francine's mind conjured up all kinds of transmission devices. "Was he wearing glasses?"

"No." Colin's smile told her he knew where her mind was going. "He wasn't wearing smart glasses. His shoes looked like they were about to fall apart. I had Jenny zoom in, but there was nothing around his feet or on his shoes that could've given him any intel."

"There is a certain muscle tension in people who are undercover that is very telling," Genevieve added. "He had none of it. His muscles were relaxed from I assume some form of alcohol or narcotic."

"Okay, so there were no people." Manny's frown intensified. "Then how the hell did they get all the jewellery and disappear with it?"

Genevieve looked at Francine. "Can I use your tablet?"

"You don't have to show us, Doc. Just tell us. I'll watch it later."

"At sixteen minutes past four drones flew past the bank towards the museum. Four of those were larger and hovered three stories above the ground."

"How silent are these things?" Manny asked.

"The smaller ones are used in stealth operations." Francine understood why Pink wanted one. "They're very quiet."

"Hell. So, if they're flying three stories up, people might not even see or hear them?"

"At night, in between buildings, I think it's probable that someone will hear them."

"Not if you're drunk and homeless," Vinnie said.

"The man showed no nonverbal indication that he'd heard anything," Genevieve said. "The smaller drone disappeared over the building, into what I assume to be the courtyard. I don't know what happened in the next seven minutes and forty-three seconds, but Colin is convinced that it got through the upstairs window and flew to the door in the side street."

"Only logical explanation, Jenny."

"Still supposition. Seven minutes is a long time. The drone could've gone somewhere else first." She cleared her throat. "The side street door opened at twenty-four minutes past four. The angle and lighting is limited, but I could make out a shape that looked like the drone, but with arms. The four larger drones flew into the museum and the small one pulled the door closed until it was only slightly ajar. Seventeen minutes later, the door opened again and all five drones left the museum—"

"Carrying their loot." Colin made fists as if he was carrying something. "I swear, three of the large drones each had a steel case in their hands."

"They don't have hands," Genevieve said.

"Clutches, arms, extensions." Colin winked at her. "Look, I'm as disgusted as Monsieur Poirier about the theft, but you have to admit it's ingenious."

"Not ingenious." Genevieve shook her head. "Only efficient use of current technology. To finish my report, the small drone pushed the door completely closed before following the other five down the street and out of sight. Not once did I, or Colin, see human interference."

"So, where did they fly to? What's the range on these things? How far can they fly?"

"As long as there is a satellite connection to the drone, somebody could operate these models from a different continent." Genevieve lifted one shoulder. "I had the same question and checked. Unlike the bigger drones, the smaller ones can fly for three hours before they would need to be recharged."

"That means they could've been in bloody central Germany by the time we got to the museum."

"And those jewels could be on their way to any place in the world by now," Colin said.

"Bloody hell." Manny rested his hands on top of his head. "Please tell me we have something else to get these guys."

"I've got nada." Vinnie scrunched up his nose. "Since yesterday, I've been phoning around and speaking to all kinds of contacts. Nobody here knows any of Haden's four pals. This morning, I got hold of an old buddy of mine who took his business to South America."

"What kind of business?" Manny asked.

"The illegal kind, old man. This dude is into drugs and guns, best business there is in South America. He deals with cartels, guerrilla fighters and other low-class criminals. But I thought it was worth the shot to find out if he knew anything about the four dudes or any art deals."

"It's not uncommon for arms and drug dealers to use art and jewels as currency," Colin said.

"Not in this case. The dude knows nothing about art and jewels being traded in his area. Then I had a lightbulb flash in my head."

"Oh, my." Genevieve leaned forward, inspecting Vinnie's face with concern. "Are you okay?"

Vinnie chuckled. "Aw, Jen-girl. I'm sorry for using such a stupid term. I meant that I had an inspired thought."

"Oh." She still looked confused, but didn't ask any more questions.

"Anyhoo. I asked the dude about drones. He says it's the best thing that happened to his business in a long time. He says he has two drones, but I'm sure he has quite a few more. From what he told me, his drones have to be much larger than the ones that broke into the Voclain Museum."

"What's he using them for?" Manny asked.

"Getting his drugs and guns across the border. There's no regulation controlling the use of drones and where they may fly. Not yet, anyway. So, he's loading a shipment of pure cocaine on a drone, flying it over the border to a drop-off point and flying his toy back home for the next delivery. Just like Amazon."

"They're delivering along the river as well?" Genevieve asked.

"No, love. Vinnie's talking about the online shop. They've been given approval to test using drones to deliver purchases."

"That makes sense. It could save a lot of time and money."

"And cost many people their jobs." Francine was still torn between hating and loving this technology. "Did he tell you how many kilos his drone can carry, Vin?"

"Not outright, but I reckon about a hundred."

"Then he's using a medium-sized drone. The smaller ones can maybe carry five kilos. The ones I'm thinking of come in different sizes, and can carry up to a hundred and fifty kilograms." She'd learned a lot from the website she'd found this morning. "Those were originally designed to deliver medical supplies to remote areas."

"And they're perfect for smuggling. Fly them low enough and they won't get caught on radar," Vinnie said. "My buddy told me that he enjoyed flying these drones. He has all the controls in his basement and flies all over the place without leaving his house."

"Bloody hell. This is a whole new world of trouble." Manny's lips flattened into a hard line. "These idiots were most likely sitting in their luxury homes in Rio, controlling the drones as if they were playing a computer game."

"It's not as easy as that." Vinnie was good with computer games. Not as brilliant as Francine, but very good. "It's skill, old man. You really need to have a light, but strong touch to keep those things from crashing all over the place."

"I still say these things need to be regulated."

"Like that's going to happen before something bad happens." Francine always marvelled at the sheer incompetence of governments. Especially when it came to technology and cybercrime. "Criminals always establish themselves and their activities long before any stupid government wakes up and smells the coffee. By then, it's too late. They're playing catch-up instead of preventing anything. The moment something new comes on the market, governments sit back and wait to see where it's going before they take action. It's their own fault for not being proactive. And that's why so many drones have been flying over big cities. Again, just look at what's been happening in Paris. The police still don't know who's been flying right above the landmarks."

"I've been briefing the president on this, but I think you should join me at our next meeting." Manny ignored her when she shook her head frantically. "Not a request, supermodel. Maybe you can get into these politicians' heads the importance of keeping airspace clear. Talking of which, do we think that this is an immediate threat to national security?"

It was quiet around the table. Francine thought about all the information she had gathered thus far. By the faraway look in Genevieve's eyes, she was doing the same. Francine could only come to one conclusion. "This is personal. I don't think it has anything to do with any government."

"Explain."

"Maybe I should start with our discoveries." Genevieve put her cutlery on her plate. "It will be more logically presented, then Francine can present her theory."

"Go for it." How could Francine take offence when she knew Genevieve was correct?

"Francine and I searched for all companies registered to Mateas Almeida, Marcos Gallo, Alex Santos, Vitor Ribeiro as well as Raul Fernandez. Gallo owns two companies, Santos two companies, Ribeiro two, Fernandez one and Almeida owned two."

"What kind of companies?" Vinnie asked.

"That's where things got interesting." That discovery had really excited Francine. "But Genevieve can explain why."

"These companies complement each other to the extent that they often are contracted to work on projects together. They mostly focus on construction, real estate and information technology. But it's a perfect symbiotic relationship. Alex Santos owns a well-established and extremely successful construction company. When his company is commissioned to build an office complex for an international company, between the four of them they provide all the designs, the workforce, the interior, the security system, even the computer system installed in specially designed rooms in the building."

"Santos' second company is an architectural firm," Francine said. "One of Ribeiro's companies is a recruitment company like Haden told us. They provide qualified workers from electricians to bricklayers. Fernandez's company provides all the IT and security for these buildings and Gallo's two companies provide whatever electrical and engineering needs they have."

"Each company specialises in their own field, but together they're a"—Genevieve looked at Francine—"what did you call it?"

"A one-stop shop."

"Does Haden have any connection to any of these companies?" Vinnie asked.

"Not as far as I could see," Francine said. "There is still a lot to check, but I couldn't find anything linking him to these guys. Just their friendship."

"Good," Vinnie said. "I like the dude."

"Make sure about this, supermodel," Manny said, ignoring Vinnie.

"Will do."

"I have to also say that the software security these companies have is far above what I'm used to." It had taken her by surprise when she'd first hacked into it. "It's sophisticated and is worth the price they're charging for it. Seriously, it was easier to hack into the bank's security cameras this morning than get into Gallo's company's system."

"Bloody hell. I long for the days where spying was done with binoculars."

"Get with the programme, handsome. Those days were over before you even started losing your hair." Francine touched the soft stubble on Manny's head. He still had a full head of hair, but kept it trimmed close to his skull.

"I started losing my hair when I met you." Manny pushed her hand away. "Did you find any red flags in these men's personal lives?"

"Gallo, Ribeiro and Fernandez are married, Gallo and Fernandez for the second time. Fernandez must be bad husband material, because he's separated. Santos has never been to the altar. Again, I haven't had enough time to do a real check, but from what I saw, these ladies are all above board. There's nothing hinky in their background or their jobs. Mind you, only Fernandez's wife works. She's a doctor. The others are all ladies of leisure."

Manny lowered his brow and narrowed his eyes. "I don't have to be Doctor Face-reader to know that you're excited about something you found, supermodel. Spill it."

"Haden was right about Santos. He's not as good as the others with his internet security. His email password took me a whole ninety seconds to crack. And I found a few treasures there." That was what she had been busy with when Vinnie had come in with two picnic baskets filled with food. "This is one of the reasons I think it's personal, not political. I read an email exchange where he was talking about his political aspirations. Gallo and Ribeiro shot him down in flames."

"Not literally, I assume," Genevieve said.

"Nope. But they told him what a bad idea it was." She paused. "This was nine months ago. Santos had been approached by a retiring local politician who wanted Santos to run for office. He thought it might be a good idea, but his childhood friends quickly told him just how bad an idea it was."

"Why?" Vinnie asked.

"Well, their reasoning was that going into the public eye would invite scrutiny. I agree with them, by the way. They also said that they'd worked too hard on their projects for some nosy reporter to find something suspicious and before they know it, their names are connected to some scandal. But that was just the entrée." She paused for dramatic effect. "They reminded Santos that they were going to have so much fun with their next projects he would forget all about being a politician."

"Did they say anything about these projects?"

"Nope." She gave Manny a dirty look. "That's when Vin arrived with the food. I need more time to search."

"I don't like the sound of this," Colin said. "We need to know what these projects are. If today's heist was one, what's the next one? How many will there be?"

"Copy all Santos' emails and send them to me. Please." Genevieve had been trying to be more polite in her requests. Francine winked at her and nodded.

"Maths is not my forte, but I counted nine companies between the five men." Manny lifted two fingers. "Tell me about the other two, supermodel."

"Ooh, you sexy Einstein. You caught that." Francine fluttered her eyes at Manny. "I made Genevieve promise to keep the best for last."

"Supermodel." Manny said this with a tired sigh.

She winked at him. "So, Genevieve and I found all those companies, right? Well, they were pretty easy to find since they were all out there for the public to see. I noticed something in one of the emails that made me wonder, so I followed that lead. I found two more companies, each with five shareholders."

"Let me guess," Manny said. "Almeida, Gallo, Santos, Ribeiro and Fernandez."

"Bingo! The first company, GRAFS, is also out there for the public to see. They are a security company offering full service, from securing all your digital data, computer and online networks to providing VIP's with bodyguards. Like I say, full service. But even more delicious than this? A weapons research and development company owned by GRAFS." Francine got up, grabbed her tablet from her desk and returned to the table, the right site already on the screen. She gave it to Manny. "Amaru Development. It was established four years ago and has been privately funded to do research and development into—"

"Weapons and drone technology." Manny lowered the tablet. "Bloody fucking hell."

"Amaru is a creature from South American mythology," Genevieve said. "It's said to be a serpent or a dragon that can cross to and from the spiritual realm."

"You don't say." Vinnie's eyes were wide. "That's cool."

Colin tapped with his index finger on the table. "I remember the name from Monsieur Poirier's pity party. GRAFS was the other security company that offered the Voclain Museum their services."

"That's right," Francine said. "GRAFS has been in direct competition with the other company for years. They often bid for the same projects."

"So they knew about the Voclain Museum." Manny rubbed his hands over his face.

Francine leaned in. "Wanna hear my theory?"

"If you say one word about aliens, I will spill my tea on your computer."

"That's stooping to an impressively low level, handsome. But there are no aliens this time. Gallo and his buds hacked the Voclain Museum's security system long before this heist. That's how they knew that little window was open. They've been watching for a long time."

"Can you prove this?" Manny asked.

"Not all of it. But I've been in the museum's system and they were hacked numerous times in the last year."

"Hmm." Manny narrowed his eyes. "Why can't all your theories be as plausible as this one?"

"Not as much fun." Francine winked and smiled when Manny turned away from her.

"I phoned Monsieur Poirier and he told me that he'd given them the blueprints of the museum so GRAFS could work on a complete security proposal," Colin said. "Not very smart, but also not unheard of."

"So GRAFS is directly connected to the museum and Amaru is directly connected to the heist." Francine leaned over until she found the right page on GRAFS' website. She tilted the tablet towards Manny. "Does that illustration look familiar?"

"Holy mother of all." Manny lifted the tablet closer to his face. "That's the small drone with the arms."

It was quiet for a few seconds. Francine was giddy with excitement about the many new directions she could go with her searches.

"I'm still wondering what happened to the Fernandez dude." Vinnie scratched his chest. "If they're so tight, why is he not showing up anywhere? This doesn't sit right with me."

"I've searched all the databases I could hack. Nothing. He disappeared in 2010." Francine didn't like this. "But don't you worry, big guy. I'll find him. Just give me time."

"Tell me you found something else, supermodel."

She rubbed her hands, her bracelets jingling. "Juicy scandals!"

"Supermodel."

"I've only checked Santos' emails as far back as four months ago. But I found something worth checking into. Three months ago, Gallo sent an email to Santos and Ribeiro, saying the red one had been caught and is safely caged. They were happy about it."

"Red," Genevieve said softly, staring at the far wall. "Rossi is the plural of Rosso."

"Which is 'red' in Italian." Francine pushed her shoulders back and lifted her chin. "I think I found us a link between the terrible five and Brigadier Clarisse Rossi."

"Where is she?" Colin asked.

"En route," Manny said. "She phoned earlier to say that she'll be here this afternoon."

"She still not happy about coming here?" Francine asked.

Manny shrugged. "I don't care. She has a lot counting against her at this moment."

"Those weapons." Vinnie nodded at Francine's tablet. "What kind of weapons are they producing?"

"That's also an interesting titbit. If I believe the website, which I don't"—Francine took her tablet and swiped the screen—"they don't produce anything. It's pure research and development. They even have 3D-printed weapons here."

"I'll have to check with my buddy if he knows anything about these guys."

"I don't think they're selling their technology to drug cartels."

"Don't underestimate those cartels." Vinnie was deadly serious. "Some of those asswipes are funding Boko Haram, ISIS and other terrorist groups."

"Well, I suppose they could all benefit from advanced weaponry."

"Hell." Manny got up, walked to the far end of the large room and back. "Doc, we need to find out what they're planning."

"If they're planning something," Genevieve said.

"Oh, they're planning something." Francine would bet her manicurist's salon on it. "I'm still saying today was just a test run."

"A frigging two-million-euro test run."

"Um, hello?" Tim's face appeared on Francine's monitor. She tapped on the tablet to complete the connection. He raised his eyebrows when he saw everyone sitting around the table. "*Bon appétit.*"

"What's up, Timmy-boy?" Vinnie enjoyed intimidating the young man.

"You have a guest waiting in the conference room."

"Who are you addressing?" Genevieve asked. "We can't all have a guest."

"Oh, I think you do. Colonel Impatient has been checking in every five seconds to see if she's arrived."

Manny stood up. "Brigadier Rossi is here? In the conference room?"

"Drinking a cup of Earl Grey tea." Tim had barely finished his sentence when Manny was at the elevator, impatiently stabbing the button.

Chapter TWELVE

"I still think I should've gone in there with the old man." Vinnie folded his arms across his chest. "I would get answers from that woman."

"You just want to scare the shit out of her because you have a man crush on Haden." Francine laughed when Vinnie's jaw dropped.

Vinnie recovered quickly. "You're just jealous that he's not thrown himself at you."

"What's a man crush?" Genevieve stopped working on her computer for a second to look at Colin.

They were in Genevieve's viewing room to observe Manny's interview with Brigadier Clarisse Rossi. After a short, but intense argument, Manny had given in to Genevieve's insistence that she watch the interview from her room. She hadn't wanted to be part of any confrontation. Manny had, however, succeeded in getting her word that she would join him if he needed her. Vinnie hadn't been impressed when Manny'd refused to let him 'put the fear of Hades' in Clarisse.

"It's an expression used when a man is infatuated by another man."

Genevieve frowned, studying Vinnie for a few moments. "But you're not homosexual."

"You bet your OCD butt I'm not." Vinnie waved his index finger at Francine. "She was being sarcastic because I like the dude."

"In a non-sexual way." Colin laughed when Vinnie made a fist and pointed it at him. "Don't worry, Vin. Just because you're good at house duties doesn't mean—"

"They're there." Genevieve gestured at the twelve monitors in front of them.

Genevieve was sitting between Colin and Francine, Vinnie was standing behind them. With the high ceilings and the glass walls looking into the large team room, it was not only larger, but definitely much less crowded than the old viewing room. Not once did Genevieve have that look of panic she got when the restaurant became too crowded, there were too many people on the street or, previously, there had been too many people in her viewing room.

Three of the monitors mounted on the curved frame showed the footage from the two cameras in the conference room and the one in the hallway. Manny had called Haden from the small conference room and they were a few feet from the door to the large conference room. Inside, Phillip was talking to Clarisse. She looked even worse than on the interview recordings Genevieve had showed them. She was wearing a simple pant suit that Francine supposed had once fitted her well. It was by no means a designer suit, but the jacket had a flattering shape that now hung off Clarisse's thin frame.

Clarisse's bedraggled looks were exacerbated by the contrast to Phillip's immaculate attire. In the two and a half years Francine had known Phillip, she'd not once seen him look anything but stylish. Today he had on a bespoke suit and a red silk tie, and Francine would bet he was wearing those Armani shoes she knew would pay most of Tim's monthly salary.

Despite his wardrobe, expensive cologne and high-class manners, Phillip had Francine's respect and admiration. He treated Genevieve like a daughter and had on her recommendation taken all of them under his corporate wing by giving them space to work. He was consistent in his values, behaviour and professionalism. He also was a master at getting people to trust him. It was clearly working with Clarisse.

She was cradling a cup, taking small, measured sips. Phillip was sitting two chairs from her, calmly drinking from his tea cup, talking lightly about the roadworks on the route from Paris to Strasbourg. Her responses to Phillip's small talk were appropriate, but she seemed distracted. Her eyes kept shifting to Daniel. Dressed in his operational uniform, he was standing by the door, legs apart, his hand resting on the butt of his holstered weapon.

Francine smiled. "Look at Daniel being all badass."

"He's not scaring Brigadier Rossi." Genevieve's eyes narrowed. "She keeps looking at him because she's confused."

Onscreen, Manny entered the conference room first, not eliciting much response from Clarisse. But when Haden walked in, her eyes flashed open and her chest rose as she gasped. Her chin started quivering and she slapped her hand over her mouth, but she couldn't contain her emotions. Her face crumpled, tears streaming down her cheeks. Manny halted as soon as her sobs became audible. His scowl intensified and he pushed his fists deeper into his trouser pockets.

"What do you see, girlfriend?"

"Remorse." Genevieve leaned forward. "Shock, guilt, relief."

"That's a strange combination," Colin said.

"She was shocked to see Haden when he came in. Almost immediately, her micro-expressions went to relief and then fluctuated between guilt and remorse."

"Guilt? Hmph." Vinnie sniffed. "She should be tried for treason."

Colin gave Vinnie an incredulous look. "Millard would love to hear you be all patriotic, Vin."

Onscreen, Haden walked past Manny and stopped next to Clarisse. The look he gave her was not forgiving. "You betrayed me. You put my life in danger."

Clarisse's sobs intensified. She hiccoughed loudly and pressed both hands against her mouth. After a few seconds, she looked up at Haden, her hands against her chest, her face wet with tears. "I did everything I could to protect you. Everything. This has to end."

The change in Manny's posture was minute, but Francine saw him stiffen. "What? What has to end?"

Clarisse didn't answer. She didn't take her eyes off Haden.

"She's begging for his forgiveness," Genevieve said softly.

"I don't know, Jen-girl. This isn't the first time a guilty person has cried hysterically, making it look like remorse."

Genevieve took a slow breath. Francine had watched this particular argument more than once. "I've agreed with you every time, Vinnie. Remorse does not mean innocence. We don't know the context of her emotions. She could be experiencing remorse because she was found out, she could be exhibiting relief for the same reason. Or relief because she will be stopped from committing more crimes."

"See? Guilty." Vinnie smirked, but Genevieve didn't respond. She was watching the videos with renewed interest.

"Why didn't you put Lieutenant Cardoso's findings in your weekly report?" Manny asked onscreen. Clarisse just shook her head. Manny's lips thinned. "What is your interest in Marcos Gallo, Alex Santos, Vitor Ribeiro and Mateas Almeida? Do you have a personal connection to them?"

Clarisse jerked and looked at Manny, the same pleading in her eyes. "I did everything to protect, not to harm."

Genevieve reached for the mouse and opened the viewing programme. She downloaded what had been recorded thus far and opened it, allowing the software to continue recording. With a few clicks, she replayed the video where Haden confronted Clarisse.

"What are you thinking, Jenny?" Colin asked when Genevieve played the two proclamations of protection the third time.

"There's more to her protecting Haden." Genevieve's soft answer was overpowered by Manny's progressively louder questions. She returned her attention to the monitors showing the conference room and pointed to Clarisse's face. "Manny's lost her. She's blocking him completely with her nonverbal cues."

No sooner had Genevieve said that than Manny threw his hands in the air and looked at the camera. "Doc! Get in here now!"

"Want me to come with you?" Colin asked as Genevieve got up.

"No. You're not needed," she said as she walked out.

"Well, ouch." Vinnie laughed. "You're not needed, dude."

Colin smiled and lifted his middle finger over his shoulder. Vinnie laughed harder.

Genevieve's statements could obliterate normal people's self-images into a million pieces. Good thing they weren't normal people. Francine had once made the mistake of saying this during lunch with Genevieve. Her friend had then spent the good part of an hour lecturing Francine that there was no such thing as normal, that she should never measure herself against others or devalue herself. It had taken Francine touching Genevieve before she'd stopped.

"She's all right." Vinnie punched Colin's shoulder lightly. "Right?"

Colin turned around, rubbing his shoulder. Vinnie's tap was another man's full assault. "What do you mean?"

"I mean"—Vinnie waved towards the team room—"with all this."

"Ask her yourself, Vin. I'm not her mouthpiece." Colin shook his head and turned around. "Do you really think she would be doing this if she didn't want to? If she wasn't all right?"

"No need to get snippy." Vinnie took a step back. "Next time I punch harder."

Even though Francine knew Colin was right, she also needed the reassurance that Genevieve was coping. After two years, Francine still found it hard to take everything Genevieve said at face value. Her whole life she'd listened to what people said between the lines. Meeting someone who never said anything she didn't mean was confusing. And wonderful.

There was no need to interpret anything Genevieve said. Only to understand it within the context of that moment. That was why Francine knew Genevieve needed Colin more than she realised, but he wasn't needed for this interview.

Onscreen, Genevieve walked down the hallway and stopped in front of the closed door. With both hands, she touched her thumbs to her ring fingers and took a few deep breaths. Then she rolled her shoulders, shook out her hands, opened the door and walked into the spacious room. Daniel stepped aside to let her past, but she didn't acknowledge him. Her attention was wholly on Clarisse.

"Maybe you can get something out of her, Doc." Manny sat down, glaring at Clarisse. Francine was sure most of the disgust on his face came from his discomfort with the tears still running down Clarisse's face.

Clarisse looked up from her lap and wiped her cheeks with the back of her hand. She didn't say anything, but shifted in her chair when Genevieve stared at her in that disconcerting way that felt like she was reading your soul. After a few seconds, Genevieve blinked once and sat down on the chair closest to Clarisse.

"Interesting." Vinnie pulled Genevieve's empty chair back and sat down. "She never sits close to strangers."

"Shush." Francine lifted her hand towards Vinnie without looking away from the monitors. Genevieve knew something they didn't.

"Who are you protecting?" Genevieve put her hand on the table, not crowding Clarisse's space, but reaching out.

Clarisse glanced at Haden. "Lieutenant Cardoso."

"Are you romantically involved with Lieutenant Cardoso?"

Genevieve's question shocked everyone. Manny muttered a curse, Haden gasped and Francine blinked in surprise.

"No!" Clarisse shook her head emphatically.

"Are you emotionally involved with him?"

Clarisse leaned away from Genevieve. "No."

"Do you have any emotional connection to him? Anything apart from your professional relationship?"

"I don't like where you're going with this."

"You don't know where I'm going with this." Genevieve's expression softened and she moved her hand a bit closer to Clarisse. Francine wondered how hard it was for her friend to show this level of social interaction. "You're protecting somebody very important to you. Someone you love."

Clarisse closed her eyes and bit down hard on her lips. She shook her head, but tears pushed through her closed lids.

"Clarisse." Genevieve's voice was gentle, patient. "Who are you protecting?"

"I can't." Clarisse folded double, hugging herself tightly. "I can't."

"We're here to help. And we cannot do that if you don't help us. Is it your husband? Children? Your parents? Your sister?" Genevieve glanced up at the camera. Francine grabbed her tablet and searched for information on Clarisse's sister. Twenty seconds later, she sent an SMS to Genevieve's smartphone. Genevieve glanced at it. "Is Celine safe? What about Evan? Ah. Marion? Where are your sister's kids, Clarisse?"

"No." Clarisse shook her head. "No, they'll kill them. They will kill them."

"Jesus, Clarisse." Haden pulled a chair closer and sat down

next to Clarisse. As soon as he put his arm around her, she turned and fell against his chest.

"I'm sorry, Haden. I'm so sorry. They sent me Marion's finger. Her finger!" Her sobs shook her body as she clung to Haden. "They said they would finish off Celine's kids, then come for mine."

"Shh." Haden pulled her tight against him and looked over her head at Manny. "We need to do something."

"I can't do anything until I know what the hell is going on." Manny's expression had softened, but he didn't look convinced. "I need to know everything."

It was another minute before Clarisse had control over her emotions. She must have been carrying the kidnapping of her sister's children all alone. Sharing that burden, even unwillingly, had to be an incredible load off her shoulders. She pushed away from Haden's chest and shook her head. "I need Evan and Marion to be safe."

Manny's eyebrows rose. "You're negotiating?"

"Agent… I don't know your name."

"Colonel Millard."

"Oh. We spoke on the phone." She swallowed a few times and lifted her chin. "Colonel Millard, these men sent me the finger of a nineteen-year-old girl. I had the DNA tested and it's hers. I don't doubt they will kill Marion and her brother."

"Who is this 'they' you are talking about?"

She glanced at Haden. "Almeida, Gallo, Santos and Ribeiro."

"Start from the beginning."

"No." She pushed her jaw forward. "I need those kids home first."

Manny's nostrils flared. Before he could say anything, Daniel stepped away from the door. He relaxed his posture and no longer looked as threatening. "Can't we reach a compromise? You tell us everything you can that will help us find your niece and nephew and we'll do our best to get them back."

Manny glared at Daniel. "We can't make promises we can't keep."

"He said we'd do our best to get them back," Genevieve said. "He didn't promise we would find them."

Manny looked at Genevieve and the corners of her mouth turned down in offence. "Of course I will tell you if she's lying."

"It's so cool when she does that." Francine loved it when Genevieve knew exactly what they were thinking.

"Make sure you do, Doctor Face-reader." Manny looked at Clarisse. "Want us to look for them? Talk."

Clarisse took a shaky breath and pulled her shoulders back. "A few months ago, Evan and Marion decided to take a break from university. My sister and brother-in-law only agreed to their plan to travel around the world because they were going to do this together. And because they promised to continue their studies when they got back."

"When did they leave?" Daniel sat next to Manny.

"October last year. They first went through the European countries they hadn't seen, then went to South America. They were going to work their way up, through Central America towards the north." She swallowed a few times. "They didn't make it that far. Three months ago, I received a video on my private email account."

"I want that video." Genevieve looked at the camera. Francine lifted her tablet, ready. "Would you give us access to your email account?"

"I tried to trace the emails." She stopped when Manny shook his head.

"Give us your email address and password," Manny said. "I have the best in the world on my team. We'll get a lot more from your emails than you could ever hope for."

Clarisse nodded and gave her email address and password. Francine accessed the account and downloaded its entire history onto their system. She planned to comb through everything as soon as they were done interviewing Clarisse.

"What was on this video?" Genevieve asked.

"It was awful." Her chin quivered, but she pressed her lips together and took a few breaths. "Evan and Marion were in a dark room. I studied that video to an inch of its life, but couldn't get anything that could give me a location. All I could see were two walls and… the kids crying."

Haden put his hand on her shoulder. "Take your time, Clarisse."

"No. I don't want to take more time. These kids have been tortured for the last three months. I want them back."

"Then talk." Manny's tone brooked no argument.

"I didn't see or hear anyone else on the video. The kids were told to tell me I should follow the men's instructions. Marion did most of the talking, Evan was too traumatised. The men contacted me after that, demanding access to the investigation into Mateas. I don't even know how they knew there was an investigation. They wanted all the information we had on Mateas and told me I had to stall the investigation."

"What did you give them?" Haden asked quietly.

"Not you." She turned to him, the pleading back in her eyes. "I did not give them you. I told them it was a joint investigation with the Federal Police. I gave them a lot of intel we'd gathered, but nothing that has been key to our case. For the last three months, I've been trying to protect my niece and nephew, you and the case."

"I never understand why people don't go to the authorities." Daniel narrowed his eyes. "You work for the DPJ. Surely, you know people you can trust, people who could help you with this."

"I used to think like you. I was always judgemental towards parents who played into the demands of kidnappers and never asked qualified people to help them. Not anymore." She pressed her hands against her eyes for a few seconds. When she lowered her hands, she looked haunted. "Almeida, Gallo or whoever did an amazing job finding a weak link in this case."

"Why are you the weak link?" Manny asked.

"I made a mistake five years ago." Her voice hitched. "I was running a task force and one of my guys shot the suspect. It was a good call, but there was space for dispute. I got there seconds after it happened. My officer was badly shaken up, not sure if he'd seen a gun when he'd pulled the trigger. We'd been chasing this man for months. He had molested dozens of children and had killed at least two that we knew of. But we'd never had enough to nail him. I checked the body and saw he had his cell phone in his hand, not a gun. But he did have a gun in his waistband."

"So you put the gun in his hand." Daniel's cheeks puffed as he slowly blew air through his lips, shaking his head.

"It saved us mountains of paperwork, saved my officer's career and got an evil man off the streets."

"How did Gallo know about this?" Haden asked.

"I don't know. Somehow they got their hands on a photo clearly showing the cell phone in the suspect's hand."

"Photoshop?" Daniel asked.

"No. You'll see that photo in my emails. It was exactly how I saw it when I got there."

"Okay, so they blackmailed you with your sister's kids and your career." Manny still showed no sympathy. "Neither a good enough reason to avoid asking for help."

"It was enough to make me wait a day. It was so stupid. That day was all they needed." Tears welled up in her eyes and she wiped angrily at them. "The only explanation I can think of is that they'd put a virus in the first video. When I opened it, I gave them access to my home. The next day they sent me videos of my kids. They accessed my husband's cell phone, then got into his computer at work. They accessed my kids' computers and sent me a video of the kids arguing."

She broke down, her breathless crying the only sound in the conference room.

Francine went into Clarisse's email account and checked everything she'd just heard. Clarisse was wiping her cheeks when Francine sent an SMS to Manny and Genevieve's phones, confirming the videos and photos. She would still have to check who had sent the emails and how they'd gotten that virus into the Rossi household. It had been brutal, but effective to go for the heart of a person when blackmailing them into violating everything they believed in. It had to have been hell for Clarisse, knowing that her and her family's every move was being watched. And that the lives of her niece and nephew depended on her cooperation with criminals.

"When did they send you Marion's finger?" Daniel asked when her sobs subsided. "And why?"

"I tried tracing one of the emails. They were alerted to it within seconds." Her voice wobbled. "They sent a video thirty minutes later. Those monsters showed Marion just after they cut her finger off."

Haden rubbed circles on her back and looked at Manny. "Will you find her sister's kids? They are innocent in all of this."

Manny glanced at the camera. "We've got something to work with now. It might help us locate them."

"Is there anything else you can tell us?" Daniel was good with people. That was why he was the GIPN team leader. And why Vinnie had gone from hating law enforcement to frequently hanging out with Daniel and the team. "Even something you think might be insignificant."

"Not regarding the kids." Her eyes were bright with tears, but she managed to contain her emotions. "As soon as they are safe, I will give you everything I have on the plans Gallo and his cohorts have."

"What plans?" Manny's tone had gone flat.

Clarisse shook her head. "Bring the kids home. Please. I'll give you anything you want then."

Genevieve got up and left the room without saying anything. Clarisse stared after her, ignoring Manny's insistent questions.

"She's shooting herself in the foot," Vinnie said. "She should give us everything now. That way we can find the kids and catch these bastards."

"She's terrified, Vinnie." Francine hoped she would never experience such fear. "She's doing what she thinks is needed to get those kids home as soon as possible."

"Yeah." Vinnie got up when the elevator door opened. Genevieve walked to the viewing room, but stopped when she saw her chair in the wrong place. Vinnie's shoulders dropped and he groaned. "Aw, come on, Jen-girl. A man wants to sit sometimes."

"Then bring your own chair." She made a show of positioning her chair in an exact spot only she could see. It took a few seconds before she was satisfied and sat down.

Onscreen, Manny and Daniel were no longer in the conference room. They were walking towards the elevator, leaving Haden alone with Clarisse. She was still apologising to him, promising him she'd done everything to keep him safe.

Genevieve opened the system's folder on one of the other monitors. "Do we have the videos from the kids?"

"Yes," Francine said. "But it's still part of her email account. I haven't separated the videos into their own folder."

"Please do that. I need to watch those videos as soon as possible. And any others you can find."

"On it." Francine got up just as the elevator doors opened. Manny and Daniel walked straight to the round table.

"Quick briefing," Manny called out and sat down. Daniel took the extra chair. Manny's brow lowered when Genevieve sat down. "Why did you walk out like that?"

"She wasn't going to tell us anything else."

"You still recording the conference room, supermodel?"

"Yes." Why did he even ask? "I know you're hoping Haden will get something else out of her."

"Unlikely." Genevieve sounded certain. "She trusts him to do his job, but not with her family."

"Else she would've asked for his help." Daniel nodded. "He was right there in Brazil. He could've helped finding them if she'd asked."

"Can we find them?" Colin asked.

"I'm sure as hell going to try." Manny looked around the table. "Who's got contacts in Brazil?"

Francine raised her hand as if she was in school. And cleared her throat. Everyone laughed. Except Manny and Genevieve.

"Contacts who can help us find the kids, supermodel."

"Oh, they can help, handsome." She flicked her hair over her shoulder. "Both of my parents have built up a lot of goodwill in the last three decades. Three years ago, my dad helped save the police commissioner's daughter. He and my dad WhatsApp each other photos of bookstores. Don't ask. They both have a thing for it. Anyway, if we can pinpoint where these douchebags are holding the kids, we can maybe get a Daniel-type team to help extricate them."

"You're not being completely truthful." Genevieve studied Francine's face.

"Dammit." Francine sighed. "I really hoped you wouldn't catch that."

"What are you lying about, supermodel?"

"I kinda helped my dad find the police commissioner's daughter." She cleared her throat and looked down at her hands. "And I also WhatsApp him photos of bookstores."

Vinnie snorted. Manny looked at her as if she'd grown a beard.

"I have a good working relationship with one of BOPE's team leaders," Daniel said.

"BOPE?" Vinnie's lip curled. "Is this another frigging acronym?"

Daniel smiled. "It stands for *Batalhão de Operações Policiais Especiais*. They're a unit of the military police who specialise in this kind of thing."

"Ooh, I checked them out when the police commissioner got them to rescue his daughter." It had been a tense four hours after Francine had tracked her kidnappers to a farm a hundred kilometres from Rio. "They are trained to rescue hostages, extract police officers or civilians who are injured in some kind of confrontation, rescue people who are caught in a gun fight and a lot of other Superman stuff."

"And they're good," Daniel said. "We had a seminar a while back and trained with them. If you can get the police commissioner to sign off on it, I'll get Davi to put his team on standby."

"Do it," Manny said.

"I will analyse the videos." Genevieve got up and walked to her viewing room.

"And I will rip that whole email account apart, looking for those bastards." Francine was determined to find the kids.

Manny put both hands on the table and pushed himself up. "Let's get this done."

Chapter **THIRTEEN**

A single beep sent adrenaline rushing through Francine's veins. Someone was using her access code to enter her apartment building.

When she'd bought this apartment twenty months ago, she'd made sure of a few things. This was one of the few high-end modern buildings in the area. It gave her access to a secure door downstairs, two security guards checking in guests and a top floor that was difficult to access unless buzzed up. With Vinnie's help, she'd also installed seven strategically placed security cameras.

When she got home five hours ago, she'd gone straight to her computer station and had been working on Clarisse's email account since then. Her computer station had three powerful computers running twenty-four seven, five monitors and speakers of the highest quality. She'd been using all the monitors, but quickly changed windows on one to view the security feed. Her mouth dropped open. "That son of a British tramp."

She grabbed the taser lying next to her keyboard and got up. Her gut had been warning her since the beginning of the case and she didn't care what Manny said. She kept her illegal weapons close at hand and was more than willing to use them.

Armed with the taser, she walked to the front door and heard the familiar scratching sound of someone unlocking her thumbturn cylinder lock. The door opened and she raised the taser. "Give me one good reason why I shouldn't aim for the other butt cheek this time."

"Bloody hell, supermodel." Manny's lips thinned and he glared at her hands. "Put that thing down."

"No." She widened her stance as if getting ready to shoot.

"For the love of all that is holy." Manny closed and locked the door. He walked towards her and pushed the taser to point at the floor. "You're not going to shoot me, so put that illegal bloody thing down."

"What are you doing here?" She relaxed her arm, searching his face. "Did something happen? Is something wrong? Did something happen to my parents?"

"Nothing happened. Your folks are fine." He gave her a confounded look. "You just have to jump from the highest building, don't you? Do you ever have reasonable, rational emotions?"

"Genevieve would say no emotions are rational. They are messengers."

"Of what?" He snorted. "Your tinfoil hat theories?"

"What are you doing here? It's not visiting hours."

Manny was about to answer, but his eyes dropped to her outfit. "What the blazes are you wearing?"

"Don't shout at me like that." She looked down. "I'm wearing a t-shirt, yoga pants and my monster slippers." She loved the oversized, screaming-pink slippers with four glittery nails on each foot.

"That is my t-shirt." He grabbed the hem of the pastel-blue shirt and pulled. "What are you doing wearing my t-shirt?"

"It's comfy." She slapped at his hand, but he didn't let go. Then she raised the taser. "Let go of my t-shirt."

He let go of the t-shirt, his eyes accusing. "You're a kleptomaniac."

"Am not."

"Really? That's your sophisticated comeback?" He stepped past her into her apartment. "How many more of my clothes have you stolen? Wait. What besides clothes have you stolen?"

"Only t-shirts that a man of your age should never wear. Really. This is not your colour." She followed him, sorely tempted to aim at his right butt cheek and pull the trigger. "Why are you here? Shouldn't you be sleeping?"

"I can ask the same of you." He glanced at his watch then at her computers. "It's quarter past one. Why aren't you sleeping? Hacking a bank to fund your designer clothes or stealing more t-shirts?"

Something wasn't right. Manny's bickering was usually without sting. Not now. She put the taser on the coffee table and walked to the kitchen. "Want some of your disgusting tea?"

"It's only disgusting because you don't know what's good for you." He followed her into the kitchen. "For example, it would be good for you to register that weapon so you have legal ownership. It would be good for you to return all my clothes. It would be good—"

"For you to stop picking a fight." She turned the kettle on and walked up to Manny. He didn't move when she stopped a few centimetres from him and looked into his eyes. "What's wrong?"

"You stealing my clothes is what's wrong."

She leaned in until they were almost nose to nose. "Did you miss this t-shirt? Huh? Did you even know it was missing?"

"Not the point, supermodel." He lowered his head to glare into her eyes. "You are stealing from me."

"Borrowing. Permanently." She felt his breath on her lips. A hot-blooded woman could only tolerate so much, so Francine did something she'd promised herself she never would. She licked Manny's nose.

"Bloody hell!" Manny reared back and wiped furiously at his nose. "What the bleeding blazes, woman! That's crossing all lines in the history of human decency."

Francine couldn't help herself. She burst out laughing. The horror on Manny's face was something she would replay in her mind for years to come. Manny stood stiffly and watched her wipe tears from her eyes. She pointed at his face, barely managing to speak through the laughter. "I see that. I see your lips twitching."

"You're infuriating."

It made her laugh harder. She leaned in and rested her hand on his stubbled cheek. "And you're grumpy. We're a match made in heaven."

Manny's eyes widened and Francine stepped away to make their tea, but Manny grabbed her hand and pulled her back against his chest. He stared into her eyes, his nostrils flaring, his movements jerky. As if giving her time to move away, he slowly lowered his head.

Francine couldn't move. She didn't know if this was a wise thing to do. All she knew was that at this very moment it felt right. Not wanting to wait another second, she raised her head and pressed her lips against his.

It was as if she'd flipped a switch. One moment, there was uncertainty in Manny's eyes, the next he took control of the kiss. His lips were soft, but firm, the kiss gentle at first. He pushed his fingers through her hair and held the back of her head in place as he deepened the kiss, his lips demanding, asking for more, for everything. His other arm went around her back, pulling her closer to him.

God help her, but Francine responded as if she hadn't kissed a man in a decade. Two years of constant verbal battles with the most exasperating male she'd ever met and two years of teasing him all came to this moment. This kiss. But she didn't want this. Not now. She pulled her hands from around his neck and pushed against his chest. He lifted his head and she stepped out of his embrace.

"No." She shook her head so hard, her hair was flying everywhere. "No, no, no, no."

Manny's lips thinned.

Still shaking her head, she walked to the kettle, slammed her hands on the counter and walked back. "Do you hear me? No."

"I hear you." His voice was cold.

"I need time. We don't have time. We need to find those kids and don't have time for funning around. If I'm going to work this"—she waved her hands up and down his body—"I'm going to need days. No. No, I'm going to need weeks."

The cold expression left his face, replaced by dilated pupils and a red flush crawling up his neck. Francine slapped his arm. "Stop being cute and sexy. We don't have time for this now. And God knows, I'm going to need a lot of time to work all of you. You'd better be ready for me, stud."

Manny threw his arms in the air and stormed out of the kitchen. Francine was thankful to have a few moments to get her libido under control. Good lord, that man had nearly kissed her last drop of sense away. She hadn't been joking when she'd insisted on time. The passion he had just exhibited was going to make her lose her mind. And her focus. After the last five hours' work, she didn't want to lose focus. She wanted to find Marion and Evan before it was too late.

She took her time making tea for Manny and yet another mug of strong coffee for herself. There were still a lot of places she needed to peek her virtual nose into and sleep wasn't an option. Manny stomped around her living area, pacing up and down the way he did when he was worked up about something. She smiled. Worked up. By the time she finishing stirring the one spoon of sugar into his tea, he seemed calmer as he walked to her computer station. She watched as he leaned over and stared at the monitors.

Deciding that now was as good a time as any, she picked up the mugs and joined Manny. "Got yourself under control, stud?"

He straightened and pushed his fists against his eyes. When he looked at her, it was with resignation. "I never thought I would say this, but I prefer you calling me handsome. Stud is just too…"

"Sexy?" She winked and held out his tea. "I'll behave if you behave."

He snorted and took the mug. "I'd rather rely on my own control than yours, supermodel."

She was glad that there wasn't any awkwardness between them. There was no denying how much she relied on the unwavering strength Manny brought into her life. She sat down and waved towards the small dining room table. "Grab a chair."

He did and sat down next to her. "What did you find?"

"That I've had to be more careful than usual. These guys have some seriously kickass firewalls and encryption going on."

"Which guys?"

"Gallo, Santos and Ribeiro. I had to dodge and duck while getting into their system so they wouldn't know I was there. I don't want one of the kids to lose another finger." She shuddered. "Did you watch that video?"

"It's godawful." Manny's nostrils flared. "Doc and I asked Haden if that was their usual MO, if they have done this before."

"And?"

"Doc says his horror is genuine. He was telling the truth when he said he didn't know anything about physical violence. In the time he'd been allowed in their inner circle, they'd only talked about heists and non-violent crimes. For them it was a game to see how much they could accomplish without getting their hands dirty."

"What does Genevieve say about the videos?" Francine had watched it only once. It had been difficult to be a witness to someone's worst nightmare.

"She didn't say anything. She refused to speak to me, kept watching it over and over."

"Is that why you're here?"

Manny rubbed his hands over his face. "There's a line nobody should cross. Children, young people should never experience something like this. Somebody needs to give me some answers. And soon. I don't know how many more times Doc needs to watch those videos or how long she'll be in her head."

"She zoned out?"

Manny grunted. "That's when I left."

Francine didn't know what it meant that Manny had sought her out. She quickly slapped down those thoughts. They would also have to wait until after the kids were safely back home.

"I knew there was something about these videos. Genevieve wouldn't just zone out if she wasn't on to some kind of key element."

"What are you talking about?"

"I haven't studied the footage. Not yet. I've been digging into its metadata, hoping to find their geolocation. I can't say that I was surprised to find nothing. Not after the impressive security they have for each company."

"What is this geolocation you're talking about?"

"Today's smartphones and other recording devices encrypt a lot of information when recording. If the device's GPS is turned on, I can get the exact coordinates of where the video was shot. I should also get the date, time and loads of other information. But that can be turned off or wiped."

"If it's wiped, can you restore it?"

Francine's eyes widened. "Look at you talking sexy tech talk."

"Supermodel."

"Okay, okay. I'll behave." Or she would try. "If Colin or Vinnie wiped the metadata, I might have been able to restore it. They know enough to maybe do it well, but they're not that good. These guys are. I got nothing off the videos."

"The photos? Those were also digital files, so they should give you something."

"Nothing. That's why I turned my attention to digging into the companies."

"Weren't you supposed to look into Clarisse's email account?"

"I did. Sorry, I should've told you. I was able to trace all the emails sent to her to internet cafes in Rio's city centre. They used two different cafes and neither have any security cameras or system to speak of. I hacked their systems with ease and looked for the computer that sent the emails, but it wasn't one of the cafes' computers. These guys most likely took their laptops, connected to the wireless there and sent the emails."

"So you got nothing."

"Continue to insult me and I'm charging my taser." She huffed. "Of course I got something. When I realised the email account and videos were not going to give me anything, I went on a scavenger hunt through Almeida and his friends' companies."

"Have you found Fernandez?"

"I'm still searching. There's just so much to look into all at the same time."

"Not criticising, supermodel. Just saying we shouldn't forget Fernandez."

"I'm not forgetting anything or anyone." She rested her hand on the computer mouse. "That's why I looked into his company as well. The one he had before he disappeared five years ago. It's still running and doing quite well. Fernandez has not been removed from the three boards he served on as a member."

"Which boards are those?"

"Amaru, the arms development company, his own company and GRAFS, the security company. Gallo has been running Fernandez's company in his absence."

"Tightly woven, aren't they?"

"That's what I'm thinking." She closed her eyes for a second. "Those videos really disturbed me. It's unimaginable that anyone could hurt a young person like this, using them as a negotiation tool. Sick. I really want to find those kids. I'm working on the assumption that Gallo, Santos and Ribeiro took them. So I went through every company I'd been able to connect to them, looking for all properties they own, lease, use, owned. Anything."

"How many properties?"

"Seventy-three."

"Bloody hell." Manny slumped in his chair. "We can't search all of them."

"Especially not since they're pretty widespread. I'm talking about houses in the south of France, a ranch in Wyoming, a villa in Miami, plenty of commercial property all over Brazil. They even have a house on St Kitts and Nevis."

"Of course they do. There they don't have to pay any tax."

"And they can hide shitloads of money in those banks. The problem is that at first, second and third glance, these guys are all clean. They really look like poster boys for education and hard work."

Manny was quiet for a few seconds. "And you got nothing on those videos?"

"I wish I did. Maybe Genevieve will do her Mozart mojo and get us what we need."

"You said earlier there was something strange on the videos. What?"

Francine lined up the first video, not very keen on watching the fear on the two young people's faces again. "I'm a hacker. Give me a computer system and I can tell you the secrets of the universe. This psychology shit does my head in. But even I know something is hinky here."

"I didn't see anything strange when I watched it. Well, apart from two terrified students."

"Just watch it again and tell me what you see." Francine clicked once and the screen filled with the two young people she felt compelled to save.

Evan was sitting cross-legged on the floor, hugging his waist. His medium-length hair was messed up, as if he'd pushed his hands through it many times. His t-shirt had blood spatter on it, most likely from his still-bleeding nose. He didn't even try to stop the slow line of blood flowing towards his chin, dripping onto the floor.

Marion was on her knees, holding her brother against her chest. He was taller, stronger and older than her, yet she was the one speaking. Not that she was doing a good job. Fear made her voice quiver, caused her to stutter and frequently stumble over words. "My name is Marion Durand. W... w... we a... a... are not t... t... too badly hurt. Evan's nose isn't broken, just bleeding. They say if you don't do e... e... exactly as they demand, we will be badly hurt. You must r... r... remember that before you do something stupid."

Marion hugged Evan even closer to her. "Please do as they say, Aunt Clarisse. They are r... r... really scary. J... j... just get us out of here."

The video went blank, but Francine continued to stare at it. The naked fear in that girl's eyes would stay with her for a long time. She turned to Manny. "I'm beginning to understand why Clarisse tried to deal with this herself."

"You're thinking like a woman, supermodel. Clarisse was trained to think like an officer of the law. It might have helped her and these kids if she'd stayed with her training."

"Do you really think you would've been able to put your emotions into neat little boxes if that were me on that screen? Or Genevieve? Or Nikki?"

Manny's face lost colour. "Don't say things like that. Not about you, Doc or Nikki."

"Vinnie? Colin?" She held up her hand when his lips tightened. "Seriously? Would you really have stayed all cold, calculated agent if Vinnie or Colin's lives were on the line?"

"I sure as hell hope so. That is what would save their sorry arses. Not getting emotional and becoming a Lone Ranger." Manny nodded towards the screen. "What do you think you're seeing there, supermodel?"

"I don't know. It's just… something is off. Why is Marion speaking? Evan should be all protective over his baby sister, hugging her. Not the other way around."

"Maybe she's an alpha female and he doesn't have a very strong character."

"We need to ask Clarisse about their personalities. Even better, Genevieve should ask."

No sooner had she said that than one of the monitors lit up, Genevieve onscreen, staring at them. "You're awake."

"Hey, girlfriend. Looks like we're all up. Wanna come over for a pyjama party?" Francine looked past Genevieve into the viewing room. When she'd left the office, Colin had been nagging Genevieve to go home. Apparently he'd not won that battle.

"I don't know what that is. And I don't want to party." She frowned. "I've discovered something. Why is Manny there?"

"Good morning to you too, Doctor Face-reader." Manny pushed his hands in his pockets. "I came to see what supermodel is working on. This case is not sitting right with me."

"Did you make sure Francine's parents are safe?" Genevieve asked.

"What?" Francine grabbed his arm. "You told me they're fine."

He closed his eyes tiredly and took a deep breath before removing her hand. "They are. I went around to my apartment and they were sleeping. They are safe, supermodel."

"It's late. Why are you in Francine's apartment?" Genevieve went still in that way she had when she was studying people. If she hadn't done that, Francine would have been fine. Now she felt like she was back in Sister Mary's office, being asked why she'd taken the convent's computer apart. Again. Genevieve inhaled sharply. "Oh, my."

"What's happening, Jenny?" Colin came into view, carrying two coffee mugs. He sat down next to Genevieve, putting her mug on a coaster. "Hi, Francine. Hey, what are you doing in Francine's place, Millard?"

Manny put both hands on his thighs, his spine straight. "We don't have time for this. We need to focus on the case."

Francine gaped at him. "You did not just say that. Oh, my God. You totally stole my lines."

"Not the same context, supermodel." Manny's cheeks reddened slightly. "Now tell Doc what you got."

Francine made sure he saw her incredulity before she turned back to face her monitors. Having Genevieve as a friend meant that there was not much that was kept secret. Before the day was over, Colin would know whatever it was Genevieve had seen in her and Manny's nonverbal cues. Then Vinnie would know and all hell would break loose. She wasn't looking forward to that. Better to keep everyone's attention on the case as long as possible. She updated Genevieve and Colin on what she hadn't found and what she had—the properties.

"Hmm. That's interesting." Genevieve bit her bottom lip. "Are any of them near water?"

"Why?" Francine was already calling up maps and checking the properties close to bodies of water.

"They're close to water and there's something about RJ."

"What the hell are you talking about, Doc? Who's close to water? Frey? What's she talking about?"

"Rio! They're in Rio de Janeiro. Girlfriend, you totally rock. I don't know if I would ever have seen that." Francine ignored all the other properties and went straight to the places listed in Rio.

"Somebody better start talking." Manny rapped his knuckles on her desk.

"There was something very odd about the recording taken shortly after their abduction. I spoke to Clarisse and she confirmed that Evan is the leader of the siblings. He has the stronger personality and apparently has a strong sense of humour. He's also very protective of his sister, which was why their parents were content with letting them travel together. They knew he would protect his younger sister."

"It doesn't look like that in the video at all."

"That was why I asked her more questions about their personalities."

"See!" Francine poked Manny in the chest. "Told ya."

Genevieve's eyes narrowed, then she bit down on her lips. Francine sighed. Her friend wanted to say something, but thought it would be hurtful or inappropriate. Fortunately, Genevieve didn't give in to her usual need for full disclosure. "The most valuable information Clarisse gave about the two was that Marion was part of her university's small acting group. It was amateur fun, but she enjoyed it and is apparently quite good. Evan has great leadership skills, he's assertive, has above-average problem solving skills, but has a fear of public speaking."

"That's why she was doing all the talking," Manny said. "But it doesn't explain how you know that they're in Rio, close to water, Doc."

"Did you watch that video?"

"A few seconds ago."

"That's not possible." Genevieve looked at her watch. "We've been talking for at least five minutes."

"Doc." Manny exhaled slowly. "We saw the video a short while ago. What gave you their location?"

"Oh. Sorry. Did you notice that Marion stuttered on certain words?"

"Yes. She was scared."

"No. She was spelling." Genevieve looked down at her

notebook resting on her lap. "She stuttered on the first letters of 'we', 'are', 'too', 'exactly', and 'remember'. Then she stuttered again on the first letters of 'really' and 'just'. I was confident in the first word, but didn't want to speculate what the 'R' and 'J' was supposed to mean."

"I suggested Rio de Janeiro, but she wouldn't even agree that it was possible." Colin kissed Genevieve's cheek.

"Okay, I have five properties in Rio that are close to the water." Francine shifted in her chair as excitement built at the prospect of being closer to finding the kids. "Alex Santos owns a condo in Lagao, a very residential area; Vitor Ribeiro owns a piece of land north of Rio; and the company owned by all of them has a property out in the industrial district. It's not close to the ocean, but there is a small lake nearby. There's also an office building and a villa with an ocean view."

"I doubt it will be the condo," Colin said. "Too easy for neighbours to hear screams. Most likely the same with the office building."

"Okay, so we now have three." Francine deleted the condo as an option. "Depending on how far the neighbours are, the villa might work."

"We'll have to check all three." Manny took his smartphone from his pocket. "I'll get Daniel to meet us in the team room."

"I suppose that means we'll be coming to you guys." Francine winked at Genevieve. "We can all be tired together."

"I'll have the coffee ready." Colin lifted his mug. "I'll get Vin to bring us some power food."

"You look happy," Genevieve said softly. Francine ignored Colin's confused look. She faced the webcam, allowing all her emotions to show on her face. Manny was busy talking to Daniel, not paying attention. And she didn't mind Colin seeing whatever he could. Genevieve smiled one of her rare smiles. "It makes me feel very happy that you're happy."

Chapter FOURTEEN

"See what we've got." Davi Pereira smiled as he lifted the controls from the desk in front of him. The leader of the BOPE team, Daniel's counterpart in Rio de Janeiro, was comfortable speaking English, even though it was mostly in confusing grammar. Davi had been on video conference with them for the last two and half hours and had chatted happily about the small drone they affectionately called Coco, a shortened form of *Socorro*, which meant 'help' in Spanish. It had played a key role in the rescue of four kidnapping victims and in arresting five notorious criminals in the three weeks since they'd received it.

The intelligence in Davi's eyes and his intensity changed him from an average-looking thirty-something male to a man Francine was sure turned many women's heads. Watching him operate the small drone to search the first two properties had made it very clear how much he enjoyed flying Coco. And his job. Where Daniel had a lighter touch, more sensitive to the people he was dealing with, Davi was a military man through and through. His focus was on the mission, keeping everyone safe and getting everyone out alive. Emotions were not his concern, having his terse orders followed was.

He leaned back in his chair and tilted the controls. "Hope we get luck."

Davi's team was four blocks away from the last of the three possible locations they'd pinpointed where Marion and Evan could be held. The piece of land outside Rio and the warehouse in the industrial area had been their first choices because of their remote locations, but they had proven to be a bust. They were about to inspect the villa.

Francine crossed her fingers, watching the centre monitor in Genevieve's viewing room. Manny was sitting next to her, Colin and Genevieve in their usual places, Daniel was standing towards the back of the room and Vinnie was pacing behind them.

From her apartment, Francine had followed Manny's old sedan in her snazzy city car for five blocks before she'd wanted to taser him again. If only to get him to drive faster. He'd glared at her when she'd overtaken him and raced to the team room. How he'd arrived only a minute after her, she didn't know. Unless he'd broken his precious road rules for a change. That might have explained the scowl marring his face when he'd entered the team room.

It had been a hard four hours since she and Manny had walked into the team room. The first hour had been spent briefing Daniel, Davi and the police commissioner in Rio, and coming up with a workable plan. After Daniel had recovered from his surprise that Francine was on first-name terms with the commissioner, he'd gotten down to business with Davi. It had been fascinating to watch them brainstorm the best approach to the properties, open to Manny's opinion and even asking Colin what approach he would take.

The first two properties hadn't held any interest for Colin. It had been the villa with its high walls that had made him pay attention, his reasoning being that security meant something needed protecting. Genevieve had pressed her lips tightly together, very likely uncomfortable with such suppositions and trying her best not to comment on it. She'd been mostly quiet, watching the men, especially Davi.

Onscreen they watched as the drone lifted off the ground and rose above the BOPE truck. Davi's truck was bigger than Daniel's, but in Rio de Janeiro it was necessary to have trucks that could withstand an onslaught from rioters or gangs whose gunfights resembled a warzone. Two smaller trucks transporting the team members were parked behind Davi's, ready to move at a moment's notice.

If it weren't for the urgency of their search, it would've been fun watching Davi operate the drone. He showed impressive skill and a light hand manoeuvring the unmanned machine to do exactly as he wanted.

They'd started at the empty piece of land when they'd still had daylight. The vegetation had been dense, but it had been quite clear that nobody had passed through there recently. The warehouse had been a bigger challenge. Dusk had made visibility more difficult and of course the building was a hindrance in itself. That was when Davi had used the thermal-imaging technology. Early on a Saturday evening, there had only been four guards, two of whom looked like they were sleeping. Davi had used software to determine the approximate height and weight of the men and had declared them unlikely to be the kids.

Francine was impressed with technology. A drone that could fit in her Prada weekend bag carried a camera that not only gave them high-definition-quality visuals, but could also with one click switch pick up heat signatures and clearly show them the people inside and outside the buildings.

At seven o'clock on a Sunday morning in Strasbourg, normal people were sleeping or slowly waking up. It was now Sunday morning, three o'clock in Rio de Janeiro, the time most people were returning from their Saturday-night parties or were already home. Watching the footage from the drone confirmed this. The residential streets of Jardim Botânico were quiet. This was one of the most affluent areas in Rio. Almost four thousand euros per square metre, this green neighbourhood that housed the city's botanical garden, a large park and even part of the Tijuca forest was only affordable to Brazil's one percent.

The drone was quiet, a humming coming through the speakers as it flew over a house the size of a small hotel. The Olympic-size swimming pool next to the house glowed from the sunken lights under the water. Soft lights illuminated the enormous property, leaving no dark corner in the landscaped garden that looked more like a royal park.

The drone continued over another two houses that were equally obscene in their size and opulence. The next property was the one they were interested in. Marcos Gallo's villa wasn't a waterfront property, but it was close to the Rodrigo de Freitas Lagoon, connected to the Atlantic Ocean by a canal. Like the other houses in the area, an eight-foot wall surrounded the entire property. The drone was around ten metres off the ground, more or less three stories. Under the cover of darkness, it would be highly unlikely that anyone would see the small drone as it slowed and hovered over the house.

The mansion reminded Francine of something her uncle would like. Ultra-modern. Floor-to-ceiling windows gave almost the entire house a view of the manicured garden. There were three floors above the ground and Francine was sure there were another two below. A mere basement level would be too pedestrian for these people. A second level below the ground would be perfect for their wine collection. Or their cocaine-packing facility.

Without a word, Davi turned on the thermal imaging. It flickered for a second before revealing five bodies in the house. One was busy in what looked like the kitchen, a second one sitting on a stool nearby.

"Are they…?" Vinnie pointed at the three remaining figures on the screen. They were in what appeared to be a bedroom, all three entangled on a bed. Vinnie stepped closer to the monitor. "They are!"

Colin chuckled and Manny grumbled something about perverted criminals.

"Don't look like they in house." On the other monitor, Davi's eyes didn't miss a thing. He sat frozen, only his hands and his eyes moving. The rest of him had the stillness of a predator stalking its prey. He moved the drone over the garden, checking each inch of the property. Apart from tiny red dots that could be rats or rabbits, there were no people outside.

While Davi and his team had geared up, Francine had called up the villa's address on Google Earth. The satellite images had shown the property from above, a beautiful piece of prime real estate. The house was built on the eastern side of the property, a large veranda lending a view to the swimming pool and the garden beyond. A hundred metres to the west of the house, Francine had seen the roof of another building large enough for three SUV's. If she had to annoy Genevieve by guessing, she would say it was a workshop or a storeroom for all the garden tools.

The drone passed over the tall trees and bushes separating the building from the main house. Even though it was a neat building, it would not do to have an outbuilding mar the view of the greenery. The landscaping made sure the view remained natural. If this building was where the kids were held, the overgrown bushes and trees made for a perfect security system.

The building came into view, low lighting in the paving illuminating the walls. It didn't provide full visibility, but would make it impossible to move around unnoticed. The building itself was a square brick structure with only one door allowing access. There were no windows, confirming Francine's suspicion that this was a storeroom or workshop.

Davi positioned the drone over the roof of the building. Immediately four red figures glowed on the screen. Francine leaned forward. One figure was walking against the north wall, his movement not as relaxed or fluid as the security guards in the warehouse. Another figure was sitting at a table, also not exhibiting any relaxed droop in his posture. But it was the two figures huddling in the southeast corner, closest to the water, that made Francine gasp.

"That's them." Francine pointed at the two shapes. "It must be them."

"Davi, the two people in the southeast corner could be the kids," Daniel said.

"Roger that. We think the other two are the kidnappers?"

"Can you move the drone so we can have a better view of their bodies?" Genevieve asked before Daniel could say anything. "Looking from above is not giving me a lot to read."

"Done." Three seconds later the drone was hovering next to the north wall.

Genevieve's eyes narrowed as she studied the monitor. "The other two are the kidnappers. Their body language is aggressive, watchful and they're keeping a distance from the two in the corner."

"Copy that." Davi glanced towards the webcam. "We move in?"

"With caution," Daniel said.

"Always, Dan. Always." Davi's teeth showed as he smiled for the first time since he'd joined them on video. "Is there other way?"

"No offence intended, Davi."

"None took." He looked away, touched his earpiece and tilted his head slightly. "Meet me in the truck for briefing. Then we're moving out."

Voices came through the system, acknowledging his order, and he turned back. "What do you want us to do with the kidnappers?"

"Hand them over to the commissioner." Daniel and Manny had agreed to that when Francine had asked. "He'll get his people to get information from them."

"Glad I'm not them." His eyes moved away, most likely to look at another monitor. "I'm leaving the drone up there to give my boys eyes. I brief my team quick on our plan of action and I be back."

Davi was the team leader, but he was also their IT expert. The way Daniel had explained it, Davi ran ops from the command centre, his truck. His team was highly trained, but relied heavily on the real-time intel he gave them during the op. Francine had to admire the skill needed to analyse data coming in from different cameras, audio being picked up and other incoming information. Working through all the data and leading a team simultaneously was an amazing feat.

Francine listened in fascination as Davi discussed a plan with his team. He listened to their input and before long they had decided on how to approach the rescue. Davi turned back to face the webcam. "Sounds good, Dan?"

"Works for me."

"Turning on body cams." BOPE had experienced a lot of scrutiny a few years ago when they'd been accused of using excessive force, even towards innocent women and children. Daniel had told them most BOPE teams resisted wearing body cameras, but Davi was proud of his team's professionalism and trusted them implicitly. He'd insisted on body cameras for his whole team, hoping to regain the public's trust by showing them good police work. It took Francine only a few seconds to have seven body cameras displaying on the monitors.

There were six men and one woman, seated in the two trucks taking them the four blocks to Gallo's villa. They stopped at the next-door neighbour's gate and one of the team members got out of his truck. After a short conversation with the security guard stationed at the gate, the officer was speaking to the owner of the house. Unlike Davi, who probably would've barked out orders and been agitated when they were not immediately obeyed, the officer was courteous and reminded Francine of Daniel.

It didn't take long to gain the owner's co-operation and soon they were pulling their trucks into the long driveway of Gallo's neighbour. The team jumped from their vehicles as soon as they rolled to a stop. The officer whom Francine now thought of as the team's PR officer walked to the front door and escorted the family back inside.

Without any more orders being given, the team immediately made their way to the wall separating them from Gallo's property. It was the wall closest to the workshop where Francine hoped Marion and Evan were. One team member leaned a ladder against the tall wall and Francine watched in awe as all seven BOPE officers climbed over the wall and dropped down in Gallo's property in under a minute. They moved with the coordination of a team that had each other's backs. Their stealth and the mysterious atmosphere created by the low illumination reminded Francine of some of her computer games.

The difference was these were real police officers holding real guns, about to rescue real kidnap victims. Moving quietly, but fast, they surrounded the building. One reported no other entry point but the door. Five team members congregated at the door, their weapons ready, their bodies taut.

"Go, go, go." Davi's soft order startled Francine. Immediately, the team took action. No one in Genevieve's viewing room said a word, everyone's attention glued to the monitors.

One team member set a small explosive against the door and stepped back. A white light burned bright around the lock for a second before another team member beat the door down with a battering ram. The door crashed into the room, followed by two flash grenades that exploded a second later.

The BOPE team rushed into the room, weapons at the ready. The man who had been sitting at the table raised his gun, but didn't have time to take aim. An officer disarmed him and had him on the floor in a flurry of movements. Two other officers rushed the man who'd been pacing next to the wall and had him on the floor and cuffed before he had time to fight or flee.

Francine searched the monitors for the body cam footage of the two people who'd been huddled in the corner. The one female officer and another officer rushed to the far corner. As the two huddled people came into view, Francine held her breath. A man had a woman in his arms, his body covering her, protecting her from whatever attack they were under. The female officer first spoke in Portuguese, telling them they were the police. When there was no reaction, she switched to English. "Police. We are police. Show your hands."

The man lifted his head and Francine exhaled loudly. It was Evan. He raised his hands slowly, lifting his arms from his sister. Marion sat up, blinking furiously, her eyes still recovering from the flash grenade.

"Please don't hurt us. We've been kidnapped. I'm Evan Durand and this is my sister Marion. Please help us." Evan was on his knees, his arms raised, but his body pushed in front of Marion.

She was sitting on the floor, her hands stretched out in front of her, shaking uncontrollably. The crude bandage on her hand was smeared with dirt. She looked around the room, toward the kidnappers. When she saw them on the floor, their hands cuffed behind their backs, she burst out in tears. Evan dropped his hands and pulled her against him, rocking her gently and whispering into her ear.

"Get them to the paramedics," Davi said. "Secure the room. The other team has secured the house and detained everyone inside."

Marion clung to Evan and he wouldn't let any of the officers separate them. This was the kind of protective behaviour Clarisse had talked about and Genevieve had known was missing in the video. Both kids were able to walk and refused help from anyone but each other. Evan tucked Marion under his arm, holding her close to him as they walked out of the workshop into the night air.

There were police officers everywhere. All the lights were blazing out of the large windows of the villa, but the officers weren't leading the young people towards the house. In the driveway was Davi's truck as well as two ambulances and three police patrol vehicles. They reached the first ambulance and Evan helped Marion to sit on the gurney. She held her hand tight against her body, her eyes wide as she stared at the paramedic.

"May I have a look?" The paramedic held out his gloved hand, his English accented, but clearly understandable.

"I think it's infected." Marion blinked away tears.

"We tried to keep it clean, but they refused to give us fresh bandages." Evan's teeth were bared. "I hope those fuckers go to your worst prisons."

Marion reached with her other hand to Evan when the paramedic carefully removed the dirty bandage. Evan took her hand and sat down next to her on the gurney, putting his other arm around her shoulders.

"Davi, we need to ask them some questions," Daniel said. "Can you get your officer to ask them if they're up for that?"

The body cam from the female officer's partner caught her looking into the camera and pointing to her ear. "I can hear you loud and clear, sir."

"Ah, could you—?"

"Let me ask them." The female officer stepped closer to the gurney. "My name is Karina. Can I ask you some questions?"

"Karina." Marion looked away from her hand. "Thank you for saving us."

"It was a team effort, but you are the reason we're here." Karina's tone was calm and friendly, putting Marion at ease.

Evan's eyes widened. "It worked? Mar's stupid acting classes worked?"

"Not stupid anymore, crybaby." Marion smiled through her tears at her brother before turning back to Karina. "I thought his idea was crazy, but we didn't know what else to do."

"It was a brilliant idea." Karina winked. "And you deserve an Oscar."

Marion's smile disappeared. "It wasn't that hard to act hysterical. I was terrified. I almost didn't do it."

"Why did it take you so long to find us?" Evan asked. "We've been keeping count of the days and it's been three months."

"It's a long story, but it's quite important that we first get some answers from you. Is that okay?" Karina waited until they nodded. She looked at her partner's camera. "What would you like to ask them?"

"Who are you talking to?" Marion looked curiously at the body camera.

Karina pointed at her body camera and her earpiece. "I'm in contact with people in France—"

"Our parents! Can we talk to them?" Evan moved to get off the gurney, but stopped when Karina shook her head.

"We'll put you in touch with your parents very soon. These people are law enforcement officers like me. They are trying to prevent a crime from happening in France and hope that you might be able to help."

"We were kidnapped." Evan's brow lowered, his lips thin. "We are not criminals. We don't know anything about crime in France."

"Could you give him your earpiece, please, Karina?" Daniel asked.

She looked undecided for a second, but when Davi ordered her to do as Daniel had asked, she reached for it. Evan glared at the earpiece before putting it in his ear. Karina's partner gave Marion his earpiece without being asked. She put it in her ear and tilted her head. "Yes?"

"Evan, Marion, my name is Daniel Cassel. Your aunt has been helping us find you." It wasn't the full truth, but Daniel was saying what the young man needed to hear. "Are you two okay?"

"Okay?" Evan scoffed. "We've been held hostage for three months! No, we're not okay."

"Evan." Marion put her free hand on Evan's arm and looked at Karina's camera. "My hand hurts, but we're okay. We were given food every day, could shower and use the toilet. We weren't tortured or raped."

"They cut your finger off, Mar. That's torture."

"But that was the only thing. And it was only that one man who was so cruel."

"Three months, Daniel Cassel." Evan's nostrils flared. "Three fucking months."

"Can we go home now? We don't have our passports anymore." Marion winced when the paramedic cleaned her hand.

"As soon as you are checked out at the hospital, we'll have you on a flight home." Daniel's tone was the right mixture of warm, friendly, serious and respectful. "Could I ask you some questions now?"

"What?" Evan would need to deal with his anger. Both of them would need counselling after such a traumatic and prolonged event, but Evan was going to have to face his rage.

"Marion, you said only one man was cruel. How many men were there?"

"Three," Marion said. "Two of them were in the work-shop with us tonight. They always took turns. We never saw anyone else."

"Do you know their names?"

"No." Evan shook his head. "Marion and I listened, but they never slipped up."

"You say you listened, did you catch anything else? Any plans they have?"

"Body count," Marion whispered.

"What about body count?" Daniel asked.

"The two who were there tonight were angry because they did most of the babysitting work. That's what they called keeping us hostage. It looked as if the other one, the guy who likes to cut girls' fingers off, was the mind behind our kidnapping and whatever else they planned. One of the two guys and the main one wanted to kill us tomorrow. The other guy didn't want to. He also didn't want the main one to cut Mar's finger off. He said they had worked so hard to move away from their past, but the other two were behaving just like the animals from their old neighbourhood."

"This was all in Portuguese?" Daniel asked.

Marion leaned against her brother. "Evan spent one summer in Portugal and decided he liked the language."

"I'm not fluent, but I understand a lot. I understood what they said, but I pretended not to understand anything." That would explain his lack of response when Karina had first told them she was a police officer.

"Did they talk about the reason they'd kidnapped you?" Daniel asked.

"No. Only that we were important for them to get the information they needed." Evan hesitated. "One of the two did say something weird. They were talking about killing us and one said that two more bodies didn't matter. After today, there would be a high body count, but they would have what they needed."

Marion groaned when the paramedic rolled a fresh bandage around her hand.

"We need to get her hand checked out." The paramedic was looking at Karina. "It has healed quite well, but there is redness and swelling that shouldn't be there. Not after such a long time."

Everyone agreed that the young people's health was top priority. Karina and her partner took their earpieces back, and

Karina got in the ambulance with Marion and her brother. The paramedic wasn't happy about the crowd, but allowed it and soon they were leaving the premises.

"Who was in the workshop, Davi?" Manny asked when the ambulance was out of sight.

"Alex Santos and Vitor Ribeiro." Davi shook his head. "Why rich CEOs kidnap kids? I see kidnappings all the time, but thugs do this. Not big businessmen. They get others to do dirty work."

"And the people in the house?" Daniel asked.

"Three men and two women. Employees of Marcos Gallo. Apparently, Gallo gives his villa to employees to have weekend sex parties." He nodded to the side of the truck. "They were busy with such a party when we breached."

Davi could not give Manny, Daniel or Genevieve answers to any more questions and they ended the very long video conference. The monitors went dark and it was quiet in the viewing room.

Manny rubbed his hands over his face a few times. "A high body count? Holy hell! And we don't know what this is about."

"And what is this thing they need?" Francine wondered aloud. What would be so important that successful men would risk their careers to commit such crimes to have it?

Chapter FIFTEEN

"Marion." Clarisse gasped and reached towards the video showing her niece and nephew's rescue on the screen against the wall in the conference room. They'd watched the footage one more time before coming to the conference room to tell Clarisse her sister's children were safe.

She clutched at her chest when her niece told the paramedic she thought her finger might be infected. Then she burst into tears, not bothering to hide her relief while watching the rest of the recording.

Francine had brought her laptop to show the video, but also to check anything they needed while talking to Clarisse. Francine was sitting next to Manny. Genevieve again had chosen a seat that gave her the best view of Clarisse and Haden next to her. Colin was sitting next to Genevieve, Vinnie on his other side. They were all turned towards the screen, watching the footage. All except Genevieve. She was watching Clarisse's reaction.

When the screen went blank, Clarisse continued staring at it. Haden was gently rubbing circles on her back. "They're safe, Clarisse. They're safe."

"Does Celine know? Have you contacted her yet?" Clarisse looked away from the screen and wiped her wet cheeks on her sleeve, smearing the last of her mascara. "I would like to be the one to tell my sister that Evan and Marion are safe."

"Our people have already been in contact with her. We're taking good care of them." Manny had agreed that Daniel would handle the notification before they allowed the kids to contact their parents. Daniel had talked about the psychological impact such a prolonged abduction could have on the kids and how important the first contact with the parents was. They'd wanted to advise the parents on the best possible way to respond. Manny's expression tightened. "We did as you asked. Now it's your turn to give us everything you have."

Clarisse swallowed a few times, not responding immediately. Haden squeezed her shoulder. "Take your time."

"Oh, no." Manny's expression turned hard. "You are not taking your time. You will answer all our questions right now. Your career is over. You'll be charged with numerous crimes before the day is over, so you might as well do whatever you can to gain some favour."

"She wasn't stalling." Genevieve pointed at Clarisse's face. "There was no calculation in her expression, no deception cues. I posit she was collecting her thoughts."

Clarisse tried to smile, but the corners of her mouth merely managed a twist.

"Her crimes are not that punishable," Haden said. "She can be fired because she didn't do her job as she was supposed to. She didn't file complete reports and she didn't report a kidnapping. Those are not crimes."

"She did do something punishable." Genevieve studied Clarisse's face. "It's all over your face. What did you do?"

Clarisse put her hands over her eyes and shook her head. "I gave them the keys to the city."

"What does that mean?" Manny asked, his tone cold. "No, wait. First question, do you know what they're planning?"

"No." Clarisse lowered her hands and faced Genevieve, as if giving her full access to determine her truthfulness. "No. I promise you I don't know."

"She's telling the truth," Genevieve said.

Manny wasn't that easily convinced. Had Manny pierced her with that glare, Francine would've confessed that she had another three of his t-shirts in her wardrobe and that she had thrown away a hideous washed-out cardigan he'd declared his favourite. But Clarisse didn't budge, didn't even wipe the single tear trailing down her cheek. After some time Manny exhaled loudly. "Okay. Start from the beginning."

She folded her hands on her lap and took a shuddering breath. "I got home one day. It was an average day at work, nothing special. When I got home at around six, my daughter was playing in the backyard with the dog, my son was watching television and my husband was busy in the kitchen. I walked into my home office and immediately knew something was wrong.

"Someone had moved my desk to the other wall. It wouldn't have been my kids and my husband refuses to go into my messy office. He's a perfectionist and has mild OCD. Being in my office causes all kinds of problems for both of us." She shook her head. "On my desk was a smartphone. It wasn't mine and it wasn't the kids'. Since my husband never goes into my office, it was safe to assume it also wasn't his. So

I checked the phone. There was one message on it. It was addressed to me. It said, 'Clarisse, check your inbox.'"

She took another shaky breath, her hands clasped so tightly her knuckles were white. "They must have known my routine, must have known I never check my private email at work. They must have been watching me. The email and SMS were sent around the time I walked in the front door."

"What was in the email?" Manny asked.

Clarisse started talking, but her voice broke. It took a few seconds before she had her emotions under control. "The video they took just after they'd taken Marion and Evan. The first video."

"Any messages with it or was it just the video?" Genevieve asked.

"Just the video." She clenched her jaw, breathing deeply through her nose a few times. "My life has been hell since that day."

"What happened then?" Manny asked.

"The moment the video finished, they phoned. They knew I had watched the video and they knew exactly who I was. If I even tried to contact the police, Interpol or anyone who could help me, they would kill Evan and Marion. And then they would come for my kids. Especially the beautiful teenage girl playing with the ugly black dog." A violent shudder shook her body. "They were watching my kids. They knew the show my son was watching and what they both were wearing."

"If not watching via camera, they could've used drones for that as well." Francine hated when the black hats got their hands on amazing technology.

"Was there anything specific about the voice that spoke to you? Anything that stood out?"

"He spoke French, but he had a strange accent. Not like a Canadian or African accent. Just strange."

"Did he give you instructions?"

"Not immediately. That terrified me. I've investigated enough crimes to know that tech-savvy criminals can take complete control of your life. I wanted to know what he wanted from me. He said that I should consult with my husband, my sister and her husband about our next steps. They would help me realise that getting any kind of law enforcement involved would be the end of the kids' lives.

"I thought that I would be able to fake my way through this, but he told me that they were watching my sister's house as well. They would know if I didn't tell them. Then would start sending pieces of my niece back to us. He said he'd wait until I told my husband and sister before he would tell me what he wanted."

"You told your family." Francine could not imagine having a conversation like that.

"It was horrible. Celine was hysterical. Her husband blamed me. My husband stood up for me, but later he blamed me as well. It's done a lot of damage to our marriage."

"Do your kids know?" Manny asked.

"No. We told them something big is wrong, but we couldn't tell them. We needed them to be strong for us. There was no way I was going to take the chance that one of my kids might innocently say something that might lead to an investigation." She sniffed. "They've been stronger than I have."

"How long after you told your sister did they contact you again?"

"A few hours. They waited until we got home and the kids were in their rooms. It was another phone call. He said that he knew Almeida was being investigated by Interpol. He knew that I'd been working with a specialised local police unit and that we were sharing a lot of intel. Since there is so much corruption in the police in Brazil, we had made this unit, this investigation top secret. The unit had their own in-house network that wasn't connected to the larger police network. We'd done that to protect our intel and it worked. This man wasn't able to get to it. Only the members of the unit had access to the network, all the files, reports, intel. And of course my team had access."

"He wanted to know everything you had on Almeida," Manny said.

"Yes. But he wanted more. He asked me what we had on Gallo, Santos and Ribeiro. I told him we weren't looking into anyone else. Only Mateas Almeida. It took me a long time to convince him, but eventually he believed that we were only interested in Almeida. It was only after this horrid event that Haden had sent me the report on his childhood friends, so I was being truthful. Maybe that's why he believed me.

"Then he told me I should make sure no one made any connections between these men and Almeida. He also wanted me to continue the investigation, but to feed it useless information. I was to give the kidnappers any and all key information I discovered and if anyone uncovered damaging intel, I had to find a way to make it harmless. Then they wanted to know who was giving me inside information on Almeida."

"She didn't tell them." Haden sounded sure.

"I didn't." Clarisse turned to him. "I swear I didn't. I don't know how I managed it, but I convinced him that you contacted me on the dark net, that you sent whatever you found from an email address that was completely untraceable."

"Which is mostly true." Haden looked at Genevieve as if to convince her. "One of the great things about Tor is that undercover cops can safely be in contact with their team and their supervisor. That was how we communicated most of the time."

Clarisse nodded. "Maybe that's why they believed me. I even went into detail how I tried to trace you, but couldn't because of the routing system of Tor. He accepted my explanation, but told me that I had to find out who you were. If I gave him your name, he would let one of the kids go early."

"A ploy." Vinnie spoke for the first time. "He would never have done that. Give away his leverage? Nope."

"I knew that. That's why I didn't say anything. For the last three months, I've been trying to protect my family—all of them—and Haden."

"You still haven't explained what you meant about giving them the keys to the city. Which city?" Manny wasn't giving Clarisse an inch of mercy.

"Strasbourg." Clarisse's head dropped and she pinched the bridge of her nose. "After I convinced him that I didn't know who my informant was, he said that he might overlook that and spare the kids if I got him the blueprints of all government buildings in Strasbourg."

"That doesn't make sense," Colin said. "That would be hundreds of buildings."

"He didn't care. He wanted all of them. Libraries, municipal buildings, tax offices, everything."

"Why?" Colin's question wasn't aimed at anyone. "Surely they don't plan to bomb all of these buildings."

"We have to let Daniel know," Manny said. "As much as it pains me, I'm with Frey on this one. Not once did I get a terrorist vibe while looking into this. Doc?"

"I'm not a criminal profiler, but from Haden's impression, these men are playing a game. Terrorists want recognition. Terrorists want to terrorise people for a reason, whether it is political, religious or another reason." Genevieve shook her head. "No, these men aren't terrorists. I'm not saying they're not planning to plant bombs in any of the government buildings, but if they do it, it won't be an act of terrorism."

"I agree," Haden said. "These guys act like typical idiots with new money—entitled, arrogant, but they don't have a terrorist-type agenda."

Francine didn't put much stock in the opinion of a man with a PhD in finance. Genevieve narrowed her eyes and stared at Haden for a few seconds. "What agenda do you think they have?"

Haden closed his eyes briefly. "I feel as if I'm naked here."

"I don't care about your feelings, Cardoso," Manny said. "What do you know?"

"After I reconnected with Almeida and heard about the 2010 heist, I looked around." Haden glanced at Clarisse. "I mentioned it in my reports."

Her shoulders dropped. "I'm so sorry, Haden."

He shrugged. "It's behind us now. Anyway, what I saw made me wonder about their true motivation for the two heists. They made it sound like it was all a game to them. But with this new information, I don't know anymore. They started GRAFS roughly a year before the 2010 heist. The little I was able to get on them made it look as if they were struggling to get clients for their security business."

Excitement rushed through Francine and she pulled her laptop closer.

"Supermodel."

"Already on it." She opened the system she'd hacked into without them getting as much as a whiff of her presence.

"They used the heist to punt their services, didn't they?" Colin asked.

Haden nodded. "GRAFS really only took off in 2010 and again got a boost after the diamond heist."

"Haden is right." Francine pointed at the large screen. "Their financial reports from 2010, 2011, 2012 and 2013. See the spikes?"

"Creating demand is one way of getting business," Vinnie said. "It's a messed-up reality in a few countries where security companies are behind many burglaries and even more violent crimes to make sure gullible rich folks need expensive security services."

"But these men are multimillionaires," Clarisse said. "Why would they want to go to such lengths for more business if it might put them in jail?"

"Here's my problem with this scenario." Colin leaned back in his chair and steepled his fingers. "The 2010 heist was worth a hundred million euros, the diamond heist sixty-three million. Yesterday's was only two million. That's hardly enough to make ripples in the art world. I don't see any of these men displaying the jewels, nor giving them to a wife or lover."

"What other reason would they have?" Manny asked.

It was quiet for a few seconds.

"Maybe it has something to do with the blueprints." Vinnie shrugged when everyone looked at him. "It's not like they've used those yet."

"Did they give any hint at specific buildings they wanted plans for?" Colin asked. "The Treasury building? One of the police stations? Eurocorps' headquarters? The Palace of Europe?"

"No. He told me he knew how many government buildings there were and he wanted the plans to all of them. He was very specific that he wanted me to get the plans directly from the city's internal system." She lifted an index finger. "He wanted buildings that were wholly occupied by government institutions. He didn't want an office building where a government agency rented only one floor."

"Directly from the city's system? Hmm." Colin stared at the ceiling. "Strange."

"Did you give him the plans?" Manny asked.

Clarisse nodded stiffly.

"I don't get why they didn't get those blueprints themselves." Francine tapped two manicured nails on the table, thinking. "Those plans are seldom behind extreme firewalls. I mean, I get they tried to hide which specific blueprint they were after by asking for all of them, but... No, it doesn't make sense."

"He told me that he didn't want to take the risk hacking into the police or a local government's systems. Was that a lie?" Clarisse crossed her arms tightly against her chest.

"Totally." Francine almost laughed at the idea. "I've hacked their company's network and they have some kickass security. In order to create such security, you need the skills to hack it. There's no way someone can build an IT security system and not know how to hack."

"Which means the dudes are setting you up," Vinnie said.

"Oh, God." Clarisse's arms tightened around her torso. "Can this get any worse? What are they framing me for?"

"*If* they are framing you." Genevieve frowned. "There is too much supposition going around at the moment."

"Based on logic, girlfriend," Francine said. "The more dirt they have on Clarisse, the more they can control her."

"Blackmail is not the same as framing someone for a crime."

Francine couldn't argue that point. "Do you think they've been trying to frame Haden?"

"You should know better than to ask me to speculate." Genevieve turned to Haden. "How did you re-establish contact with your friends?"

Haden looked at the far wall, a sad smile lifting his lips. "When I first got to Rio, I made sure to be at a function Almeida was going to attend. You know, I was actually glad to see the bastard. And he was glad to see me. He was the one who got me back into the group. That night we arranged to meet for a beer later in the week. He never gave me his personal phone number, but he did give me a burner phone. Just like old times, he said. Just us boys.

"It was an old phone, no internet connection or GPS or smart technology. He phoned me a few days later and said the others wanted to meet me, have a little reunion. It was the first time I went to his estate."

"They were smart." Francine had to respect their caution. "Those old phones can't be hacked and they can't be traced to within a few centimetres. Provided the phone is turned on and has a signal, it will be traced to the closest tower. With a smartphone, you can trace the person to his exact GPS location, you can remotely turn on his camera to see what he or she is seeing. Oh, the options are legion. They were very clever using those phones."

"That was the only way we stayed in contact. That was how we arranged our meetings. And it was always out of the public eye. The five of them didn't allow any connection between themselves apart from doing business together. For an outsider, they appeared to be business acquaintances, nothing more."

"They've been playing this game for a long time then," Colin said.

"The more I think about it, the more convinced I am that they knew I was working for the police or the DPJ. I'd become far too confident in my undercover skills and missed it. They played me and I wouldn't have known until I was dead. Or implicated in some crime that I would have no way of proving my innocence in." He looked at Francine. "I'm so sorry for what happened to your dad. But I'm not sorry it brought him into my life and brought me here. Safe."

Francine's lips pulled into a tight line. She was not her parents. She was not going to forgive a man for standing by while her dad suffered.

Manny moved his leg until it brushed against hers and left it there. She closed her eyes for a second, forcing her focus back to the case. Later, she would find a way to make Haden pay for what he'd done. She certainly had the skills to charge a few new pairs of Gucci summer sandals to Haden's account. Maybe also a matching handbag. And that pair of Louis Vuitton ankle boots she'd seen in their new collection. And a hot chocolate fountain.

"Why isn't there anything in your reports about the arms development company?" Manny's question to Clarisse caught everyone off guard. Especially Clarisse. Her eyes stretched wide, her eyebrows raising.

"She doesn't know about this. The surprise is genuine and there's no guilt." Genevieve stared a while longer, nodded and relaxed. "She doesn't know."

"Of course I don't." Clarisse was now giving herself a full-body hug. "What arms development company?"

"Almeida, Santos, Gallo, Ribeiro and Fernandez share ownership of a company whose main aim is research and development," Genevieve said. "The drones used in yesterday's heist bear close resemblance to the illustrations of the prototypes on their website."

"Fuck." Haden pushed his hands through his hair.

"What did you know about the heist?" Manny asked.

Haden snorted. "Apparently, not much. I knew there was going to be a theft. I didn't know of what. It could've been an armoured truck carrying cash, gold, diamonds, anything. It could've been a bank robbery, an art heist, a kidnapping. I didn't know."

"He asked you what you did know," Genevieve pointed out softly. "Not what you didn't."

"What I did know? It was going to take place this week. I didn't know which day. The theft was going to bring us all around one million euros."

"Well, that was a big, fat lie," Vinnie said. "How were they going to divide two million's worth of old jewellery between five people and get one million euros each?"

Haden's fists pressed against his thighs. "Yeah. Like true friends, they were going to split everything in equal parts. Just like old times. At least I knew they were lying about that. The old times we shared were not as good as they seemed to recall. We did a lot to help each other, but Marcos... um, Gallo, Santos and Fernandez always did a lot to help themselves as well. They were always looking out for numero uno. Only when it would've been too obvious did they share."

Manny rapped his knuckles on the table. "Focus."

Haden took a deep breath and exhaled slowly. "I rented the van, but Gallo was going to organise the driver. They were talking about being specific with instructions for the driver. In hindsight, I suppose they told him to wait at a rendezvous where the drones would deliver the jewels to him. He would then take it to the container that I organised. And voila! A few days later their loot would arrive wherever they wanted it."

"But why such a big container?" Vinnie asked. "Those little jewels don't need that much space."

"Maybe they stole something else." Haden shrugged.

"No," Manny answered immediately. "I've been monitoring all reports. Apart from the usual petty thefts, nothing else has come in."

"How far back did—" Genevieve stopped when she registered Manny's irritated expression. "You were thorough."

"You bet your bloomers I was. And yes, Doc, I know you don't wear bloomers." He rubbed his hands over his face. "Bloody hell. This is not getting us anywhere."

"Clarisse has more information." Genevieve tilted her head while studying Clarisse. "When someone presses their hand against their mouth or, like she's doing now, pinches their lips together with their fingers, they are trying to prevent themselves from talking."

"Talk." Manny pressed his fists on the arms of the chair as if he was going to push himself up, his elbows flaring. "Now."

Clarisse gave a half-laugh, then sighed heavily. "Why not? My career is over in any case. And I'll most likely be sitting in prison for quite a while."

"Your family is safe," Haden said. "Remember that."

"There's that." She swallowed and straightened her shoulders. "I have recordings."

"Of what?" Genevieve leaned forward. "Video recordings?"

"Some. Most of it is audio though. After that first call, I attached a small recording device to the phone. Every time they called, I recorded the entire conversation. I was hoping to hear some background noise or something that would lead me to the kids, but I didn't want to listen for that while I was talking to them. I listened to those recordings a million times, but couldn't find anything."

"You're being hyperbolic to make a point," Genevieve said. "I do believe that we might learn a lot from those recordings, even if there aren't any background noises. What about the video you mentioned?"

"That is CCTV footage that I obtained illegally." She looked at Manny. "Might as well go down for that as well—abusing my authority for personal purposes."

"What footage?" Genevieve asked.

"Five days after they sent Marion's finger, I was walking to the office—"

"In Paris?" Manny asked. "They were in Paris?"

"I only saw Gallo, so I don't know if all of them were there." She shuddered. "I went into a cafe for coffee when he sat down next to me. Very casually, as if we had arranged to meet. I didn't recognise his voice. He wasn't the one who'd been phoning me. But I knew his face. After the first phone call, I checked all the names that man had asked about. The man in the café was Marcos Gallo. He asked me if I'd had the package tested. He was referring to Marion's finger. I told him I'd had it tested and that the results showed it was Marion's blood group and preliminary results showed it was her DNA."

It was quiet for a few moments while Clarisse took a few calming breaths, her arms still wrapped around her torso.

"He then told me that if I dared do any further investigation, he would send Marion to me bit by bit, then he would start on Evan. Then it would be my kids." Her voice hitched and she cleared her throat. "He told me to get those plans to them and to shut up. That day I sent him the plans, but I also got into the city's CCTV system and downloaded the footage from that street. And all the other streets and places where I could find him."

"Where is the footage?" Genevieve was sitting straight, her eyes wide with anticipation.

"I have an account in Tor. It's all stored there."

"Will you give us access?" Francine asked.

"Of course."

"To everything you have?" Manny raised both eyebrows in warning. "Or are you still holding something back?"

"No. This is everything. Everything I know. I'll give you my Tor email account details as well. There you'll find all the communication between myself and these men. All my sent messages are saved, so you'll see the emails with the buildings' blueprints I sent." Her shoulders dropped. "You know everything I do. Or you probably know more."

Genevieve got up. "I need to look at the videos. We need to listen to the recordings."

"I'm making lunch. It's time we ate something." Vinnie smiled sweetly at Genevieve. "I'll make something that will give you lots of energy and you can eat while working."

Genevieve nodded once and left the room. It took another minute to get the Tor account details from Clarisse. Francine's gut was telling her this was the break they needed. She just hoped they would find out what these horrid men were planning in time. Millions of euros' worth of jewels stolen under one's nose was one thing. A high body count was something she didn't want to take to bed with her.

Chapter SIXTEEN

"There are over three hundred blueprints here." Francine had hoped for fewer. Significantly fewer. But when she'd opened the compressed file Clarisse had sent to Gallo, it had given her much more than she'd wanted. "It's going to take hours to go through these."

"We need to find a way to eliminate some of them." Genevieve glanced at Francine before returning her attention to the CCTV footage playing on the monitors in front of her. They were in Genevieve's viewing room. Shouting back and forth was simply not Francine's style, so she'd taken her laptop and told Genevieve to scoot over.

That had resulted in the response Francine had expected. Outrage. She'd laughed and Genevieve had grumbled because Francine was teasing her. Again. Francine had asked if it was okay for her to sit at the end of Genevieve's wide desk. Genevieve had suppressed a shudder before she'd agreed to it. By now, Francine knew those kind of reactions were nothing personal.

She'd put her laptop down and continued working. Working on her laptop wasn't her preferred method, but since it was connected to her souped-up computer system, she had no problem poking around where she wouldn't dare with a shop-bought computer.

The moment she'd accessed Clarisse's dark net account, she'd looked for the videos and sent them to Genevieve, knowing that her friend was burning to watch them. While Genevieve watched the videos over and over, at normal speed, slowed down, sped up, and again at normal speed, Francine had read through all the email communication on Clarisse's account. There were seventeen emails, all of them between Clarisse and the men. They never signed off their emails, so Francine had no idea who'd sent them. But she was willing to bet a pair of Prada boots that Gallo had sent most of the emails.

She'd had a bad feeling about the number of building plans sent in the compressed file, but still had hoped that her gut would be wrong. It wasn't. If the 'high body count' was going to take place today, she didn't have hours and hours to pore over these plans. "Okay, how are we going to narrow these plans down to only a few possibilities?"

Genevieve glanced longingly at the monitors where she'd paused the footage and sighed. "I'll rewatch these videos later. Show me the emails."

"Gimme a minute."

"You always say that and you always take much longer." Genevieve leaned back in her chair while Francine connected to Genevieve's computer and displayed the emails on the monitors. She split the screens so all the correspondence was there, next to each other. Genevieve glanced at her watch. "I apologise. This time it took you fifty seconds."

Francine waved her manicured finger at her best friend. "Never underestimate my mad skills, girlfriend."

Genevieve shook her head like she often did when Francine said something Genevieve considered frivolous. A small frown pulled her brows together as she leaned forward and started reading all the emails.

They were alone in the viewing room. Manny and Daniel were in the team room discussing the case. Colin had taken his phone and disappeared so he could talk shop. Manny had scoffed that Colin just didn't want them to see his true colours when he was talking to his thieving buddies. Colin had given him the finger as he'd walked to the elevator. He was indeed going to contact his 'thieving buddies' to find out if anyone knew about any heist planned for today.

Vinnie had still not returned with lunch, even though he'd promised to be back in twenty minutes. He was ten minutes late. Francine was tempted to reprimand him in a Genevieve tone for giving an ETA and not keeping to it. She smiled at the thought, but her smile disappeared when she noticed Genevieve's expression. "Do you see something I didn't?"

"The first, fourth, fifth and tenth emails were written by the same person. All the others were written by another individual. It's clear in their sentence structure, their vocabulary. The second sender is much more proficient in French. The other one made typical second-language speaker mistakes."

"Does that help us?" If it did, Francine wasn't seeing it. They needed to know where this horrid event was going to take place today.

"No, it doesn't." Genevieve's jaw tightened.

"Then we go back to what we know." Francine had a plan.

"Good idea. Watch the videos with me and tell me what you see."

It wasn't what Francine had had in mind, but it couldn't hurt, so she nodded. Genevieve's eyes lit up and with a few clicks of the mouse she got the video to play from the beginning. While checking the emails, Francine had only glanced over as the videos had been playing. She was impressed that Clarisse had taken security video footage from numerous sources and had edited it to make one chronological movie. Some parts of the footage came from new-generation security cameras, the images clear, the recordings high-quality. Others were grainy, black-and-white images from cheap and outdated cameras.

The first video showed Gallo getting out of a taxi and walking a few metres to an American-style coffee shop. He was dark-skinned, but his Portuguese heritage showed in his European features. Despite his average height and build, he stood out. His dark blue slacks, sports jacket and trendy scarf made him fit in well with the other fashion-conscious pedestrians. But it was the air of authority and success he exuded that made heads turn. Especially women's.

The view changed the moment he stepped into the coffee shop to a camera from within the establishment. It was mounted behind the counter and had a full view of the place. The coffee shop was not crowded, but had enough people to give it a cosy atmosphere. Couples, friends and one family occupied the tables and couches. Only one table had a woman sitting alone. It was Clarisse. A clean plate was on the table in front of her and she was sipping coffee from a super-sized mug, typical in American chains. Gallo walked straight to her table, sat down and loosened his scarf. At first, Clarisse's face was filled with irritation, but when she looked at him, her hand flew to her throat, the other holding her mug in a tight grip.

For more than two minutes, Gallo appeared to be chatting

amicably to a friend while Clarisse's fear increased. Her breathing had shallowed and Francine was sure that if this wasn't a black-and-white video she would've seen Clarisse's face losing colour. When Clarisse looked like she was ready to faint, Gallo nodded and patted the back of her hand holding the mug. She jerked and spilled some coffee onto the table. He laughed softly, said something else and left. Clarisse sat frozen, her eyes wide and unblinking for a few seconds. Then she pushed her coffee away and rested her head on her arms.

The video cut off there, moving to a street camera showing Gallo leaving the coffee shop. For the next few minutes, a few cameras caught him walking down the street, turning left, then right until he entered a high-end menswear store. Clarisse had also accessed the camera from within the store, showing Gallo fitting two suits, spending an outlandishly long time in front of the mirror turning this way and that before shaking the shop owner's hand. He changed into his own clothes and paid for his purchases, most likely having the suits shipped to Brazil.

From there, street cameras caught him walking around for another six minutes. It was fascinating in a disturbing, yet compulsive way to watch someone going about their everyday life. Francine strongly believed all humans were voyeurs at heart and her interest in what Gallo was about to do next just proved it.

The video jumped from one street camera to the next, showing him entering an elegant restaurant. Again Clarisse had accessed the security cameras inside the restaurant and had a good-quality frontal view of him as he took a table by the window.

He ordered and took out his smartphone while he waited. His tea and a pastry arrived and he barely acknowledged the waiter, still tapping on his smartphone. Francine would've given her favourite red Jimmy Choo handbag to know what he was typing. And who he was communicating with. After a few minutes, he put the phone down, poured himself a cup and pulled the plate with the pastry closer. The next twelve minutes were dreadfully boring, watching him sit there, tapping on his smartphone, drinking another cup of tea, not once even looking out of the window.

When he paid and got up to leave, Francine wanted to cheer. Another street camera caught him leaving the restaurant, then sauntering down the street until he spotted a taxi and waved it over. He walked a bit faster to reach it, got in and the taxi drove off away from the city centre. Once the vehicle was out of sight, the video stopped.

"That's it?" Francine asked.

"That's all there is."

"Do we know where he went?"

"We can ask Clarisse, but if it's not on this video, I don't think she was able to track him to his end destination."

"Or maybe she didn't want to." Francine blinked a few times. "Did you see the fear on her fac… of course you saw her fear when he spoke to her. God, Genevieve. This woman has suffered so much."

"These men were successful in finding the weakest point in a strong woman's life. We never know to what extremes we would go when our loved ones are threatened." Genevieve blinked a few times and did her finger-thing.

"Hey." Francine put her hand on the armrest of Genevieve's chair. "We know you love us, and believe me, we all know how hard it is."

"Loving someone"—Genevieve cleared her throat—"loving you isn't hard. Knowing your life might be in danger is impossibly hard. I have this ridiculous desire to lock Nikki up and never allow her to go anywhere. It's irrational and most vexing."

Francine smiled. "That's love, all right."

"Well, it is inconvenient and exasperating." Genevieve gave a small smile. "It sucks."

Francine burst out laughing. Never before had Genevieve quoted one of Nikki's favourite sayings. Nikki would love this. "Yup, it really sucks. But that's what we do. We love."

"Is that what you're feeling for Manny?"

"Whoa!" Francine reared back. "No. Oh, no, girlfriend. We are so not talking about this. Oh, no. No. No."

Genevieve's smile widened. "You're exceeding your usual overreaction."

"Because I don't want to freak out right now. Let's please get back to this case. Please."

"Will you allow me to talk to you about this later? I find this most intriguing."

Francine wanted to melt into a puddle and flow away. But Genevieve would find her and analyse the puddle. So she waved her hands around. "Fine, fine, fine. But not until I bring up the topic." And not until she was ready to hear the truth. Because God knew, Genevieve would have no qualms saying exactly what she saw on Francine's face. And Francine wasn't quite yet ready for that.

"Agreed. Now tell me what you saw on the videos."

"Nothing out of the ordinary." Francine had been looking really hard. "Except of course when he was in the coffee shop with Clarisse. But apart from that, his behaviour was typical of a businessman visiting Paris. He went shopping for new suits, had tea and some pastry in a fancy restaurant and got a taxi to somewhere. Did you see something?"

"No. Yes. I don't know." Genevieve tapped her index finger against her temple. "There's something there. I just don't know what it is yet."

"Hmm. Okay. We need to Genevieve this."

"Did you just use my name as a verb?"

"Totally." Francine laughed at the look of distaste on Genevieve's face. "Usually I only use it in my head, but it sounded good. I might use it again."

"Oh, please don't." Genevieve had a similar expression of resignation as Manny had when Francine aggravated him. "What did you mean when you used my name like that?"

"We totally have to be systematic. Take everything we have from the top." Francine tapped with a nail on her lips. "We've just watched this video. We know Gallo was in Paris about three months ago. We know Almeida and his four buddies have eleven companies between the five of them, two of which they own together."

"Is this what I do? List everything in such a manner?"

"Yes. Now, help me list more shit… information we have on these guys."

Genevieve hesitated. "Can I instead ask questions?"

"Not really the rules of the game, but okay. Ask away."

"What do we know about the companies?"

"They are medium-sized companies that achieved great success by co-operating with each other." Francine snorted. "More like they bribed their way into all those contracts to make sure they were working together."

"But none of their financial information reflected any wrongdoing."

"I think we didn't dig deep enough. Hmm. What did you find when you looked at GRAFS and Amaru?"

"The same. Successful companies with clean records."

"But don't you find it interesting that one of those companies is the arms research and development company and the other is the security company?"

Genevieve froze. Her eyes moved towards the wall and after a second she tapped her temple again. "It's there. I know it's there."

"It will come to you." It always did.

"I hope so. For now, I would like to see everything you have on those two companies."

"Give me a minute." Francine winced. "Maybe a bit longer."

Genevieve gave a half-laugh and turned back to the monitors. Within seconds the video was playing again, this time in slow motion.

Francine's fingers flew over the keyboard as she bypassed all the security these guys had implemented to keep their systems safe, to keep someone like her from nosing around their business. It took her ten minutes, but when she sat back in her chair, she had everything.

"You have to see this, girlfriend." She looked over to find Genevieve sitting scarily still, staring at a paused scene on the monitor. Gallo was pouring himself a cup of tea, the teapot horizontal, dark liquid streaming from the spout into a bone china cup. Francine touched Genevieve's chair and pushed a little. "Are you with me?"

"Hmm? Yes." Genevieve turned her body towards Francine, her eyes glued to the monitor for a few more seconds. "I'm sure it's there."

"You'll find it." Francine had full confidence in Genevieve. "But first you'll have to bow to my superiority."

"Why ever would I do such a thing? I'm far supe… stop teasing me."

"No." Francine winked and pointed at the far left monitor. "I checked both companies' banking history and compared it to their accounting logs."

"You got access to that? Didn't you say they had excellent security?"

"What did I tell you about doubting my skills?"

"I wasn't doubting your skills at all. I just thought you didn't want to take the chance that they might know you've been in their system."

"Mad ninja skills, baby. They will never know I was there." She saw the look of Genevieve's face and winced. "Sorry. I'll slow down with my expressions."

Genevieve pulled her shoulders back. "No, don't. I will learn to understand what… mad ninja skills are."

"You'd better ask me. If you Google this, you'll just be confused. Want to hear about ninja skills or hear what I found?"

"Oh, please. Tell me what you found." Genevieve's relief was almost comical.

"Okay. The arms company seems to be very much in the background. A quick check through the managing director's emails tells me their focus is completely on research and development. They're not trying to sell anything to anyone. It seems like they live up to their mission statement about living their passion for science. I checked the emails of the managing director for the security company and guess who that was until five years ago?"

"Raul Fernandez."

"Exactly. They waited for about six months after Fernandez lost any and all digital footprints before making Gallo the managing director. At a quick check of those emails, it seems like they're really pushing to get more high-end clients. This company is funding the arms company in most of its research. But what is really interesting is this little document." Francine opened the document that had caught her interest.

"A client list. These are the companies they provide security services to?"

"Not just companies." Francine wiggled in her chair, unable to contain her excitement. "Museums like the Voclain Museum, galleries, governments, local authorities, huge private entities like this oil refinery in Venezuela and this gold mine in South Africa. See? They're targeting the really big guys, worth millions of euros."

"Why do the last three names have asterisks behind them?"

"Yeah, I saw that too. I don't know yet." She followed a hunch and did another search through GRAFS' accounting logs. "Well, lookee here. They're not clients. All the others are."

"So they have the city of Paris, another South African gold mine and a luxury cruise line as potential clients?"

Francine went into Gallo's email account. She didn't have to look far. She brought the email up on a monitor. "Yup. Gallo is emailing his sales manager here. He wants the proposals perfect for next week."

Genevieve touched her chin. "Next week? That seems suspiciously soon after this high body count they're planning."

"They could be planning an attack on some landmark like the Louvre, the Eiffel Tower or a really touristy place like that. The damage would be not only to an important building, but also to the people. If they're planning to bomb it."

"No. I maintain that there is no bomb threat."

"Hmm." A thought popped into Francine's mind and she pressed her hand over her mouth. "Wow. Hmm."

"What?"

"Let me check first." She didn't want to get this wrong. Knowing exactly what she was looking for, Francine worked her way through GRAFS' and Amaru's financials, development programmes and email communication. After what felt like only a few minutes, but was more like forty, she sat back, staring at her laptop screen in disbelief. "Well, give me a broom moustache and call me Magnum."

"That's an extremely odd thing to say." Genevieve sounded concerned. "You're not making sense."

"I know!" Francine bounced in her chair. "But this makes perfect sense. Okay, check this out. Amaru has been working on the drones at the same time as GRAFS has been working on a security system protecting the airspace around buildings from these drones. It's just like I told you about the hacking. In order to build a system that can really keep hackers out, you need to be a top hacker. They are developing the crime and the prevention."

"Makes sense."

"This will be 2010 all over again. Just like Haden said. Oh, my God. This is such a wicked, evil plan."

"Wicked and evil both have the same meaning." Genevieve inhaled deeply, held her breath and exhaled. "You're being hyperbolic."

"And I have reason. In 2009, Amaru developed a superior security system, especially for museums, art galleries and large jewellery stores. Soon after the 2010 heist, GRAFS' sales shot through the roof. They were selling this system to all the local museums and places. Their reputation for excellence soon drifted abroad and they got clients from the USA, all over Europe, even Russia. Their system is really good. They weren't selling an inferior product."

"Again, this makes sense." Genevieve nodded. "After the drones flying over Paris a few months ago, the drone flying close to the White House, the Voclain Museum heist and whatever they have planned for today, they won't have trouble finding clients for this security system."

"And they'll be able to charge a lot of money for it. The demand will be there and they'll be the only place on the market with the supply."

"Sounds good." Manny's voice right behind Francine made her jump in her chair.

She swivelled around, clutching her chest. "You sneaky sneaker. You almost turned my luscious mane gray."

"Your mane?" Manny slowly shook his head. "Do you know what they are planning yet, supermodel? Daniel has organised for his and a second team to be on standby."

"I'm sorry, handsome. Genevieve and I are working our sexy tushes off trying to figure it out."

"We'd better hurry it along. It's already noon and I don't want us to have another Voclain Museum situation where we walk in after the fact." Manny looked over to Genevieve, his eyebrow lifting. "Is she on to something?"

"Why?" Francine turned to see Genevieve rocking in her chair. She'd pulled up her legs, wrapped her arms around her knees and began to softly keen. It might be minutes or hours before Genevieve came out of her shutdown. "We'd better get busy until she can tell us."

Chapter SEVENTEEN

In the beginning, Francine had been concerned that Genevieve would hurt herself in some way while in a shutdown. It had taken a while for her to understand that this was Genevieve's safe place. Most times Genevieve didn't retreat there voluntarily. When her senses were overstimulated by sights, sounds, emotions or anything else, her brain needed to escape from that. Frequently, while working on a case, Genevieve also shut down when her brain had recognised a pattern or some key information and it wasn't reaching her thinking brain.

Until she'd met Genevieve, Francine hadn't given much attention to how the brain worked. Now it fascinated her. Especially when Genevieve had explained that every non-neurotypical person handled stress differently. What worked for her was mentally writing Mozart compositions. Other people on the spectrum had their own unique ways of dealing with physical or mental pressure. Francine often wished she could hug her best friend, put her arm around her or touch her. When Genevieve was keening like she was now, Francine really wanted to hold her tight. But it would be the worst thing she could do.

So she looked up at the man still standing behind her chair. "Well, bring a chair closer, stud. Let me tell you what else I've got."

"No." Manny towered over her, his expression growing even more severe when she giggled. "You're not calling me that."

She fluttered her eyelashes and blew him a kiss. "I promise to keep your studliness our secret."

"You're an aggravating female." He pulled Colin's chair closer. "What did you find?"

Francine showed him the emails and the folder with over three hundred blueprints and told him everything she and Genevieve had discussed. They brainstormed a few ideas, but Manny became annoyed when Francine included secret government experimentation and alien invasion in her theories.

"What? We're missing something and I'm trying to get the creative juices flowing so I can put all these clues together."

"And you need aliens for that?"

The rest of his tirade was interrupted by a Skype call on her laptop. Her dad. She tapped the answer button and smiled at the sight of her dad. "Hello, Daddy."

"Fifi. We miss you." He was using his smartphone and held it up as if taking a selfie. "Can you see us?"

"No, I only see you." The image shifted to the left and half of her mom's face came into view. "A little more and I can see both of you."

Her dad moved the phone as instructed until she could see two smiling faces on her computer. "Can you see where we are?"

"The cathedral." It was easy to recognise the imposing building behind them. "Visiting again today?"

"It's beautiful inside," her mom said. "Those windows are true art."

Their last case had sent them from one Gothic-era church to the next. It was the same case that had caused Genevieve such anguish, and had taken away a lot of the beauty of these churches for Francine. She hoped that one day she could go inside again without remembering that case. Her parents looked happy, but she still worried. "Is everything okay?"

"More than okay," her dad said. "We're loving every minute here. Nikki has been keeping us company. She said you are very busy on a case."

Guilt washed over Francine. "I'm so sorry I'm not visiting with you. It's just…"

"No guilt, Fifi." Her mother's face was stern. "We know you do important work. Now tell me, is your man with you?"

Manny cleared his throat and pushed his chair closer to her to come in view of her webcam. "Hello, Aggie. Tomás."

"Manny! So good to see you." Her dad brought the phone closer to his face, cutting her mother out of the picture. "You look tired."

Francine winced. She had also noticed that the dark rings under Manny's eyes were really bad today, but she hadn't said anything. At least she had makeup to hide hers. She cleared her throat. "Daddy, I have a question for the two of you."

"What can we do to help?" Her mother pushed her dad's arm until she came into view again.

"Daddy, you knew Mateas Almeida and his family quite well. Did you know his friends? Those men who were at the house when you took the video?"

Her dad shook his head. "I only saw them a few times. And they were always somewhere on the estate, too far to really see."

"Were there always only four men? Before Haden joined them?"

"Yes. Oh, wait." Her dad scratched his chin. "Now that you mention it, until a few years ago, there was another man with them."

"Do you remember what he looked like?" Manny asked.

"I'm afraid not. Like I said, they were always far away on the estate. I can tell you he was a man, he was about the same height as Haden, had dark hair, and… if I remember correctly, he had a white patch of hair just above his right ear. But that's all I remember."

"That's a lot of help. Thank you, Daddy."

"Are you looking after yourself, Fifi?" Her mother stared into the camera. "I know how you are."

"I'm showering, eating and sleeping, Mom."

"And working hard." There was a lot of pride in her dad's voice. "Your mother and I have arranged to have a month's holiday. So you just take your time and find the bad guys, Fifi. We will be here when you're done and then you can take us to all those restaurants you've been talking about."

"It's totally a date, Daddy." She loved how easy-going they were. "You'll think your taste buds have gone to heaven."

They laughed.

"Love you, Fifi. Goodbye, Manny."

"Goodbye, Aggie. Tomás."

"See you soon, Manny. Love you, Fifi."

"Love you two more than my collection of shoes."

Again they laughed. The scene shook and changed a second before it went dark.

"I like them." Manny slumped back in his chair. "Solid people."

A lump formed in Francine's throat. She swallowed it away and put her hand over Manny's. "That means a lot to me. Thank you."

Manny was about to respond when Genevieve jerked. Her eyes were clear when she looked at them, comprehension filling her expression. Francine pulled her hand back to her lap and Genevieve lifted an eyebrow. She groaned when she lowered her legs and immediately rubbed her thighs to restore blood circulation.

"You got something, Doc?"

She lifted one finger and reached for her keyboard and mouse. A few seconds later, the video of Gallo in the restaurant started playing. The moment he lifted the teapot to pour himself a cup, she paused it. The same still frame she'd stared at before. To Francine's surprise, she didn't zoom in on Gallo's face or any of other people in the restaurant. She zoomed in on the teapot.

It didn't take long for Francine to spot it. "Oh, my God! How on earth did you see that?"

"See what?" Manny was squinting at the monitor.

"May I?" Francine pointed at her laptop. Genevieve nodded and Francine went into her friend's system and enlarged the reflection on the teapot. "That's what, handsome."

"It's mighty blurred." He squinted some more.

"Give me a sec." Francine took a screenshot and uploaded the still to her photo manipulation software. It took three minutes to reverse the image and for the programme to sharpen the image.

"Bloody hell. You got a shot of his smartphone."

"Not just his smartphone." Francine couldn't believe what she was looking at. "We got him in the middle of sending an email."

"'C.R. will not step out of line again. Got her hook, line and sinker,'" Manny read. "Holy mother of all. He's talking about Clarisse Rossi. Can you trace this email, supermodel?"

"Can a dog bark?"

"Yes. But how is that relevant?" Genevieve asked.

Francine didn't answer. She was too busy doing what she loved most. Breaking into cyber places to do good. "Why on earth he was using a Gmail account is beyond me. Just because the account name is made up of a series of numbers and letters does not protect him. Why didn't he use a Tor account?"

"Are you complaining, supermodel? Because it looks to me like you're having a fine time hacking his Gmail account. As far as this Luddite knows, hacking a Tor account would've been much more difficult."

"Oh, pooh." She waved one hand at him in a shushing gesture. "Don't get all logical on me. Ooh! We're in. Let's open his last email." She clicked on the email that was received two hours ago. "It's from Ribeiro. Well, I'll be damned. Who's Vincent Buisson?" Francine, Manny and Genevieve stared at the email on the monitor. It consisted of only one line. *'Everything is set. Vincent Buisson will visit soon.'*

"That name has not come up anywhere," Genevieve said. "Francine?"

"Nope. But we can find out who this mystery man is in a nanosecond." She opened the programme she'd written that would search all the law enforcement databases—FBI, CIA,

FSB, Interpol, Scotland Yard and every other law enforcement agency that had internet access. It took three point one seconds for her to find Vincent Buisson. She clicked on the first link, feeling like she was on an Easter egg hunt.

Not much surprised her, but she didn't expect the window to open on a Strasbourg correctional facility's system.

"He's a prisoner?" Surprise tilted Manny's voice. "What the hell? Who the blazes is this man?"

"What are we looking at?" Colin walked into the viewing room.

"Vincent Buisson." Genevieve looked at his face. "You didn't find any useful information?"

"No. There's nothing big going down today." He glared at Manny sitting in his chair, pulled another chair up to the other side of Genevieve and sat down. "Two guys plan to rob some rich socialite of all her jewellery tonight, but it's a burglary. Nothing like what we're looking for."

"Did you report it?" Manny asked.

"No, Millard. I'm helping them and getting a cut. Of course I reported it. Daniel knows and he's passing it on to the right people."

"No need to get snippy."

Colin ignored him. "Who is Vincent Buisson?"

Genevieve gave Colin a quick overview of what they'd found. She looked at the monitor. "He was convicted of manslaughter and sentenced to twenty years. Isn't that a bit harsh?"

"He was drunk when he caused a car crash and killed a family of four." Francine despised drunken drivers. "The kids were two and four years old. Oh, my, they were a Member of

Parliament's family. It was his daughter, son-in-law and grandkids. I suppose the court was encouraged to make an example out of this man." Francine flipped through his file and got to Vincent Buisson's photos. The first photo must have been taken shortly after his accident. His face was badly injured, one side swollen from surgery, three deep lacerations on the other. She looked closer at his medical report. "He needed reconstructive surgery after the accident. They had to rebuild his left cheekbone, put screws in his jaw to keep that together and put a metal plate into his forehead. He broke one arm and had a deep cut in his thigh, but most of the damage was to his face."

"Are there photos of him before the accident?" Genevieve had a strange expression on her face.

Francine looked for more photos, but only found ones taken a year ago. She flipped to the next one and gasped. "Oh. Oh. Oh."

"His hair." Manny touched his head on the same spot. "A white patch above the right ear. Just like your dad said, supermodel."

"What did your dad say?" Colin asked.

"He said Raul Fernandez had a white patch of hair just above his right ear."

"When did he go to jail?" Genevieve asked.

Francine checked. "The same year as the heist, the same year Raul Fernandez disappeared and left his company without a leader. 2010."

"Bloody hell. But why has he gone through the entire legal process as Vincent Buisson? Isn't his name Raul Fernandez?"

"False identity?" Colin suggested. "If he was the person

who pulled off the 2010 job, he could've entered the country on a false passport. A good forger could've created a whole identity for him, including a childhood, education and work history. No one would've suspected anything. And when he was caught after the accident, his forged identity must have passed scrutiny."

"Or they could've been so proud of themselves for landing someone they could make an example out of, they didn't check close enough." Francine had seen how arrogance and greed corrupted officials. That was why she didn't trust the law. With the exception of Manny. And Daniel. And Daniel's team. But that was it.

"It would also explain how and why there's no digital footprint of Raul Fernandez after 2010," Colin said.

"And why Haden never saw him again." Manny slumped in his chair. No one else said anything. Francine fiddled on her computer. It helped her think. What had Ribeiro meant when he'd said this Buisson would be visiting soon? Was it code for something else? She entered the address of the prison where Fernandez AKA Buisson was being held into a mapping programme and opened the link. The prison was on the outskirts of Strasbourg, the aerial view showing a beautiful old building.

"Is that the prison?" Genevieve sat up straight in her chair, her eyes wide.

"Yes," Francine said.

"The prison where Raul Fernandez is?"

"Yes."

"Is that prison one of the blueprints Clarisse sent to the Tor address?"

An uneasy feeling flittered around in Francine's stomach. She opened the folder with all the blueprints. "It's here."

"What about the Voclain Museum? Is that blueprint also there?"

After a few seconds Francine clicked and highlighted the file's name. "Also here."

"Can you bring both the plans up, one next to the other on neighbouring monitors?" By the time Genevieve finished her request, the two prints were on the two centre monitors.

"Holy hell!" Manny stood up. "It's the same."

"Not exactly the same." Genevieve looked from one to the other. "But a very close likeness. It appears that the architects of both buildings were inspired by the same castle-like design."

"They used the Voclain Museum heist as a practice run." It felt like Francine had just downed four double espressos in one go. She bounced in her chair. "They're going to bust Fernandez out of prison."

Chapter EIGHTEEN

"What on God's green earth is that?" Manny stared wide-eyed at Francine as the GIPN truck swerved around another vehicle. Francine was sitting next to Pink in the tech truck, working in tandem with him, trying to get a handle on what they were about to go into. Manny and Vinnie were in the back of the truck with them, Daniel in front with the driver.

Francine shook out the cape she'd taken from her large Burberry handbag and draped it around her shoulders. She'd bought this a few weeks ago and now seemed the right time to wear something to bring her extra luck. Taking care to fasten the three buttons around her neck, she looked over her shoulder and pointed at the logo on her back. "See?"

"You have to be bloody kidding me." Manny's mouth dropped open, then he scowled at Vinnie and Pink when they laughed. "The frigging woman is wearing a Supermodel cape. There's nothing funny about it."

"It's hilarious." Vinnie chuckled as he strapped another gun holster to his thigh. Despite the lightness Francine's new clothing had brought, it was still a dire situation. Sirens rang out around them and the truck was driving at a speed Francine was sure was pushing its road-holding limits. Vinnie didn't seem to mind the rough ride. "You're the one who calls her that, old man. Deal with it."

Pink put his fist around the microphone in front of his mouth and wiggled his eyebrows. "You just need one of those spandex bodysuits."

"No, she doesn't." Manny's glare went from Pink to Francine. "She needs to wear her normal clothes and stay in front of her computer. In the team room."

"Oh, we are so not having that argument again." It had taken Francine five minutes to calm Manny down when Pink had asked her to join him in the GIPN tech truck. Since they had no idea what Gallo and his friends had planned for this prison break, Pink had thought it wise to have Francine close by. Even Genevieve had agreed that it was a smart move, especially with the escape plan most likely including drones and other technology Gallo had access to.

The last thirty minutes had been intense. Manny had updated Daniel, who had immediately alerted the prison warden. Fortunately, it hadn't taken much to convince the warden and he'd ordered a lockdown.

It had been seconds too late.

While Daniel had been on the phone with the warden, Francine had watched on the street cameras outside the prison as eighteen drones flew down the street and over the high walls. She'd hacked into the prison's security cameras and had put the footage up on the twelve monitors in Genevieve's viewing room. They'd watched in horror as all the prisoners had opened the numerous bags the drones had dropped in the exercise yard. Out of each bag had come knives, guns and smartphones.

Some inmates had grabbed the phones and run. Others had pocketed knives, but the most frightening thing had been to watch these men grab the guns, expertly check if they'd been loaded and put them to use. Within seconds after the drones had disappeared towards the east of the city, four men had been shot, many stabbed and fights had broken out everywhere.

The warden had reported problems with their online system. It did not permit them to lock down all the doors and gates. That was when Pink had requested for Francine to join him in the tech truck. They'd lost precious minutes when Manny had insisted that she would not set foot near the prison. Well, that had sealed it for her. No one told her she couldn't do something. She'd ignored his blustering, grabbed her laptop and her bag and was outside before Manny could stop her.

Genevieve and Colin had stayed behind to monitor the video feeds coming in from the prison, the CCTV cameras Francine had been able to access on the streets surrounding the prison and the footage from the body cameras on the GIPN team. Genevieve's sharp eye would not miss even the smallest change in body language and Colin could spot a thief or someone about to commit a crime from a mile away. Their place was in the viewing room. Francine's place was in the tech truck.

"We will discuss this later." Manny glowered at her before looking at the rows of monitors secured against the side of the truck. "What's the situation?"

"They've secured and locked down three sections, but another two remain open." Pink tapped away on his keyboard. "This is not a very sophisticated virus they've installed."

Francine looked at the strings of code. "It never needs to be sophisticated. It just needs to find a way in."

"How did they get into our system?" On the video feed, the warden was a short man who looked more like a businessman than someone in control of almost two thousand criminals. He'd given them full access to his system and had surprised Francine with his co-operation.

"An email with an attachment, a flash drive that lies around until someone checks to see what's on it," Francine said absently. "There are many easy ways to get into even the most secure system."

"Have you had any recent problems with the system?" Pink asked.

The warden shook his head. "No. Six months ago we had a few renovations done to the building and upgraded the system after that."

Francine's eyes widened. "Who provided your system?"

"Pegasus Security."

"Oh, my God." Francine couldn't believe this. "It's the same company that did the Voclain Museum's security. GRAFS really want to destroy their competition."

"Did you submit the updated blueprints to the city after the renovations?" Manny asked.

"Of course we did." The warden crossed his arms.

Francine snapped her fingers. "This is the reason why Gallo wanted Clarisse to get the blueprints directly from the city's system."

Pink scratched his chin. "The city might've updated the blueprints in its internal system, but it wouldn't necessarily have updated the public records."

"Can you fix our system?" the warden asked. "We need to lock down the other two sections."

"Working on it." Francine's fingers flew over her keyboard, just like Pink's. A few seconds later, they both lifted their hands at the same time, looked at each other and grinned widely. "Done."

"Thank God." Onscreen, the warden ordered a man sitting at a computer station to lock down sections D and F.

"Have you located Vincent Buisson yet?" That had been the first thing Manny had asked. It was also the reason Manny was wearing a bulletproof vest and had a second handgun strapped to his thigh and enough ammunition to take on a small Brazilian gang.

"Not yet. His cell is in section D, one that is…" The warden stared at monitors on the desk in front of him. "It's a riot there. You guys need to hurry the hell up and assist my men. They're spread too thin at the moment."

"We're two minutes out," Daniel said from the front. The prison was located on the outskirts of the city, making the twenty-minute journey an impressive feat considering the distance and traffic.

Francine grabbed onto the desk in front of her when the truck slowed down and stopped. On a monitor to the left of them was a split screen giving them a full view of the truck's surroundings. She stared at the grocery shop a hundred metres away. "We're not at the prison. Why did we stop here?"

"To keep you out of the line of fire." Daniel came from the front and opened the side door. "We're catching a ride in. You two monitor things from here."

Francine was convinced there were specialised classes in the police academy teaching men how to give orders. Daniel's tone, body language and warning gaze bore great similarity to what she frequently saw in Manny whenever he ordered her around. Or when he *tried* to order her around.

Manny was halfway to the door when he turned back and glared at Francine in exactly that manner. "Stay. Be safe. Don't do anything stupid."

"Look at you talking dirty to me." She flung one side of her cape over her shoulder, trying for as much flair as possible, and winked at him. "We have my cape for super-duper protection. You just make sure you keep your tasered butt safe, handsome."

For a second they stared at each other until Manny slowly blinked, turned around and muttered, "Aggravating female."

The door slammed behind him, leaving her and Pink alone in a truck filled with the latest in technology. Francine rolled her eyes. "He's so in love with me."

Pink burst out laughing and shook his head. "The two of you are so wrong for each other, it might just be right."

"Where are we?" Francine was more interested in the action taking place on the monitors and in where they were parked.

"Four blocks away from the prison. The parking lot is best if we need a fast start." Pink nodded towards the driver. "Claudette could get us out of here in seconds if need be."

Claudette was a petite woman who handled the truck as if it were a toy. She also considered the vehicle her own and didn't allow anything to draw her attention away from protecting her truck and everyone inside. That gave Francine peace of mind while she turned her concentration back to her laptop. It was connected to the truck's system, but she still had the benefit of all the extras she'd put into her device.

In a few seconds, she set up a search that would trace the exact origins of the virus that had opened the virtual prison doors for Gallo. Leaving it to run, she glanced at the monitors. In the three sections the warden had first locked down, most prisoners were in their cells, all the doors locked. In section B, three men were on the floor, one holding his stomach, blood pooling around him. The other two weren't moving at all.

"They're at the gate." Pink pointed to the monitor directly in front of him. Manny, Vinnie and the others had already exited the two GIPN SUV's and were waiting for the first gate to close behind them so the second one in front of them could open. The GIPN team was in full uniform, their identities obscured by the masks and helmets they wore. Manny was also wearing a helmet, but he would not engage in securing the prisoners.

The first gate sealed and the second slid open. As soon as there was enough space, the team made their way into the premises. A guard was waiting for them at a door and closed it behind them when the last man entered the building. Francine switched to the interior cameras and found the team on the fourth screen. Manny had broken away from the team and was asking one of the guards to take him to the warden. The guard pointed to the right.

Francine could no longer take the panic that built up in her. She phoned Vinnie.

He clicked on his earpiece after the first ring. "Whaddup?"

"Vin, don't let Manny walk around alone."

Onscreen, Vinnie's head swivelled to where Manny was walking down a long corridor. Vinnie tapped Daniel on the shoulder, nodding towards Manny, and took off. "I got the old man's back."

"Thanks, Vin."

"Thank me by staying out of my kitchen, you evil destroyer of good cooking." He tapped on his earpiece to end the conversation. He jogged up to Manny and slapped him on his back. Manny staggered a few steps forward and said something that made Vinnie laugh. The prison security videos were high-quality technology—the visual and audio were great—but there was so much noise coming from the prisoners and the guards, hearing anything below a shout would require audio software and an hour or more isolating sounds.

On the other screens, most of the prisoners in section F had voluntarily gone back into their cells. Unfortunately, there were still more than a dozen running around with guns. Two inmates had overpowered a guard and had taken his assault rifle. Those two were now in the kitchen, taking up position behind a barrier they'd built with the steel tables. Pink was in constant communication with Daniel, feeding him the information in a code that had nothing to do with computers.

It was clear how well Daniel, Pink and the others functioned as a team. They trusted each other's read on a situation implicitly and they relied heavily on the intel Pink provided. It took them only two minutes to reach the kitchen and another few seconds to confirm their plan. It was almost an anticlimax to watch the smooth actions as Daniel threw a flash grenade into the kitchen. Immediately, the team flowed into the room, overpowered the two prisoners, took the weapons off them and had them cuffed.

Francine's attention went back to Manny. He was no longer in the room with the warden. Her heart sped up as she searched the feeds for him and Vinnie. She wasn't surprised when she found them in section D. That was the one section still not completely under control. It was also the section that housed Raul Fernandez. Pink directed his team to back Manny up. They left the two inmates to the guards and jogged out of the kitchen.

Section D was not a sophisticated architectural marvel. Like the other sections, it had a central communal area flanked by cells on three sides, three stories high. A man was lying in the communal area under a table, blood surrounding his head. Another was lying in the opposite corner, holding his leg, looking around wide-eyed. Francine didn't want to zoom in to confirm that his leg was bleeding profusely. She wanted to watch the screens in case Manny and Vinnie needed her help.

They met up with two heavily armed guards and walked into the communal area. Manny and Vinnie went to check the man under the table. It was quiet enough in the communal area for their footsteps to reach the tech truck. Manny sat on his haunches next to the man, careful to avoid the blood pool. The corners of his mouth turned down as he put his fingers to the man's neck. Manny shook his head. "Dead."

"With half his face shot off, I'm not surprised." Vinnie looked around the area. "The warden dude said Fernandez is not in his cell and they haven't seen him since the drones dropped the bags. Are there any hidey holes where he could wait until opportunity frees him?"

One of the guards looked up from where they were talking to the prisoner with the leg injury. "Not here. We've secured the kitchen, the laundry room and the bathrooms. There's nothing else in this section."

The other guard tied a bandage tight around the prisoner's leg. "We need to get him to a doctor."

"As soon as this section is completely cleared." The first guard pressed down the button of his two-way radio. "What's the report on prisoners unaccounted for?"

"Section F, we're still missing two. Section D, five." The voice coming through was clear.

"Does that include Fernandez?" Manny asked.

"Who?" The guard frowned.

"Vincent Buisson."

The guards spoke into the two-way radio again.

"Yes, he is one of the five prisoners unaccounted for."

"We need to find him."

Daniel and the rest of his team came into the large open space, their weapons ready, their gazes moving the whole time, looking for potential threats.

"Section F has been secured." Daniel stopped next to Manny. "I just got word they found the other two."

"Five missing." Vinnie rolled his shoulders. "Let's go get 'em."

"Easy there, cowboy." Daniel looked at his smartphone. "The blueprints show a service entry to the east. How frequently is it used?"

"We never use it," the second guard said. "It's been sealed."

Daniel lifted one eyebrow. "Let's check it out."

The team moved to the kitchen, Vinnie and Manny following. If Manny hadn't been there, Vinnie would've been in front. Of that Francine was sure. In practiced movements, two team members flanked the doors, another one carefully opening it. The video from the kitchen showed the space was deserted and Pink relayed that information to Daniel. Yet the team was watchful as they walked through the kitchen towards the service door.

Manny moved next to Daniel and scowled when he saw the door. "Bloody hell. Does that look sealed to you?"

"Not my definition of sealed." Daniel pushed the door and it swung wide to the outside.

Even more alert now, the team made their way outside, each one focussing on a specific area, keeping an eye out for any movement. Francine saw it first. "Behind the truck!"

The team must have heard her through Pink's mic and reacted immediately, dropping and rolling away, coming up with their weapons aiming at the truck. From behind the truck, two prisoners shot at the team. Had the team not heeded Francine's warning, the shots might not have gone wide. Daniel and Vinnie returned fire, hitting one of the prisoners in the chest. His legs collapsed under him and he landed on his back, his head bouncing hard off the concrete. He didn't move.

The second man's eyes went wild. He had a gun in each hand and was shooting without taking proper aim. One lucky shot hit Daniel on his left triceps. Daniel stilled for a second, the barrel of his gun wavering. Manny's lips thinned, his eyes hard. On a deep inhale, his trigger finger contracted slightly. A heartbeat later, the second prisoner was lying next to his friend, shot in the heart.

Francine didn't know when she'd grabbed her head, but she was sitting with both her hands gripping her hair. She let out a shuddering breath and dropped her hands to her lap. "There are still two more out there. And Fernandez."

"They know." Pink switched to different cameras in that area, looking for any suspicious movement.

Mozart's *Eine Kleine Nachtmusik* filled the tech truck. Francine grabbed her smartphone and swiped the screen. "Why don't you Skype me?"

"Why should I?" Genevieve asked. "Don't distract me. Manny and Vinnie are busy and you need to stop Raul Fernandez."

"I… what?"

Genevieve's deep sigh sounded over the line. "You need to stop Raul Fernandez. I was watching the street cameras to avoid seeing Manny and Vinnie engaged in a gun battle."

"Fernandez is out? He's on the street?" Francine reached for her laptop.

"He's wearing a dark suit, dress shoes, a striped tie and sunglasses. He's in the parking lot where you are parked."

"He's here?" Francine's high-pitched question got Pink to bring up the footage from around the truck onto the bigger monitor. "Oh, my God! I see him. He's walking towards that snazzy Fiat."

"You must tell someone to stop him." The rest of Genevieve's sentence got lost as Francine tried to think of the best way to deal with this situation.

Fernandez walked to the dark blue Fiat and leaned down just enough to reach the bottom of the right fender. She wasn't surprised when he straightened, unlocked the car and got in as if he did that numerous times a day. She scanned the parking lot for anyone closely resembling Gallo, but only saw two teenage girls, a woman and an elderly couple. And cars. Plenty of parked cars.

It barely registered with her that Pink was informing Daniel about this development. A plan was forming in her mind and she knew the taser incident would have nothing against what she was about to do.

She grabbed her handbag and ran to the door. "I'll be on my phone."

"Francine!" Pink jumped up. "You can't go!"

"I can." She opened the door. "You can't. Stay here. Monitor everything and help me."

"Manny will kill me," was all she heard as she ran across the parking lot, her cape billowing behind her. She didn't have much time. The dark blue Fiat was already pulling into the street. She ran to the sporty red car she'd spotted from the truck, digging through her handbag with one hand. She reached the car the moment her fingers closed around the square device.

A girl never knew when she might need to break into a BMW. Not that it was her true reason for getting the handheld device that would give her access to any keyless car. She'd been curious if she could hack a car with this toy a friend of hers had refined.

Most thieves needed to be in the car to hack the computerised system. The device she had opened whichever door she pointed it at and, by the time she had her butt in the seat, would have a fully computerised car under her control. Her carjacker friend Raya had sworn up and down it would work.

Since it was the first time she'd used the device, it took her a full forty seconds to get in the car, throw her bag on the passenger seat and pull into the street. By that time, the Fiat was already out of sight. She put her phone in the holder against the dashboard, put it on speakerphone and called Pink. "Where is he?"

"West."

"On it." She turned right, the power of the engine obeying her heavy foot with a roar. "Smart bastard."

"What? Me for having your back or him for using a nondescript car and leaving the city?"

"Him. You, I'm just thankful for."

"You owe me big time. Manny…"

"Oh, pooh." The car sailed around a bend. Francine loved the road-holding on a BMW. "I see him!"

"What the bleeding, fucking hell are you doing, supermodel?" Manny's angry voice boomed through the interior of the car. Pink must have patched him into the call.

"Catching bad guys, handsome." She wasn't planning on catching anyone. She was just going to keep an eye on the bad guy until Manny and the team came. "Unless you get here before I catch him. Pink, do you still have eyes on him? On us?"

"No. Another ten kilometres and you'll be out of the city limits. You ran out of street cameras a few kilometres ago."

"Shit." She was disgusted with herself when she realised she liked knowing someone was watching. "Wait. He's turning right."

"North?"

"Yes."

"He's heading for the forest area. It will be easy to lose a tail with all those small roads."

"Do not engage, supermodel." Manny was back. Furious. "Do you read me?"

"Are you going to shout at me or are you going to come and save this damsel in distress?" She didn't wait for an answer. "Pink, you've got me, right?"

"GPS reading, hacked your camera. I've got your back."

"He's turning again." Francine followed the Fiat onto a narrower road lined with trees. "How far out are you, handsome?"

"It will take us another five minutes to catch up to you, Francine," Daniel answered.

"Go faster, criminal." Manny's tone was clipped. "You always complain I drive like your Auntie Teresa."

"My Auntie Helen, and you do drive like her." Even Vinnie's voice sounded strained. Francine's hands tightened around the steering wheel. "Hold on, destroyer of meals. We're coming."

Francine was keeping a good distance between her and the Fiat, not wanting to create suspicion, but also not naïve enough to think that Fernandez hadn't noticed the red BMW by now. How could he not when he was driving an illegal hundred and sixty kilometres an hour and she was keeping up with him? He rounded a bend and left her sight for a few seconds, obscured by the dense vegetation that grew so close to the road.

When she came around that bend, he was waiting for her. He'd slowed down to an almost crawl and she was on top of the Fiat before she could brake. The crash felt more like an explosion. The airbag deployed, pushing Francine against the seat and obscuring her view. It was terrifying not to see anything while the car spun a few times. It felt like the back tires hit the gravel on the side of the road and the car skidded to a halt.

Francine's heart was pounding as she pushed the airbag away from her. Her borrowed BMW had stopped on the shoulder of the road with a metre to spare before a bridge. Had it been closer, she would've hit the first concrete pillar of the bridge and it might have sent her careening down the steep side of the road.

"Supermodel! Bloody hell. Francine!"

"I'm here." She touched her forehead and felt blood. "I'm off the road, close to a bridge. Fernandez's car is parked on the bridge. I don't see him."

"Stay in the bloody car! Criminal, move it!"

Strangely enough, Manny's anger calmed Francine, gave her comfort. It was immediately replaced by an injection of adrenaline when the driver's side window exploded into a million little pieces. The side of her face stung as little shards embedded themselves in her cheek.

"Who are you?" A man pulled her door open. "Why are you following me?"

Francine reached for her handbag to find the stun gun Manny had made her promise to get rid of, but she was viciously pulled from the car.

That was it. No more being defensive. She was going on the offence.

One glance at the man gripping her arm was all she needed to know she'd indeed caught the bad guy. Instead of fighting off Raul Fernandez, she allowed him to pull her from the wreck.

She used that momentum to throw herself at him and they both fell onto the road. Without waiting, Francine lifted her elbow to drive it into his throat. Prison life and growing up in the favelas had taught him dirty fighting and he rolled away. When he came up into a crouch, he had a knife in his right hand. Francine only had her cape. And a lot of built-up emotions. She jumped up, rested her weight lightly on her feet and settled into the fighting stance an old boyfriend had taught her.

"You're fucking with the wrong people, whore." He lunged towards her, but she easily moved out of his reach. Another trick her ex had taught her in his home gym was to never respond to taunts. That in itself would frustrate the assailant until he made a mistake.

She didn't have to wait long. Fernandez lunged at her again. She stepped into his attack, grabbed his knife-wielding arm and pushed it past her. Then, turning into him, she pulled on his arm and, with their combined momentum, hauled him against her shoulder, straightened her knees and threw him onto the road.

Fernandez landed hard, but was immediately back on his feet. His face was red, twisted in an ugly expression of hate and anger. At least his knife had been knocked out of his hand and was lying out of his reach.

When he came at her this time, he didn't attack her. He grabbed her cape and pulled. The collar tightened around her throat and she reached for the three small buttons that were secure in their holes. But they twisted out of reach when Fernandez jerked her hard towards the side of the road. Not wanting to risk permanent neck injury or a broken hyoid bone, she followed. He reeled her in and walked to the shoulder— the steep and rocky side of the road that ended about four metres lower in a ravine of rocks. If he flung her over the side, she might not die, but there would be permanent damage.

With one hand she tried to break some of the tension on the cape and with the other she tried the buttons again. Her boots were slipping on the road as she braked, fighting for more time. One button slipped out of its hole all by itself and Francine grappled with the next one. The cape was so tight around her neck, breathing was also becoming a challenge. Fernandez was shouting more obscenities at her, his demeanour verging on a psychotic break.

The second button slipped through its hole when Fernandez pulled her past the front of her borrowed BMW. All she could think of as she tried to prevent this lunatic from giving her a rocky death was that she had unfinished business with Manny. She also wasn't finished being a friend to Genevieve, shopping with Nikki and ruining Vinnie's meals. And she still wanted to spend time with her parents. She wasn't ready for this day to be her last.

That was all she needed to put more effort in resisting Fernandez's momentum when they reached the shoulder of the road. Only another metre and with one strong pull, he could hurl her to her death. She dug in deeper to push the last button through, but it wouldn't give.

Then the worst and the best thing happened at once. Her nail broke. And the button slipped through its hole.

Fernandez had been pulling at her cape with all his strength and had no time to counter his momentum when the cape slipped from her neck. As the heavy, black silk material came loose in his fist, his eyes widened and his arms windmilled a second before he lost his footing and fell backwards over the edge.

Francine fell to her knees, both hands around her throat. She swallowed at the pain and wondered where the hell Manny was. No sooner had she started contemplating buying a stronger taser than two SUV's screamed to a halt next to her.

"Francine!" Manny was out of the SUV and running towards her before it came to a full stop. "What the bleeding fuck did I tell you?"

"That I look beautiful in your t-shirt?" Her voice was raspy and tears formed in her eyes from the pain of speaking.

He knelt down beside her, his hands on her shoulders. "Are you okay?"

She nodded. "Fernandez might not be okay. He went over the side there."

Daniel and Vinnie immediately went to where she was pointing, guns drawn.

"He's definitely not doing okay." Vinnie came back. "We might have to scrape him off the rocks down there. Way to go, kitchen Godzilla."

She lifted her middle finger and gasped. Tears came to her eyes and Manny's hands tightened on her shoulders. "What's wrong?"

"I broke my nail." And her nail bed was hurting worse than her throat.

Manny reared back. "Oh, for the love of all that is pure and holy. You disobey my orders, steal a car, wreck that car, get into a physical altercation with a man who wants to kill you, win said altercation and you cry over a broken nail!"

"I'm not crying." She angrily wiped at her eyes with the backs of her hands. "And my nails are important, you Neanderthal."

Manny got up and held out his hand to her. "I see you are still in fighting form."

"Never doubt it, handsome." She took his hand and let him pull her up. She moved in closer, all sarcasm and playfulness gone. "Thank you."

"Always, supermodel." Manny dropped her hand. "But so help me God, if you ever pull a stunt like this again, I will toss your arse in prison along with the thief and the criminal and I will throw the bloody key away. Are we clear on this?"

"Crystal." She flicked her hair over her shoulder and raised her chin. "And just so you know, that cape came in quite handy in the end."

"There are still two inmates running around somewhere." Vinnie crossed his arms.

"Make that three fugitives." Dan rested his hand on his hip holster. "Davi says they can't locate Gallo. All the law enforcement agencies in Brazil are on the lookout for him, but he's vanished."

Francine had almost forgotten about the other men in Brazil. "What about Santos and Ribeiro? Have they said anything? I need to phone the police commissioner."

"No. You need to have your head checked out." Manny's lips twisted when Vinnie chuckled.

"Look at you seducing me with your silver tongue." Francine gingerly touched the side of her head. "It's just a scratch. I'd rather visit my manicurist."

Manny shook his head and turned to Daniel. "Do we have people looking for the other two escaped prisoners?"

"Yes." Daniel's phone pinged and he looked at the screen. "The prison is completely secured. They're now going through each cell looking for the guns, knives and phones."

"At least we stopped a full-on riot," Vinnie said.

"That we did." Daniel nodded. "A good day's work."

Francine agreed and disagreed. Something told her Gallo would not take well to the news of his childhood friend's passing. Not when he'd gone to such lengths to break Fernandez out of prison.

But the adrenaline was wearing off and she was beginning to feel every little scratch and bruise. And her nailbed was throbbing. She needed to go home, lick her wounds and order a new cape.

Chapter **NINETEEN**

"Franny!" Annoyance deepened Vinnie's voice as it overwhelmed all the conversation in Genevieve's apartment. "Remove your father from my kitchen!"

"Oh, dear." Francine's mom smiled apologetically at Phillip and looked towards the kitchen. "You should never have told him, Fifi."

Francine winked at her mom. "No, I should've. I really should've."

Genevieve's apartment was filled with people. Phillip had joined them for Vinnie's celebratory dinner and had been chatting with her mom and her dad. Well, until her dad had decided to inspect the mouth-watering aroma coming from the kitchen. Genevieve and Colin were seated on the other sofa, talking to Manny about their search for the escaped convicts.

"Franny!" A slap sounded from the kitchen. "Get your dad's priestly hands away from my cooking."

She laughed and walked to the kitchen. "What's the problem, big guy?"

"This man"—Vinnie pointed at her grinning father—"wants to add cinnamon to my Auntie Teresa's lamb stew."

"But it will enhance the flavours." She kept her tone sincere and convincing. "I read it on a blog somewhere."

"Out! Both of you out!" He swatted her dad with a dishcloth. "I can see where your daughter inherited her destructive tendencies. Like father, like daughter."

Francine's dad laughed and patted Vinnie on his shoulder. "And I can see why Fifi trusts you with her life."

"Huh?" The change of topic caught Vinnie unawares and for a moment Francine thought he might blush. He didn't. He pushed his chest out. "We're family. We watch out for each other."

"Good man." Francine's dad patted his shoulder again and walked past Francine, winking at her.

She stepped closer to the stove, but Vinnie blocked her way. "I've had enough harassment from your family for one day."

"Actually, I don't remember if I thanked you for, you know. Coming to my rescue and watching out for Manny."

Vinnie lowered his head until he looked her in the eye. "No matter how many times you try to destroy my cooking, I will always have your back." He straightened. "Fifi."

She laughed and slapped his arm. Then she got serious, her tone dark. "Call me Fifi again and I will put turmeric in every single spice jar you have in this kitchen."

They stared at each other for a few seconds and burst out laughing. It was good to have things back to some form of normal.

It had been three days since the prison break. After her injuries had been tended to, she'd gone home, fallen into her bed and slept for twelve hours straight. When she'd woken up, she'd taken a long shower and dressed in one of the outfits she kept for days when she needed to feel armed against the world.

Wearing low-slung designer jeans, a red silk shirt and red high-heeled Zanotti boots, she'd left for an emergency appointment with her manicurist. Her nailbed was thankfully no longer sensitive and her nails were a fabulous deep purple. It suited the soft purple mohair sweater she was wearing today.

Once her nails had been restored to their former glory, she'd joined Genevieve in the viewing room. Together they'd spent two days scouring all the videos they could find, looking for the two escaped prisoners. They'd found one. He'd made the mistake of stopping at a store a few kilometres from the prison to buy a cheap mobile phone. It had taken Francine eight minutes to track him to his exact location and send Daniel and his team there.

A man convicted of running an underground fight club that had led to the deaths of four men was still at large. Francine had looked into his case file and had showed it to Genevieve, who had confirmed her bad feeling. Not only was he good at organising illegal and deadly fights, this man had an astute business mind. He'd used the money he'd gained from the fights to invest in property. Francine had found three apartments in France in his name, but nine other properties across Europe belonging to a corporation that was owned by another corporation owned by the prisoner.

One of the European properties, a villa in Spain, had been sold to him by none other than Marcos Gallo. That connection had sent a shiver down Francine's spine. It had exacerbated her feeling that they'd not seen the last of Gallo. Not by a long shot.

She mentally shook herself and walked back to the sitting area. Having her parents join them for dinner was a very special occasion and she didn't want to spoil it with dire predictions.

Her dad was laughing at something Phillip had said and her mom was talking to Genevieve about the park they'd visited today. Francine sat down next to Manny on the second sofa and listened as his and Colin's debate about restoring art to their owners decades after it had been looted by warmongers turned into a heated argument. The name-calling had just started when Vinnie announced that dinner was served.

Vinnie and Nikki had set the table. With two extra people, they'd had to move the chairs in to make a place for everyone. Genevieve stopped in front of her chair and her breathing hitched. She blinked a few times and put one hand on the back of the chair she always sat in. The other hand was pressed against her stomach, her thumb and ring finger pushing hard against each other. Francine wondered if she was writing Mozart or focussing on her breathing to accept the change in space around her chair and plate. Whatever it was, it worked. She took a deep breath and sat down. Then she spent three minutes aligning her plate, cutlery, glass and napkin in the exact places they needed to be.

When she was ready, everyone else had already piled their plates high with Vinnie's delicious cooking. It always amused Francine to watch how Genevieve carefully measured each spoon onto her plate, making sure her vegetables never touched her meat and all dishes served separately stayed that way on her plate too. It was time-consuming, but it seemed like a calming ritual, one that brought a small smile to Genevieve's mouth when her plate was just so. Only then would she start eating.

"Okay, I like just can't wait any more for you guys to tell me." Nikki interrupted the conversation about the weather prediction for the weekend. "Were those paintings real? Were they really the ones stolen in 2010?"

"They were." Phillip dabbed at his mouth with his napkin. "I spoke to the Paris Museum of Modern Art this morning and they're ecstatic. They're bringing in another expert, but so far they've verified all four paintings."

"What about the fifth painting?" Nikki asked.

"The Braque? It's still missing."

"The police have searched Almeida's house, but couldn't find it anywhere," Manny said. "They also went through Ribeiro, Santos and Gallo's properties, but didn't find it."

"A pity." Phillip smoothed the napkin on his lap. "This has made international news and people have been asking when the four paintings will be on exhibition again. They're planning a grand opening of the exhibition in the summer and have invited all of us."

"Are you going?" Nikki asked.

"Yes, but I don't have a date." Phillip lifted one eyebrow. "I was wondering if you—"

"Yes! Ooh. Yes." She jumped up, ran to Phillip and threw her arms around his neck in an awkward hug from behind. "It will be super cool. We can tell everyone you're my dad."

Phillip's eyes widened, then his expression softened. "We can do that."

"Yay!" She sat down again, completely unaware that Phillip was swallowing and staring at his plate. Often Francine wondered what any of them had done in their previous lives to deserve such a bright ray of sun in their midst.

Phillip cleared his throat. "An international memo has also been sent to all the museums and galleries warning them of

GRAFS. All the places that had hired GRAFS to do their security are now scrambling to find reputable companies to take over that role."

"Are we reporting back?" Francine's dad asked. "Is this what this dinner is about?"

"You have important news." Genevieve stared at his face. "Not good news."

"Unfortunately, you are right." He shifted in his chair. "I spoke to Rio's police commissioner last night. Alex Santos asked for a lawyer the moment he was arrested in the workshop. He's not given them any information and his lawyer is one of the top defence attorneys in Rio. Alex is now out on bail, but the commissioner told me that the case might not go the way we would like it to go."

"Why not?" Nikki asked.

"Well, Vitor Ribeiro made bail the same day as Alex. He went home and ordered his favourite meal to be delivered to his house. He died before he finished eating it."

"He was poisoned?" Francine couldn't believe this. "Why would Gallo and Santos kill their childhood friend?"

"He'd agreed to testify against the other two. He was supposed to give his statement the next day." Francine's dad shook his head. "I spoke to Haden and he's devastated by all of this. He told me that Ribeiro was always the weaker of the five friends. He followed the suggestions of the others, easily influenced. It was most likely easy for the police to convince him to turn against his friends, especially since he was happily married and had two children."

"Wasn't Almeida also poisoned?" Colin asked. "Have you heard from the medical examiner yet?"

"Look at you, being the contact point for everything, Daddy." Francine smiled at her dad.

"Yes, I spoke to the medical examiner. They tested Mateas' stomach contents as well as the orange juice he'd had for breakfast and it was laced with cyanide."

"It's heartbreaking that friends can do this to each other," Francine's mom said.

"They were never friends, Mom. They were survivors of circumstances, but not friends. There was never loyalty between them."

"I don't agree with that." Genevieve looked at the wall hung with her African masks for a moment before looking back at Francine. "I definitely don't agree about never being loyal to each other. For the last five years they'd been conspiring to break Raul Fernandez out of prison. In this time, something must have happened to put stress on their loyalty. Almeida's change of heart about the antique jewellery heist and the prison break could have been the last stressor that fractured their loyalty."

"Well, I think Gallo is mentally unwell." Francine was convinced. "Haden told us he was the mastermind of all the plans. I won't be surprised if he was the one who poisoned Almeida and Ribeiro."

"That's speculation, Francine. You're above that." Genevieve's tone held a reprimand. "Without any more speculation, do we know where Gallo is?"

"He disappeared." The corners of Manny's mouth turned down. "The police can't find him anywhere and he's not been spotted at airports."

Two days ago, Francine had again looked into the four men's personal and business finances. Gallo hadn't waited to be caught before he'd made his move. The same day the two young people had been rescued and two of his friends had been arrested, he'd emptied all his bank accounts. His real estate business account, his international real estate account and all his personal accounts had been drained and closed. Francine happily speculated that all that money was now in an offshore account that could not be traced or touched by any authorities.

"At least Evan and Marion are back home safe," Francine's mom said.

"And Clarisse is under house arrest." Manny scratched his chin. "The Paris police department don't know how they're going to deal with this PR mess. Haden is also under investigation, but he should be cleared without any problem."

"What do you think will happen to Clarisse?" Francine didn't like the idea of this woman being sent to prison. She'd already suffered so much.

"I don't know, supermodel." Something in Manny's tone belied his words. Francine wondered if he'd made calls to some of his many influential contacts to ask for a favourable review of Clarisse's case.

Francine leaned closer and dragged her manicured nail down his arm. "You're a cuddly-wuddly teddy bear."

"Get off me, female." He pushed her hand away. "Don't aggravate me."

"Isn't it amazing how a visit to a grieving widow's cellar uncovered such a web of crime?" Francine's dad interrupted before Francine could continue provoking Manny.

"The butterfly effect," Nikki said. "One tiny little flap of tiny little wings."

"I've always found that theory preposterous." Genevieve aligned her knife and fork in the centre of her empty plate. "A butterfly could never create enough air movement to lead to a tornado on the other side of the planet."

A debate about that theory started and soon the topic of Brazilian childhood friends, a prisoner still at large and a mastermind on the run was forgotten. A few times, the room became loud with laughter and Genevieve clutched Colin's hand. Yet she didn't leave. Being part of such a great group of people brought positive energy into Francine's life. She knew Genevieve experienced it as well. Just in a different way.

After dessert and coffee, her mom and dad made their excuses. The last two evenings Francine had kept them up late, entertaining them in her favourite restaurants and chatting until both her parents could no longer hide their yawns. Phillip offered to drive them to Manny's apartment since he also needed to turn in early. Tomorrow was a working day and they all had to start early. There were criminals to catch.

After five minutes of hugs, her parents left Genevieve's apartment. They'd offered to find alternative accommodation, but Manny would not hear of it. Neither he nor Francine had told her parents that Nikki had moved back into her room and Manny had been spending the last two nights in her loft apartment. But the way her mom was looking at her tonight, she was sure they knew.

Genevieve knew, which meant Colin knew. He hadn't said anything and she knew he wouldn't. Not until she said something. With a bracing inhale, she stood up and held her hand out to Manny. "Well, come on then, handsome. I'm not done with you yet."

Manny's cheeks turned red. "Bloody hell, supermodel."

Colin snorted as Manny got up and led Francine to the door. She ignored Vinnie's calls from the kitchen to explain what she'd meant. When his questions became infused with stronger language, she laughingly pushed Manny out of the front door in time to hear Nikki ask what the fuss was all about. Francine closed the door behind her and prayed the elevator would arrive before anyone came bursting out of the door.

"That was mighty brave of you," Manny said when Francine repeatedly pressed the elevator button. He pushed his hands in his pockets and leaned against the wall.

"Like you were going to say anything."

"It's none of their business."

Francine froze for a second, then slowly turned to him. "Really? You're going to try to keep secrets from one of the top nonverbal communication specialists in the world, a man who sees more than he lets on, a girl who has you eating out of her hand and someone I know you consider a close friend?"

The elevator arrived and the doors opened with a ping. Manny followed her in, grumbling about nosy friends. "They should keep their minds on work. Put their skills to use finding Gallo and the other prisoner."

"Oh, pooh!" She stepped closer and pulled his jacket's collar. "That's tomorrow's worry. Tonight we have other things to focus on."

"Like what?"

"My new cape was delivered today. I'll model it for you."
She winked slowly. "But then you must model yours."

"Mine?" His eyebrows rose. "You got a cape for me?"

"Yes. With Super-stud on the back."

~ ~ ~ ~ ~

Be first to find out when Genevieve's next adventure will be published.
Sign up for the newsletter at http://estelleryan.com/contact.html

~ ~ ~ ~ ~

Listen to the Mozart pieces,
look at the paintings from this book
and read more *drones, the 2010 heist and Léger at:*
http://estelleryan.com/the-leger-connection.html

Other books in the Genevieve Lenard Series:

Book 1: The Gauguin Connection

Book 2: The Dante Connection

Book 3: The Braque Connection

Book 4: The Flinck Connection

Book 5: The Courbet Connection

Book 6: The Pucelle Connection

Book 7: The Léger Connection

Book 8: The Morisot Connection

and more…

~ ~ ~ ~ ~

Please visit me on my Facebook Page at
www.facebook.com/EstelleRyanAuthor to be part of the
process as I'm writing Genevieve's next adventure.
and
explore my website at www.estelleryan.com
to find out more about me and Genevieve.

Manufactured by Amazon.ca
Acheson, AB

14171842R00185